D1374467

The Pollinators of Eden

The
Pollinators
of
Eden

by John Boyd

Weybright and Talley

New York

Copyright © 1969 by John Boyd

All rights reserved, including the
right to reproduce this book or
portions thereof in any form.

Published in the United States by
WEYBRIGHT AND TALLEY, INC.,
3 East 54th Street,
New York, New York 10022.

Published simultaneously in Canada by
CLARKE, IRWIN & COMPANY LIMITED,
Toronto and Vancouver.

PRINTED IN THE UNITED STATES OF AMERICA

To Lynn Gillaspy, as a warning

Go, and catch a falling star,
Get with child a mandrake root . . .
And find
What wind
Serves to advance an honest mind.

> John Donne

The Pollinators of Eden

Chapter One

FROM: Surgeon General, NASA, Houston, Texas.

TO: Director, Institute of Advanced Studies, Santa Barbara, California.

SUBJECT: Psychiatric case history, Freda Janet Caron.

DIAGNOSIS: Humanism with nymphomanic omniphilia.

REFERENCES: (A) Letter dated 8/12/37. Doctor Hans Clayborg, IAS, to Secretary of Agriculture. (B) Directive #27, U.S. Attorney General.

In accordance with reference (A) and in compliance with reference (B), the case history of the subject patient, a female Caucasian, aged 24, formerly employed as a cystologist for the Bureau of Exotic Plants, is herewith submitted for extramedical recommendations.

Subject patient's traumatic episode occurred May 16–17, while accompanying Scientific Expedition C, for Charlie, to the planet called variously Flora, the Flower Planet, or the Planet of Flowers. However, deep narcosis analysis reveals that events contributing to the patient's hospitalization commenced in January with the arrival from Flora of the first section, A for Able, at the Fresno facility's Navy landing. . . .

BLOND AND OVATELY WILLOWY, FREDA CARON STOOD ON THE control-tower bridge and searched the morning blue above the San Joaquin Valley, using Commodore Minor's binoculars to scan the sector he pointed out. Thus she caught the first glint of

1

sunlight against the USSS *Botany* when the transport swung stern down to commence its earth approach and saw the first prick of its contrail when the ship plummeted into the atmosphere. She was focusing on the droplet of vanadium 320 beneath the rosette when the bridge lookout called, *"Botany, ahoy!"*

As its retros slowed it in the thickening air, the starship became a dot in the sky that inched southwestward over the landing pad as its contrails dissipated eastward. The dot swelled. Her ears caught the rustle of its retro-jets, which rose to a keening and faded as the launching pad's concavity focused the whine back onto its source, dampening the shriek to a rumble that hardly shook the control tower one thousand yards from the pad.

Silver, slim, the shape of the *Botany* was emerging to her angle of sight as it sank into a self-compressed cushion of air. Below her, the decontamination chamber, exit nozzle flexing from its huge carapace, was trundling over the hardpan toward the pad. All the technology of man, it seemed to her, had gathered to this segment of time wherein the earth received her children from space, and Freda thrilled at the sight until . . .

Above her, the *Botany*'s landing pods unfolded, outward and downward, on extenders which resembled the ribs of a windstripped umbrella, and its grace was altered to the grotesquerie of a praying mantis. Even its silver dulled to slate when the vessel sank below the skyline of the winter-greened Coastal Range, and that which had sailed as companion to the stars was squatting a captive of earth.

Now, inside the ship, she knew, the weight of passengers, coiled inside eggs of water, was triggering their expulsion into chutes, marked 1, 2, 3, from decks A, B, C. They would awaken while sliding down curving tubes whose branches connected at lower levels, and they would plop, 1A, 2B, 3C, into bins on the floor of the decon chamber, sorted and graded by rank and serial number, academic degree and Social Security number, line or staff officer, scientist or assistant. In her mind's ear, she could hear the plop, plop of the falling pieces which had composed

2

Section Able of the Flora Project. But the pieces were friends and associates: they were named Rex and Hal and Kenneth. Among them was a very special piece, whom she had already sorted and graded and selected to be her husband.

Paul Theaston was coming home from Flora. Had it not been for their wedding in June, Freda herself would be leaving in April, with the Charlie Section, for the Planet of Flowers.

Flora, the Planet of Flowers. It, at least, had escaped being numbered!

Freda recalled the telecast months before when the Royal Space Navy captain, who had discovered the planet, denied himself a place in history when he refused to follow the standard procedure of explorers and put his name before the planet's orbit number. She remembered his exact words: "When they call the Grand Canyon 'Powell's Ditch,' then I shall permit this planet to be named 'Ramsbotham-Twatwetham #3!'"

She was remembering the telecast as the *Botany* settled so gently to the pad that its strut joints barely flexed. Before the gyros whirred into silence, the decon turtle had scuttled up, its exit nozzle nudging for the airlock distended from the crotch of the spidery extenders. Beside her, the Commodore exploded with admiration, "Barron always brings them down as lightly as a falling rose petal."

Freda smiled agreement, knowing that the old space dog was simply following Navy etiquette. Commodore Minor well knew that a box no bigger than a man's head had controlled the descent of the ship, that a reserve apprentice spaceman could have conned the craft as well as Captain Philip Barron, USSN.

Freda thanked the Commodore for his invitation to the bridge and promised that she and Paul would join him for lunch. She left the bridge for the reception area below.

Decontamination usually took half an hour. Waiting in the section reserved for management, she was grateful that rank had its privileges. Across the areaway, families of enlisted men and nonprofessionals crowded into a roped-off area in a melee of jostling elbows, a miasma of evaporating deodorants, and a din

3

of crying babies. She was already edgy with anxiety: there seemed to be some law, she thought, which stated that anxiety increased with the square of the nearness to reunion with a loved one.

To compose herself, Freda reviewed the wedding plans she was saving to discuss with Paul: guest list, engravings, cake and gown design—all the delightful trivia of a formal wedding. For the most part, she didn't absolutely need Paul's opinions or decisions, but she wanted him to feel that he was contributing more to the wedding than the body he would place before the altar. Then she ran through the agenda backwards, but her jitteriness increased and went into overdrive when she heard the clunk of the turtle locking onto the exit ramp.

Navy protocol aligned the procession that filed down the ramp into the waiting room. Heading the contingent of ship's officers came Captain Barron, striving simultaneously to adjust to earth's gravity and to maintain military bearing. As he strode toward the elevator, his rigid bounce reminded Freda of a man walking on two pogo sticks. Staggering, cantering, bouncing, gliding, the ship's officers followed, all beautifully tanned by the sun of Flora. Next came Doctor Hector, Project Able's scientific director, his lanky frame gallumphing across the floor as he waved a greeting to Freda. Behind him came the remaining scientists, department heads all, but Paul Theaston was not among them.

Paul Theaston, her fiancé, had not returned from Flora!

She knew immediately that he had merely stayed over with Section Baker; her friends had all greeted her with smiles. But her former anxiety deepened into disappointment. No doubt, since he was the project's only morphologist, he had been unable to complete his work goals in the four months assigned to a section. Now, he would be returning only days before the wedding. All the prewedding tasks would be hers, demanding twice the time she had scheduled, taking from time she had planned to use crossbreeding Martian lichen with terrestrial rock moss.

She stood for a moment to watch the tide flow down the ramp and crest over the crowd opposite, eddying around cries of

4

"There's daddy!" and "Over here, honey!" With an ear trumpet, she was positive she could have heard the slurp of kisses and the plop of withdrawing lips. With disgust and envy, she was watching when Hal Polino, Paul's assistant, literally swirled from the crowd, pirouetting to clear two earthenware pots he held, one under each arm. Each pot contained a tulip in full bloom, and he had seen her, was coming toward her with a grin. "Keep your lips puckered, Doctor Caron. Paul is sending me as his proxy."

"If you enjoy public displays," she snapped, "look behind you! Where's Paul?"

"The lucky stiff got an extension through Section Baker, to finish his study of orchid pollination."

Polino noticed her disappointment, and his grin changed to a smile, his eyes softened. "Anyway, he sent you these, a gift from fairyland to the most beautiful plant scientist on earth. My words, not his. Paul's message is on the name plates."

She glanced at the flowers Polino held. Their stems were a foot long and greener than the stems of earth tulips. Their blooms were of a yellow that was iridescent. Three inches below the carpels there was a bulbous swelling, serrated with flutings. On placards stuck into the loam of the pots Paul had lettered, *"Tulipa caronus sireni."*

"If Paul thinks he can placate me by naming a tulip for me, he'd better reconsider his approach."

"These aren't ordinary tulips, Doctor. Listen."

Polino bent his head and whistled a wolf's call against the bulb of the tulip in his right arm. Holding the pot away from him, he swirled once in a complete circle and held the pot toward her. Low, but very distinct, the flower trilled a wolf whistle. It was realistic to the point of bawdiness, and Freda laughed.

"The ovary sac is an air chamber with a plastic memory," Polino explained, "and that's why Paul gave it the name 'siren.'"

Freda took the tulip from his hand and looked down into the bloom. It was a male, all stamen and no stigma. "This plant is heterosexual," she said.

5

"Completely so," Polino agreed. "I'm carrying the female next to my heart."

Astonished, she glanced at the female. There was a vestigial stigma at the lip of the oviduct, but no stamen at all. For her the air chamber had become merely an oddity. The two plants had achieved a stage of heterosexuality which put them eons ahead of their terrestrial cousins.

"Are you returning to the base with the rest of us?" Polino asked.

"No, Hal. Paul and I had a luncheon date with the Commodore, and I plan to keep it."

"I have a package for you in my gear which includes a letter. Paul wanted me to hold it until after the briefing, because he wants you to see the briefing first. Besides, he gave me twenty dollars to take you to dinner tonight. There's a postscript to the letter he wants me to give to you verbally, because he's afraid if you read it cold, without my persuasiveness, you'd think he flipped his lid."

"We'll discuss that after the briefing," Freda said brusquely. "Meanwhile, you take the female tulip to my office, in greenhouse five, and hang it. I'll bring the male tulip."

It was an order from a superior, and Polino recognized it as such. "Yes, ma'am," he said, and turned toward the bus ramp.

She had been angered by Paul's presumption in virtually ordering her to dine with a mere assistant, particularly with one who used such expressions as "flipped his lid" and called his administrative superior a "lucky stiff," and she had been abrupt with the student. Walking toward the elevator, she felt a tinge of remorse which she recognized as a feminine weakness. When Polino turned away, his sad brown eyes had reminded her of her childhood's only pet, a cocker spaniel which had died while still a puppy.

In the elevator her anger softened in the presence of Paul's gift. The tulip was adorable, and if she judged Paul's behavior without rancor, she had to admit that he had acted intelligently when he suggested dinner with Polino. On twenty dollars the student would be compelled to take her to some obscure restaurant in the Italian section of Fresno where it was unlikely she would be seen dining with him. As Paul well knew, Doctor Gaynor, Chief of the Bureau of Exotic Plants, disapproved of management fraternizing with lower-echelon personnel, even when such personnel were graduate botanical students attached to the Bureau. Doctor Gaynor would particularly disapprove of a female department head dining with Hal Polino.

Although Hal Polino was handsome and Italian, his major faults were lack of methodology, irreverence toward authority, and odd enthusiasms, particularly his interest in twentieth-century folkways. He played dissonant jazz on a guitar, wore a plaid cap when he drove; and, Paul had told her, Polino's "pad" held fewer professional journals than it did the philosophical works of Ayn Rand, William James, and Hugh Hefner. In her official capacity as Administrative Director of the Cystological Section of the Bureau of Exotic Plants, Department of Agriculture, Freda was called upon to make value judgments as an administrator as well as a scientist. In both capacities she was in full agreement on Hal Polino, despite Paul's regard for the boy. Polino was certainly not junior-executive material; in fact, she doubted if Hal Polino would ever have a name plate on his desk.

As she stepped from the elevator and strode across the rotunda toward the officers' mess, she was wondering so strongly why Paul had entrusted a message to his student assistant that she was beginning to suspect a plot: Hal Polino might have invented the entire stratagem simply in order to date her and enhance his prestige as a "Latin lover" in the eyes of other students. The idea was worth further analysis, she thought, staring down the beginning leer of a sailor who approached down the corridor.

As he passed, an air current created by the sailor's passage in the corridor played against the tulip's air chamber. Suddenly it emitted, low but piercing, a wolf whistle. She heard the sailor stop behind her, sensed him staring in disbelief, and she distinctly heard him mutter, "By the fondling flares of Orion!"

Freda was happy that the sailor could not see the grin which

7

came to her face. He would have accepted it as a further invitation and, once the word was passed, she would be fighting off landing parties from the naval contingent attached to the station.

Commodore Minor was sympathetic over Paul's absence and amused by her anecdote on the tulip and the sailor, but Captain Barron, who had joined them for lunch, was depressed. Two of his ratings had jumped ship on Flora. "Both ten-year men with families on earth," he commented in amazement. "We expect to lose a few apprentices who bluff their way past Navy psychologists and join the Navy with the intention of getting off earth."

"That would take a rather high order of intelligence, I imagine," Freda said.

"Most of the deserters are eggheads," the Captain commented, "who haven't the guts to compete in a technological society."

Commodore Minor whistled the first four bars of "Anchors Aweigh" into the tulip's air chamber and fanned it with his hand, and the tulip responded with the same four notes. "Try him again, Commodore, and let's see if I can harmonize."

Singing to the tulip's whistle perked the Captain up slightly, but his problem still gnawed.

"I can't blame the boys. We've forgotten what pure silence is like on earth. It's a pleasure to hear nothing but the sough of wind through trees or to look up at night and really see the stars, but now I'll have to organize a search-and-seizure party for the Charlie Section. We can't use heat tracers. The trees give off as much body heat as animals. Even probabilities based on the deserters' profiles are out. One of them was a chief computer's mate who knows how the brain operates."

"Have you thought of bloodhounds, Captain?" Freda asked.

"Freda, that's the first usable suggestion I've had!"

"Freda has a beautiful I.Q., also," the Commodore said.

"What gripes me," Captain Barron said, "is that this breach of discipline will put Flora off limits, and I wanted to recommend the planet for Navy Rest and Recreation."

"If Paul Theaston breaches discipline, Freda," the Commodore said, "I'm putting my chit in as a substitute for the deserter."

8

"Flora isn't that attractive," the Captain demurred.

Freda appreciated their banter, but she wanted to set the record straight. "We scientists have a different discipline from the military, gentlemen. To us, Flora is an object, not a subject. We are as indifferent as a surgeon would be to the body of a beautiful woman he was operating on."

"Now, Freda, I'm sure Paul didn't feed your profile to a computer before he proposed, so he's not completely indifferent to beauty. He even timed the flower to arrive during its blooming period."

Age had not weakened the Commodore's perceptiveness. She chided herself that she had not been first to recognize Paul's consideration, and she, too, was sure that he had not fed her profile to a computer. She had not matched her profile with his, either, although she had secretly matched his with someone else's —proving a compatibility which had assured her "Yes" to his proposal.

With relief, she welcomed Captain Barron's remark, "But the blooms are permanent on the flowers of Flora."

Analyzing her sense of relief, Freda reasoned that remorse was allied to fear, and fear was allied to doubt. Somehow Captain Barron's words restored her belief in Paul's insensitivity, which bolstered her confidence that he would never defect from earth to the planet Flora.

After Doctor Gaynor, in his official capacity as Bureau Chief, had welcomed the audience to the briefing, and after Doctor Hector had commenced with the films taken on the planet, Captain Barron's remark kept running through Freda's mind. If the blooms were permanent on the flowers of Flora, were the plants pollinated even as they were germinating? There was a logic to plant fertilization: a permanent bloom deviated from that logic as completely as human behavior on earth deviated from the logic of the reproduction patterns of other animals. She had to force herself to concentrate on Doctor Hector's voice.

Concentrating on Hector's voice was difficult. "Oohs" and

"Ahs" arose from the audience when a new scene flashed on the screen, and the photography was distracting. Colors were far too exaggerated, either from poor camerawork or the quality of Flora's sunlight. Freda suspected the former. The cameraman was running amok. He would sweep a full circle around the horizon to show the parklike landscape, tilt the camera up to catch a cloudscape, swing down to a grove of trees lining some valley brook in the distance, then zoom in to focus on a particular tree bole, as if conducting a seminar in the texture of tree bark. He did not show details of flowers, he composed still lifes of flower arrangements, shooting the same bed four or five times from different angles. His alternation of panoramic sweeps with static pauses was enough to give one a headache, and she made a note to herself to ask questions from the floor concerning camerawork at the next administrative meeting. She was not one to quibble with other departments, but Personnel should be restrained from employing cameramen who were obviously refugees from underground movie productions.

But she was too tactful to raise a question about her strangest and strongest distraction—Doctor Hector himself. In the classroom, his voice rustled with a flow of data so precise, valid, and constant that, when studying under him, she had developed the agility of her writing hand by taking notes. Now his remarks were as passionate and as irrelevant as a lover's. When she found a fact in the flow of his poetry, she pounced on it.

One fact came with startling abruptness during a peroration on swimming in the streams of Flora. ". . . floating down those tunnels of green lined by gray colonnades of boles, or trailing a phosphorescent wake at night, somehow renews the innocence of boyhood, its joys amplified by the dreariness of the years between, and with no bees to sting one's bare behind. There are no insects on Flora."

His remark shook her. If there were no insects, why did blooms exist at all? Why a visual lure for pollinators that didn't exist? Of course, she would find out from the seminars given by specialists during the following week, but she liked to establish her guidelines during the briefing. Hector was exasperating with all his fury and no sound data. Obviously the blooms were lures, but for what? Apparently for the members of Project Able, she thought ruefully, since they had inspired such poetry and camera art. Flora had sex appeal.

"A perfectly balanced plant ecology," Hector was saying. "Absolutely no menace to life. You can't fall down and break a bone: the turf's too springy. You can't starve: the berries, fruits, and nuts ripen continuously. An acid quality of the grass hastens decay, so the lawns are never littered. Since the axis tilt is slight, the climate is constant and there is no need for clothes in the temperate zones. There are no beasts of prey, no animals at all, in fact, save the one tropical spot on the globe, an island we named Tropica, where we will now go to join Paul Theaston."

Freda was happy to flee the camp and its poetry to the nononsense comments of her fiancé. Paul would give her facts, she knew. Her pet name for him was "The Prince of Pragmatism."

Getting to Tropica proved another problem in cinematics. In a helicopter approaching low over the ocean, the cameraman shot interminable footage from the moment the island's sixteen-thousand-foot peak, snowcapped and trailing clouds, rose beyond the horizon. Project Able's geologist, sounding awed, explained the tiered formation as they neared the island: a coral reef had formed around a volcano, and, at intervals of epochs, succeeding upheavals had lifted succeeding coral reefs, one above the other, to form a seven-storied mountain. Now its layers supported the parent cone, which soared eight thousand feet above the topmost plateau. Tropica was colorful, Freda admitted. With coral escarpments surrounding terraces covered with growth, it was pink and green topped by white above the blue sea.

She had found the design for her wedding cake!

As she expected, Paul let his camera do most of the talking. Her tulips were on the lowest level, and Paul had set up a sound-and-motion-activated camera to study a female tulip's pollination, germination, and seeding. His only preparatory remark, apart from pure explanation, was simply, "What follows is the most remarkable example of plant-animal symbiosis I have ever encountered."

Even that was an understatement. As the sound recorder focused on the flutings, sighings, and cluckings normal to the tulip, Paul remarked, "As nectar clogs the seed duct, the tones change." She listened, noting that he had underexposed the color of the tulips to avoid distracting attention from the process itself, and she heard a distinct tone change. The sounds in general grew higher-pitched, more melodious, although the lower notes gained huskiness.

Now the tulip was trilling in the breezes, piercing the air with beckonings so enchanting and resonant that she cupped her ear and leaned forward, fearing lest she miss a nuance or intonation. Then . . . some oafish enlisted man whistled a wolf's call, and laughter broke the spell.

Her vexation subsided when a furred animal bounced onto the screen, a shrewlike creature, roly-poly in its plumpness, with a face which bore the wide-eyed innocence of a koala bear. "I've named this the koala-shrew," Paul said, as the animal, no larger and more attractive than a kitten, sat back on its haunches, its forepaws quivering, to listen. A breeze stirred the air chamber of the tulip, sounding a note sensual in its urgency and its invitation. Bouncing and tumbling, the koala-shrew scampered to the source of the sound. In a movement so deft and gentle it was dainty, the tiny forepaws reached up to bend the bloom downward. The koala-shrew snuggled its face closer to the beckoning flower, and a serpent's forked tongue flicked out and slithered into the bloom of the plant.

When Paul replayed the process of pollination in slow motion, Freda averted her gaze from the screen. She felt she had witnessed a violation, and the faces in the darkness around her substantiated the feeling. They were leaning forward with the avidity of lewdness, like so many voyeurs in the shadows.

Later she watched as the seeds germinated and were expelled from the sac of the plant, to glide and loop for distances of forty feet, according to Paul. "They must strike the ground with enough force to penetrate the turf," he added, "or the acid in the grass will destroy them."

Freda was happy to get to the higher levels, where the orchids grew, some as tall as eight feet. The heavy, straight stalks were not characteristic of their terrestrial cousins, but the flowers and tendrillike branches were unmistakably and exquisitely those of orchids.

In the beginning, Paul's lecture on the orchids was straightforward, without the continental rhapsodizing, although he skirted the edges of propriety with one observation that brought titters from members of the audience who grasped his meaning. "This is a segregated plant society. The female root system demands a growing radius of at least four feet from the stalk, so the males are relegated to the outer circles in less desirable growing areas. The bifurcated root system of the males demands less growing room, and an inspection of the system reveals tubular appendages, which reveals that the ancients used scientific precision when they named the plants 'orchis.'"

When Paul entered the female groves, he pulled aside the tendrils to reveal a hiplike swelling on the stalk of the plant, approximately one-third of its height from the ground. "As Boyle remarked, it's difficult for an orchidologist to refrain from comparing orchids with the animal kingdom. What you see here is a seed pod, but the cellular striations around this portion of the stalk suggest muscular tissue. A single seed at a time is germinated, and all births are Caesarean.

"I've not been able to determine how pollination occurs. On the mainland, seed-feeding birds and air currents do the job." (Ah, there is the answer, Freda thought.) "But here the birds avoid the orchids, and the pollen nectar cannot be airborne. I am extending my tour of duty to determine how pollination occurs.

"I have named this species 'hipped orchids,' but there is another enchanting aspect to these flowers. When the girls are ready to be courted, the nectar makes them hang their heads and blush from shyness. Observe Sally." He reached up and pulled the flower down to the level of his own head, watching as the nacrelike shimmering of the orchid gradually diffused into pink.

"Oohs" and "Ahs" and spontaneous applause broke from the audience as the house lights went up. Freda arose and walked down the aisle, disturbed and pondering. Paul had not reached up and grabbed the stalk of the flower in his palm merely to lower it. He had cupped his hand around behind the stalk and drawn it down to his shoulder, in the manner of a man drawing a girl's head down.

Preoccupied, Freda forced a smile when Hal Polino came over with a manila envelope. "Here are Paul's notes on the Caron Siren tulip, Doctor, and his mash note to you. As I mentioned, there is a lengthy postscript he wanted me to add verbally."

"What is it?" she asked.

"You're supposed to read the letter first. The postscript is the reason for Paul buying our dinner. He doesn't want the conversation overheard by technical people."

"Then drop by the greenhouse later and pocket the money. . . . By the way"—she added a sentence quickly to show her goodwill—"I want to thank you, Hal, for hanging the tulip."

"No strain. No pain. The temperature in the glasshouse is almost the optimum for the tulips, so the plant is safe. . . . But, Doctor, no dinner, no message."

His eyes were not pleading now, but confident.

"Very well, you Valentino of the working girl, but don't let the rumor that I whistled at a passing sailor get you started in the wrong direction. It was the tulip who whistled, not I."

"Oh, hell," he exploded, clapping a hand to his forehead. "I should have known the scuttlebutt was wrong. I should have known Galatea was impervious to mortal longings."

Almost laughing at Hal's fallen crest, she said, "I'll be ready at seven," and walked across the lawn toward the distant greenhouse, recalling that she had referred to the tulip as "who." Some of the insanity of Flora must have communicated itself to her during the briefings.

In a mild way, she had been touched by Hal Polino. Before he learned the truth about the whistle, his expression had been similar to Paul's when Paul looked at the orchid he called Sally.

Paul had not inspected the blossom with the eyes of an empirical scientist; he had ogled it with the longing of a lovesick adolescent.

Chapter Two

PAUL'S LETTER WAS BY NO MEANS THE "MASH NOTE" OF HAL'S peculiar vernacular, nor had Freda expected one. She would not have elicited a proposal of marriage from a sentimentalist lacking restraint and self-control. She had seen one marriage wrecked from rampant emotionalism born of sensuality. Pulling the bit on an overeager stallion was not her ideal of romance. She was pleased with the formality of Paul's opening paragraphs.

> My dearest Freda,
>
> Enclosed are my notes on the *Tulipa caronus sireni*. By now you have seen the briefing and understand my reasons for accepting a second tour of duty, but not *all* of the reasons.
>
> Hal will brief you on what I choose to call Hypothesis X, concerning the pollination of the orchids of Flora. Hal himself suggested it in one of his fanciful moments, but I support it for reasons of my own. I dare not put the hypothesis onto paper. If the paper were lost or stolen, it would be sufficient evidence to send me to Houston, permanently.
>
> Hal Polino does not have the bookkeeper's mind which the methodology of science requires . . .

"Bookkeeper's mind!" She liked that! If the accurate tabulation of scientific data deserved such gratuitous dismissal, then Doctor Freda Caron was wasting her time outside a kitchen.

> . . . nor does he have the power of analysis, the genius for synthesis, to compare with a Freda Caron, if this "cat" may comment on a queen. Yet, when his whimsies drift in the right direction, Hal is capable of inspired suggestions.

16

Now she saw what Paul meant. Mere accumulation of data *could* be tedious, particularly when one could not foresee directions. But she disapproved of his use of Hal's argot, even facetiously, since it suggested student influence over the teacher.

But there is empirical evidence to substantiate Hypothesis X: tendrils grow from the hipped orchids in pairs, on opposite sides of the stalk, and the leaves along the tendrils are of the same striated cellular structure as that of the female hips—muscle cells. In addition, the tendrils of the male, as well as the stalk, are much thicker than the female's.

You can see immediately that the project needs a cystologist. If you wish to delay our wedding and come with Section Charlie to Flora, you have my consent and blessing. . . . Incidentally, if you need my advice on wedding plans, feed my profile to the computer and get my decision by proxy.

Back to the orchids. You have, by now, inspected the tulips and know these plants are aeons ahead of their earth cousins in evolution. Mark you, the beauty of the tulips is but a shadow of the beauty of the orchids.

Each orchid in the segment of the grove I have chosen to study has its own personality. They are lovable. Sometimes the wind blows a tendril across my face in a certain way, and I am intrigued by the thought that they are capable of loving me.

There was no doubt about it! Hal Polino had inveigled Paul to read outside of his field, perhaps even poetry.

But this thought is purely intuitive and less than supported by evidence. Birds shun the groves, and a basket of koala-shrews I loosed among the orchids ran squealing in terror over the edge of the escarpment and fell to their deaths, over a thousand feet below.

17

Probably, Freda thought, the koala-shrews were fleeing from the pressure on their eardrums caused by the increased altitude.

I had brought the shrews as an experiment. With my limited laboratory facilities, I believe I have detected hemoglobin in the sap of the orchids. Are the plants, then, carnivorous . . .

It would be easy to detect if the plants were meat eaters—feed them radioactive beefsteak and trace the hemoglobin.

. . . or so highly developed along lines of evolution that they are part animal? If the latter is true, then it would directly support Hypothesis X.

Frankly, there is a logic here, beyond human logic. A question which on earth might seem sacrilege comes easily to the lips on Flora: is the goal of life the superman or the superplant? It is written, "God is no respecter of persons," but He certainly respects species.

Freda smiled ruefully. Paul *had* been reading outside of his field.

Our heliologist says that the sun here is much older than the sun of earth. Flora is in her death throes. If I were Evolution, seeking a life form to survive the contraction and explosions of the universe, I would choose a seed. Incidentally, the orchid seed I have enclosed is the only one I have been able to find, and it is partially eaten by the grass.

She was positive now. These speculations were alien shoots grafted onto Paul's stalk by Hal Polino. Paul would have to be rid of this influence. At tomorrow's conference, she would suggest a quarterly rotation of students—to broaden their academic backgrounds—and the present quarter ended next week.

18

But the great mystery was, and still is, how do the orchids pollinate? Sometimes I feel that they are deliberately concealing their secrets from me.

Whatever Hypothesis X might be, Freda thought, Paul had already revealed enough to get himself committed to Houston!

I have thrown nets over females in estrus . . .

Ah, there was the Freudian slip to end all slips. Flowers in estrus!

> . . . only to find the nets torn aside. I have strung nets for night-flying birds and caught nothing. I have dug pits deep enough to trap cattle and covered them with the living grass, but I have captured no animal. Whatever the pollinators are, they have vision, for the orchids are so beautiful that they expand human awareness. Whatever the pollinators have, they have olfactory organs, for the female orchids exude a perfume so enchanting that if I could bottle it and ship it home it would devastate the ecology of earth in nine months. And the pollinators must have intelligence, for I have come to a flowering garden—a virtual Eden—with the equipment of a technological society, and still the question abides.
>
> What are the pollinators of Eden?
>
> Love,
> Paul

An interesting letter. But Freda could see behind Paul's open-faced, Anglo-Saxon scrawl the fine Italian penmanship of Harold Polino. She laid it aside and picked up the packet of tulip seeds plus the carefully wrapped but tattered orchid seed, which resembled a partially husked black walnut.

Freda deduced that the seed had been much larger—at least as wide around the girth as a tennis ball—and ovate. Despite the wrapping, it exuded the faint odor of vanilla, and she recalled that vanilla was processed from orchid seeds. Possibly a grove of Florian orchids on earth would be of commercial value to a manufacturer of food flavoring.

She placed the remnant of the orchid seed in the refrigerator and returned to Paul's field notes on the Caron tulips.

One item intrigued her. "Plant the seeds six inches apart, and as soon as the tulip's sex is determined, separate the males by at least three feet. Apparently their root systems drain some element from the soil, for they do not thrive in close proximity with each other. Spot them among the females." In this respect, she noted, the tulips were opposite from the orchids.

Automatically she began to record his data into a logbook. As she wrote, she was aware of sounds—the drone of a jet plane, the hum of traffic drifting up from the Paso Robles Freeway, the distant whirr of her air-conditioner. She was reminded of Captain Barron's admiration of the silence of Flora. His feeling was probably related to the Freudian wish to return to the womb, which was probably a misinterpretation on Freud's part of a racial instinct from prehistoric days, the desire of the caveman to scramble back to the safety of the cave. But progress was outside the cave, where the sunlight and the strange noises were.

Personally, she loved the sounds of civilization. For her, society hummed as pleasantly as a dynamo, and she was proud to be a part of its machinery.

An evening breeze stirred, and behind her the female tulip laughed. Freda smiled at its imitation of her laughter at the spaceport, for the sound was joyful, and she entered into the log, "Plastic memory of female specimen exceeds five hours."

She closed the door—temperatures dropped rapidly with the declining sun—and walked over to type the label for the logbook. She typed, "*Tulipa caronus,*" and halted, thinking: In the classical sense, the siren was a sweet singer, but time had warped the connotations of the word. She was not a vamp who lured men to their deaths; if they chose to die of frustration, she might aid and abet, but the decision was their own.

She decided to drop the term "siren" from her tulips. Paul had grown a little fanciful on Flora. His major influence had been Polino, but the planet had furnished the environment. As she pasted the label on the logbook, she was grateful that the Space Administration permitted no more than two tours of duty on an unclassified planet.

Even with two tours behind him, she wouldn't be surprised if Paul Theaston returned wearing long hair and strumming a lyre.

She carried the female plant to the photo table, poured plant dye into the loam around its roots, and set the fluoro camera for five-minute exposures. She had two hours before Hal Polino called for her, time enough to check the plant's rate of osmosis.

She cut a blade from its lower stalk, and the movement of her hands caused the tulip to sigh deliciously.

Under her electron microscope, the leaf pattern showed no difference from that of its terrestrial cousin, although she compared the blades only in her memory. The veinlike pattern of osmosis ducts appeared the same to her casual inspection, but the feel of the blade in her fingertips was more rubbery than that of an earth tulip.

Ordinarily Freda would have preferred to eat a sandwich and spend the evening with the tulips, but Hypothesis X had aroused her curiosity. She was looking forward to dinner with Polino. It was against her sense of justice to condemn Paul's assistant for exercising undue influence without a trial, so she would try him first. She bent to the tulip and said, "Good night, dear one."

As she opened the door to leave the room, the tulip answered, "Good night, dear one."

She smiled as she closed the door, thinking there was also a matter of name-calling she wanted to settle with Polino. To her the word "Galatea" sounded suspiciously like Italian for "jelly-fish."

As Freda showered, she caught herself humming a currently popular revival of a folk song, "Sock It to Me, Baby," and her voice dwindled into a self-conscious silence, more from wonder at herself than from the ribaldry of the tune. Rarely had she felt so exuberant, and her happiness disturbed her.

A moment's analysis told her what prompted the caroling: an afterimage of the Caron tulip was casting a golden light through her mind. "A thing of beauty is a joy forever," somebody had said, and for the past quarter hour the saying had proved to be true.

As she prepared her toilet, spending less than five minutes on her makeup, the laughter of the tulip kept returning to her, pleasantly at first. After she slipped into her green cocktail dress and stretched on her bed to relax a few minutes, the memory of its laughter touched her with sadness. She submitted her changed reaction to analysis: when Polino had met her at the spaceport, she was anxious about Paul and disappointed over his absence. When she laughed at the male tulip's wolf whistle, her laughter had been a release of tension as well as a reflection of merriment. This afternoon all the anxiety had been filtered from the tulip's imitation, and she had heard herself laughing as a child, as she had before her parents had divorced. She had not laughed with such spontaneity since she was ten, and her sadness had been a nostalgia for the lost innocence of childhood.

She had tidied her emotional closets when Hal called for her in the afterglow of sunset, and she could appreciate the sincerity in his voice when he said, "In your dress of green with your hair of gold, Doctor, you're as fetching as a Caron tulip."

She smiled in spite of herself and said, "Save your apple-polishing for the senoritas in Old Town. Here, hold my wrap!"

"May I call you Freda, Doctor Caron, because I didn't come prepared for a formal dinner?"

She didn't approve of first names between department heads and graduate students, although the practice was general, but she didn't wish for him to be inhibited tonight. She preferred that he behave around her in much the same manner as he acted with Paul. "You may call me 'Freda' after we get off the station. And I'm glad you're not prepared for formalities tonight, because

I have some heavy labor for you. We'll stop by the greenhouse and hang the female tulip I am fluorographing."

As they walked along the flagstone path to her office, he said, "I was able to get reservations at the Napoli."

"The Napoli!" Indeed he had chosen a restaurant where they would not be seen by station personnel—it was too expensive. "Twenty dollars won't cover the tip at the Napoli, Hal. We'll go dutch."

"No, ma'am," he said firmly. "There was once a kitty in the students' dorm. For three years it sat there, growing with each quarter of the school year, waiting for the first student to take you out on a date. Tonight I walked off with it."

"You have won a bet on me?"

"Not without an argument. Some claimed unfair tactics, since they knew you wanted to hear about Paul—Doctor Theaston— but I convinced them it was my Italian charm. However, there were bylaws adopted when the pool was formed. The winner had to promise a blow-by-blow description of his night with you in a motel."

"You know very well there'll be no motel."

"Right," he agreed. "But they'll get the description they paid for. So, as long as your reputation's ruined anyway, you may as well relax and enjoy the whole evening."

As he opened the door for her, she said with feigned indignation, "You're not trapping me with your specious logic. . . . Look, Hal!"

He had flipped on the lights, and her first glance revealed that the female tulip was dead. It had fallen toward the fluoro screen, spewing its seeds as it fell. Some had struck the fluoro screen, but most of the tiny black seeds trailed across the white linoleum.

"It *fell* dead," Hal said.

"Gather the seeds, Hal, and put the corpse in the freezer. I want to look at the fluoro prints."

"Done in by plant dye," Hal said sadly as he picked up the

seeds, "after less than a day on earth. I always said this was a tough world."

Freda removed the roll of prints from the camera and took them to her desk. The last pictures, taken before the plant collapsed, showed a network veinal system outlined by the fluoro screen. The lines were not osmotic channels, because they had resisted the stain. The system rose upward from the base, spread outward along the branches, and joined in a cloudy nexus beneath the air chamber, diverged again, and rose upward.

"I counted thirty seeds," Hal said, placing them in a humidor on her desk.

"There should be thirty-two. But I'll find the missing pair in the morning. Put the corpse in the freezer; I'll take it over to the lab tomorrow."

Behind her, Hal lifted the pot and bore it toward the refrigerator, moving with stateliness, softly chanting a Te Deum.

"Quit the clowning," she said. "You make me feel like a murderess."

Hal slammed the refrigerator door and turned back to her. "What's your theory, Doctor? Plant stain shouldn't kill a flower."

"I have no theory, but the likely place to look is in the tulip's cellular structure. It has a network, here, that resembles veins."

He looked down. "Or a nervous system with a ganglion. . . . Let's go, Doctor. We might lose our reservation."

As they turned to go, Freda looked at the male tulip for a long moment before she switched off the light. "If there's any way this flower can be adapted to earth, I'm going to find it. The Caron tulip will be the heritage I leave for future Theastons."

"Sometimes, Doctor Caron, you sound as much like a woman in love as a plant scientist."

When they passed through the gateway onto the parking lot, Hal said, "Now, Freda, you're technically off base."

"I'll concede the parking lot— But look at all the cars. After four months away, you'd think the bachelors of Section Able would be on the town."

"After a man has said good-bye forever to a woman he has

loved, it takes him at least a week to get back into the mood for chasing flippers."

"What's a flipper?"

"It's a twentieth-century term for girls who flirt. Derives from the word 'flippertogibbet,' meaning fool around with a flipper and she'll have you hanging from the gibbet of marriage."

"Don't you find it a waste of time, digging up all these oddities?"

"Now you're being Doctor Caron . . . Freda would only be pleased that she's being taken out despite her escort's memories of Flora."

"Thanks for the compliment, then, Hal," she said as he held the car door open for her.

After he seated her, he went around and got into the driver's seat, arching back to reach into his pocket for the car keys. He should have taken the keys from his pocket before he got into the car, she thought, but she held her tongue. Tonight she was plain Freda.

"Ordinarily," he apologized, "when I get into a small car with a beautiful woman, I have the instincts of an octopus, but out of respect to the memory of my late friend and mentor and your fiancé, Paul Theaston, I intend to conduct myself with propriety. It's my way of putting in my chit for the job of sideboy since Paul has defected to Flora."

"You aren't really serious?"

"He *could* be seduced. He's a specialist, and they're like monks, carrying a cross of innocence to the Calvary of womanhood. Flora's a female planet. You heard Doctor Hector babbling. What's a lady of sweet silences to an inexperienced man would be a dumb broad to me. . . . I can speak freely around you, Freda. Your intelligence is attested by computers."

"Thanks, boy."

"Knowing females, I landed on Flora like a karate expert walks onto a mat. But, seriously, I think Paul's safe. He has no weaknesses, and he has you."

"Thanks, boy."

25

His voice sank to a low, husky whisper as his arm snaked across the seat behind her. "Strange evils lurk in the colors of Flora. I know, for I'm a Green Hornet."

"Down, boy," she said, moving away. "Now, tell me, Green Hornet, what's a Galatea?"

"Galatea was a statue so beautiful her sculptor fell in love with her, and his love gave her life. But Venus de Milo was jealous and got Galatea stoned—"

"Oh, that's Greek mythology. You're Italian."

"Rome conquered Greece. Anything a Greek can do, Italians can do better."

"Another question. What's this Hypothesis X Paul tells me about?"

His features, visible now in the neon glare of downtown Fresno, grew serious. "You aren't ready for that idea, Freda. I want you to fungo a few easy ideas first, to get your mind limbered up. Hypothesis X is a high and inside fast ball that could low-bridge Einstein."

Freda had no intention of conducting a study of the comparative abilities of Greeks versus Italians, but she conceded the laurels to the Italians in the matter of obtaining reservations at Italian restaurants. They were conducted to a window table by a phalanx of centurions, seated to rest by an extremely unctuous maître d', and presented with a view of the lights of Fresno twinkling forty floors below and stretching as far south as the topmost towers of Bakersfield, whose lights were visible beyond the horizon. Even so, her attention was drawn away by the wine-pouring of a waiter who must have learned his trade conducting the Milan Symphony Orchestra. When Freda commented on the camaraderie of paisanos, Hal dismissed her admiration. "A Swede could do it the way I did it. How do you like the wine?"

"Exquisite. How did you leave Paul?"

"Buck naked in a breeze from a helicopter. I didn't get to work with him on Tropica because Hector assigned me to the continent after I helped Paul set up camp. After that, I only saw him twice, once to pick up soil samples and once to pick up your package. That soil, by the way, is loaded with rare earths. Some of the plants glow for a while after sunset, and on my second visit I mentioned that if the plants could emit light, they could possibly receive it. Personally I knew of maple trees with a psychic lure, but Paul jumped on my idea of light reception. By then, he was hung up on the pollination bit, and he figured the orchid blooms could be visual lures for other orchids."

"But it wouldn't explain the fragrance," Freda said.

"There is none. Just a musky odor. . . . More wine?"

"Please."

As Hal poured, she was remembering Paul's lines, ". . . the female orchids exude a perfume so enchanting . . . it would devastate the ecology of earth in nine months." If Hal spoke the truth, and he should have no reason to lie, his remark meant that he had not seen the female orchids. Casually she asked, "Where did you talk to Paul when you landed?"

"Usually by the helicopter. We landed on a stretch of bare coral near the edge of the escarpment."

"Did you ever go back into the groves with Paul?"

"Never did. As a matter of fact, I once accused him of having a still back in the groves. He said they all looked alike. See one orchid, you've seen them all, he said. Besides, he liked the view from the escarpment, and it *was* impressive. A thousand feet, straight down, and across the terrace, about three miles, rose another escarpment, this one about six hundred feet."

Hal paused as bowls of minestrone were wafted before them. She sipped the soup, thinking: If Hal spent only an hour at a time with Paul, he could not have exerted a tremendously erratic influence on his teacher. Hal was bent in benediction over the soup, which was delicious, and suddenly he raised his head. "Why did you ask if Paul ever took me back into the groves?"

"Oh, I'm just generally interested. You were saying something about maple trees."

"Oh, yes!" He grinned. "You know, psychologists have a theory about something called abreaction, where a fellow works out his fears in his behavior. They say that a man such as I am, who appreciates women—"

"Like a karate expert walking onto a mat," she interrupted him, partly as Freda, from sheer impishness, and partly as Doctor Caron, to point out the inconsistencies of thought.

"Touché," he almost shouted in glee, waving his soup spoon in his right hand and reaching out impulsively to take her hand with his free one. "All joking aside, there's two of you—Freda, warm and witty, and Doctor Caron, the authoritative perfectionist. Never desert Doctor Caron, Freda, for she will carry you to the heights of policymaking, and her advice is needed in the halls of the mighty, but never forget Freda, Doctor Caron, because she's a lot more fun."

He withdrew his hand. Such a pretty, impulsive speech, she thought; and he was sincere. But, judiciously, she was not affected by his charm: the more attractive Hal was, the more subversive Polino was.

"Anyway, the theory holds that a great lover is actually a latent homosexual, which is about as sensible as saying that you became a botanist cause you subconsciously wanted to practice animal husbandry."

A mere graduate student daring to attack an entire science, Doctor Caron thought; but, to Freda, he made sense. She listened closely, disapproving of the way he waved his spoon for emphasis. Bad table manners indicated a lack of restraint.

"Back on the continent," he continued, "I used to go up to a grove of maple trees once in a while to read. All those dancing daffodils can get distracting, and the grove gave me a quiet place. There's nothing sexual about a tree. Even on Flora they're hermaphroditic."

Ah, there was the source of Paul's flowers in "estrus."

". . . After a week in the sanctuary, I began to favor a particular tree. This is normal! You've had a favorite tree . . ."

Indeed she had, Freda thought. There had been an elm grove she had fled to for comfort and solitude, as a girl, when her parents' quarrels had risen to hysteria. She would always love elm trees.

"In the beginning, I thought nothing of it. It was comfortable to sit between its roots and lean back against its bole. It was just a tree tree." He paused for a moment; a dreaminess came into his eyes. "But it *was* beautiful, in a masculine way. Strong-limbed, sturdy. It was the sort of tree that a blue jay would trust.

"One day I was sitting under my tree reading, when a naval rating wandered by. None of us wore clothes, but I could tell he was a navy man from the decal on his arm. He had come up to look for acorns. . . . They are large and edible on Flora . . . and he was cracking one between the heels of his palms as he wandered over to see what I was reading. He started to sit down on one of the roots of my tree, and I ordered him away. In very specific terms I told him what I'd do if a certain part of his body touched the tree. He walked away, looking back at me and saying, 'Okay, matey! *Okay!*' as if he knew I was squirrely."

"How interesting," Freda remarked as she forked into the lasagne the waiter placed before her. It was as light and as fluffy as a soufflé, without a hint of garlic, and the Chianti complemented it perfectly.

Hal shifted from a soup spoon to a fork and into high gear. "When it struck me that I would have killed the sailor for fooling around with my tree, I got scared and fled the grove, figuring I was ready for Hollywood. Later, thinking about it, I figured the headshrinkers were still wrong, but the point is—they scared me."

His fork beat like a metronome. "I had let the Freudians of earth defile my mind. I had dishonored the grove with my fear!"

"Mmmm, good! . . . I don't follow you," Freda said.

"What I mean, all that clings to a tree is not necessarily fruit, and I had felt—"

"You're right, Hal," she interjected, partly in agreement but mostly to break the rhythm of the fork, "nuts cling, also."

"What I felt with the maples was spiritual communion. That's all! The sailor's naked behind was desecrating my shrine, for, in rites beyond ritualism, I had achieved rapport with the spirit of the grove. Freda, you observe before you the last surviving druid priest."

She was observing that and more. "Logic beyond logic" was another airy phrase Paul had borrowed from this boy. Harold Polino was the moral equivalent of the Napoli's lasagne, she thought, but, as Paul had said, he did produce usable insights.

"Do you think Paul would be as impressionable?"

"No, Paul's a morphologist. He studies the structure of plants. He's not primarily interested in their spiritual qualities or their personalities. He might favor a certain orchid in a grove. So would you. So would I. On the scale of plant evolution, the orchids are demigods compared to the trees. I'm not saying he's completely indifferent to plants. But it would have to be a very dark night before old Paul would try to make love to a mandrake root."

"Eat your lasagne before it gets cold!"

Rebuffed by her tone, he withdrew into his lasagne, and she let him eat, slowly sipping her Chianti. She was drinking more, by far, than she usually drank, but it was not impairing her judgment. The wine only relaxed her, made her feel more open. When he was almost finished, she said, "If you think my mind is stretched sufficiently, I feel ready for Hypothesis X."

"Let me refill your glass," he said. "You'll need it."

"You're the doctor," she said curtly.

"Got your seat belt buckled, Freda?"

"Belt's buckled."

"All right, here comes Hypothesis X." He almost smirked as he pronounced his sentences slowly and carefully. "Your boy, Paul, believes the orchids are ambulatory. He's convinced that the male orchids do a little nocturnal woo-pitching. He thinks they walk by night."

Chapter Three

HAL'S GRIN COULD NOT CUSHION WORDS THAT KNOCKED THE EU-
phoria out of her.

All evening she had toyed with ideas, formed theories, framed
explanations, not a one of which would have earned her a merit
badge from the Girl Scouts; but what Polino suggested, she had
not even considered; her fiancé was a stark, raving lunatic!

"Did *you* give Paul that idea?"

"I can't claim full credit." He was actually modest. "But on my
last visit, Paul kept harping about pollination, and when he
showed me a bifurcated root system, I told him that if the sun
lived long enough, the orchids would grow feet. Paul launched
from that pad, I guess; but, believe me, Freda, I never thought
he'd take me seriously."

She knew Hal spoke the truth, not through observed evidence
but from a deeper knowledge contained as much within the
nerve ends of her body as the neurons of her brain—a knowledge
beyond knowledge. Hal's motives were clear to her now. This
marvelous boy had brought her here, beguiled her with tall
stories, teased, shocked, and delighted her, to fungo her emotions rather than her mind, to prepare her for this final shock.

Paul needed her on Flora!

Paul's offhand invitation for her to visit Tropica was a plea
for help.

Paul needs me, she thought. Wrong! Paul thinks he needs
me. What Paul really needs is institutional care. . . . He had
tried to hint to her in his letter that unless she came for him,
for him it was either Flora or Houston.

Any man with a shred of sanity left would prefer Flora to
Houston, so what was Paul worried about, if it weren't that

shred of sanity? Personally she preferred the sulfurous stench of the sunlit side of Venus to any spot you could name in Texas, but right now she wanted her euphoria back.

She shoved her empty glass toward Hal, pointed to the bottle, and said, "Kill it!"

"We'll split this one and order another."

"Then split it!"

He split it, and there was still enough left for two full glasses. In the manner of Italy, Hal said, they locked arms across the table and took a sip, bolstered on each other's stanchion, and Hal said, "Ciao!"

Still hooked to her arm, he added, "Your eyes are pools of blue water. I'd like to take off my clothes and dive in."

"I'll drink to that," she said, and did so, adding, "Chow chow!"

Her expression unhooked him. "What the hell's chow chow?"

"Chopped green tomatoes. But we're not here to discuss recipes. Paul needs our help. The problem is: how are we going to smuggle a maximum-care psychiatric ward to Flora without letting the National Space Agency know what we're up to?"

"He isn't crazy *yet*, Freda," Hal reassured her. "He's just beginning to flip. If he could solve the one problem—how the orchids pollinate—he might be as normal as you and me, unless the orchids *do* walk. Then we're crazy and he's sane, and he *could* be right."

"He wanted me to relieve him on Tropica," she pointed out.

"I couldn't think of a better place!" Hal said.

"If it weren't for our confounded wedding, I'd like to go to Flora. I think I could show Paul a thing or two about pollination."

"I don't know." Hal shook his head dubiously. "Paul's so damned pure. Why don't we both go to Flora and show him how it's pulled off?"

"No, Hal. You haven't got your Ph.D. yet, and Paul and I aren't married."

"In my circles, both of those problems are purely academic."

"But you don't understand, Hal. I'm a virgin."

32

"If you're bragging, I'll go along with your little joke. If you're complaining, I'd like to assure you that there's no conflict between sex and morality—one girl's defloration is another girl's efflorescence."

"You still don't understand, Hal. It's not ethics. My analyst tells me I have a deep-seated phobia for human contact."

"Freda, I hate to make generalities, but anything a psychiatrist tells you is probably moonshine. I can prove you have no such phobia. Drink that bottle of wine, and wait."

"No, we'll split it," she protested. "After all, you're driving."

Leaning back while Hal poured, her mind was acutely clear and functioning at the highest level. She knew, for instance, why Italian restaurants always had red-checked tablecloths: volatile Italians were always spilling their wine.

Considering the problem of the tulips with the omniscience she now owned, Freda realized that the vein patterns she had seen on the fluoro screen could have been exactly that. If so, the plants were little animals. Little animals had animal instincts. Paul said the tulip males mixed with the females. It might be possible to train the tulips to pollinate directly—stamen to oviduct—as the sun trained sunflowers to follow the sun. Her ideas needed refining, admittedly, but they sparked her with inspiration, and the course she must take lay suddenly as clear before her as the Great Circle route from Fresno to the Witwatersrand.

Lowering her voice, she leaned forward. "We've been assuming too much here, with too little information. I'm going to hand-pollinate those tulips, get me a bed started, and give them controlled opportunities to breed. If they could do it with koala-shrews on Flora, they can do it with Freda Caron on earth! Then, I'm going to insert their solution on a seven-foot level into the computers, and solve all of Paul's problems right here on earth. When he lands, I'm going to present him with a typed and bound thesis, *Methods of Pollination Used by the Orchids of Flora*. My thesis will serve two purposes—to restore his sanity and to show him who's the boss."

33

She was waving her fork at Hal, an act that indicated to her that she was coming under the influence of Chianti. "Dinner's over, Polino," she snapped. "Let's go."

Riding home with the top down diminished Freda's euphoria and restored her wariness. By the time he pulled the car up into the circle before the Bachelor Ladies' Quarters, she had readied a counteroperation to forestall Hal's Operation Anaconda.

When he inquired with a veiled threat, "Is it merely 'Good night, Doctor Caron,' or has Galatea come alive?" she answered promptly, "Keep your seat."

She slid out, snapped the door shut smartly, and swung around in front of the car to come and stand beside and above him. "First, you're not a Greek. You're a Latin, and Latins are lousy lovers. I don't say this from personal experience—I read the graffiti in the ladies' lounge. . . . Now, keep your hands beneath the dashboard."

Dazed, he followed her instructions. She reached down, clamped his head top and bottom, then bent and kissed him with a succulence that left him rigid with shock. Quickly she released him and said, "Good night."

He almost yelped, "Good night."

She ran up the steps, turned, and waved at the boy, who still sat dazed, and entered the building. She was amused at his reaction and amazed by her own. In a spirit of playfulness she had acted the wanton, but she had not expected to send him into adrenalin shock, and she had certainly not expected his shock waves to ripple back and shiver her own musculature.

Tomorrow she might regret her coltishness, but tonight she had given the lie to a psychiatrist who had once said, "Miss Caron, you abhor physical contact. This fits you ideally for the plant sciences; but it will make a marriage difficult for you, unless you find a man as austere and as self-disciplined as your father."

But maybe he had not lied, she reconsidered. Paul's profile had matched her father's precisely, and she was genuinely fond of Paul.

Smiling to herself, she brushed her teeth. She had discovered nothing about Hal Polino at the dinner that she didn't know already. She liked the boy, but he was a bad influence, and not merely on Paul's methodology. Another six months in the student's company might find Paul sneaking off to Old Town with the boy on field trips to prove there was no conflict between sex and morality. Hal Polino had been given his trial, he had been condemned, and her conscience was assuaged by judicial procedure. Crawling aboard her bed, Freda muttered aloud, "Hell, I didn't even violate his constitutional rights!"

After three cups of black coffee for breakfast, Freda went to her office and carried out two searches for the missing seeds. Her first search was logical, figured from the recalled trajectory of the other seeds and from the possibility of ricochets from the fluoro screen. Her second search was general, section by section of the floor, and Mr. Hokada, her field foreman, reporting for duty, found her on hands and knees. She rose to tell him she wanted the two acres between the greenhouse and the fence plowed and gave him the dead tulip to take to the laboratory for chemical analysis. The two seeds must have stuck to the bottoms of Polino's shoes, she concluded, as he retrieved their podmates.

Next she sat down and carefully phrased her recommendation that student assistants be rotated on a semester rather than a term basis. The reason: "To give them a broader and more general overall view of the interrelationships existing among and between the various departments of the Bureau of Exotic Plants, from an administrative point of view, and to achieve an in-depth awareness of the function of the plant sciences as an integral but distinct subphylum of the full spectrum of the biological sciences, their methodology, procedurology, and history in the development of the technological society, from an educational point of view."

That should rid Paul of Hal Polino! She was a success at the suggestion box, and most of her success, she felt, came from the clarity of her wording.

She wrote an additional memo suggesting that noise dampers be placed over compressors in the greenhouse air-conditioning units, since the noise was distracting. Doctor Gaynor had a tally sheet in his office which listed the number of contributions to the suggestion box, as well as the number acted on by management personnel. Freda habitually placed at least two suggestions in the suggestion box at each administrative meeting. Currently her name led all the rest in both number of suggestions submitted and in number acted upon by the Suggestion Box Committee.

All during her busy morning she had been sustained and soothed by the cluckings, cooings, and whistlings of the surviving tulip. When time for the meeting approached, she left for the administration hall with little remaining of her hangover except a throbbing in her temples and a tendency for the world to expand and contract slightly.

She stopped by her room to wiggle into her tailored jersey, the conservative dress Doctor Gaynor favored in female department heads—thinking an added advantage might accrue to her in the student-rotation program. It was possible that Suzuki Hayakawa might be assigned to her, and she could use Suzuki's deft hands in the cross-pollination program she planned for the tulips. It would be a task, if all sixty-two seeds germinated, but Japanese girls were docile, cheerful, and obedient. Her present student assistant, Mary Henderson, presently on term's-end leave, was not trustworthy. Mary was a girl who would plant marihuana in the alien daisy patch if supervision grew slack.

For Freda it was a morning of triumphs. Doctor Gaynor opened the administration session by listing the schedule for the week's seminars by resident specialists on their findings on Flora. Next, a procedural question was raised relating to a complaint from the San Joaquin Land Company regarding the control of pollen. During last fall's harvest, it had been discovered that pollen from an alien corn had crossed the fence into the San

Joaquin Land Company's cornfield, and the resulting hybrid had damaged their milling equipment. Freda rose to suggest that glycol carburetors be affixed to the nozzles of the irrigation spray to form a film over the Bureau's pollen to prevent it from being airborne. Her suggestion was so apt and prompt that it was greeted by applause and passed unanimously.

Next, during a lively discussion concerning the placement of refuse bins, Freda saw Doctor Gaynor's secretary walk to the podium and hand him a slip of paper. He glanced at it, then rapped for attention and rose to announce: "My secretary, Mrs. Weatherwax, after two years on a standby status, has finally handed me a suggestion that student assistants be rotated on a semester rather than a term basis. As long as this does not conflict with the continuing project, I consider this action eminently advisable. Heretofore, I have not installed the policy by directive. I wanted the suggestion to spring from my management team, to reassure me of your awareness that the Bureau functions not only as a research-and-development arm of the Department of Agriculture, but as an educational facility as well. I shall recommend to the Suggestion Box Committee that this suggestion be passed forthwith, to enable us to commence graduate-student rotation with commencement of the next semester. For this long-awaited recommendation, I wish to commend Doctor Freda Caron."

As the audience cast glances in her direction, Freda knew a rough morning was slipping into a sweet afternoon. She had no idea how sweet until Doctor Gaynor announced, "After we've adjourned, I wish to see Doctor Freda Caron, head of the Department of Cystology, and Doctor James Berkeley, head of the Department of Psychiatry, in my office."

Since she couldn't assist in the placement of trash bins, Freda left the hall and went to take an aspirin, continuing on to Doctor Gaynor's office. Mrs. Weatherwax, small but motherly, gray but efficient, waved her into the inner office with a smile of greeting. Inside, she found Doctor Berkeley had arrived ahead of her and was slumped in a chair, working a crossword puzzle.

"Hi, Freda," he said. "Reach any decision, yet, on my memorandum of last November?"

"No, Jim," she answered, but he had already slunk back into his crossword puzzle.

Despite a course in "The Evaluation of Management Personnel," Berkeley confused her. He did not fit the patterns of behavior analyzed in her class. He was a psychiatrist of the Frommian school who wished to practice the art of loving, he had told her, but he lacked sex appeal, and no one would cooperate. He had been rejected so often that his libido had turned inward so completely that his wife had divorced him and threatened to sue him for alienation of his affections.

Freda suspected him of fetishism or a peculiar sense of humor. Once he had wandered into her greenhouse looking for a woman's garter. When she asked which woman, he had replied absently, "Any woman's."

He had never tried to touch her, overtly or covertly, but he had sent her an interoffice memo requesting permission to pinch her thigh. At first slightly peeved, she had considered turning his memorandum over to Doctor Gaynor; but, after reflecting, she tore it up. Not only would public knowledge of the memorandum embarrass her, it might inspire Doctor Gaynor to attempt to show her shortcuts to higher policy levels.

Now, the author of the memo, rejected again, sank into the depths of his crossword puzzle.

Doctor Gaynor, slender, silver-haired, handsome, entered briskly, nodded to their greetings, and pulled up the chair behind his desk. He abstractedly studied his manicure, pulled a buffing brush from his desk, and buffed his folded hand. In his presence Freda grew more alert to details, and she noticed that his pale-blue suit matched his pale-blue eyes and that the irregular silver threads in the weave matched the silver of his hair. In the ladies' lounge, the cryptic lines had once appeared, "If Charlie Gaynor isn't red-haired, *something* is being dyed."

Looking now at his silver threads among the blue, Freda had the sudden intuition that the note had not been wrong. Gaynor

38

was much younger than his appearance. The hair on his head was dyed to match the platinum sheen of the thread and to lend the authority of age to his office.

Doctor Gaynor looked up suddenly. He put the fingernail buffer back into the drawer with a military snap, spread his arms wide to grip the edge of his desk, and leaned forward, looking briefly at Doctor Berkeley and at Freda with the half-proud, half-doting air of a teacher regarding his favorite pupils. "I consider you two tops on my team. When I am called to higher responsibilities in Washington, I expect one of you to take over this Bureau. But, before I leave for the Department, I want to leave something down here for you to remember me by. . . ." He paused for dramatic effect. "This morning I got a call from Clayborg at Santa Barbara."

"Who is Clayborg, Doctor Gaynor?" Freda asked.

Doctor Gaynor seemed surprised. "Doctor Hans Clayborg, at the Santa Barbara Institute for Advanced Studies. The world's leading expert on entropy. He specializes in galactic-energy loss. Doctor Clayborg has been up all night reading the minifacted briefs on the Flora expedition, and he's wild with excitement. He suggested that I petition the Senate's Planet Classification Committee to declare the Planet of Flowers an open planet—at least for experimental studies—until the International Agency acts. The Institute doesn't function except in an advisory capacity, but he says he'll personally lend his weight to the petition."

"That would give us a jump on the Russians," Freda said.

"Exactly. And from all reports, that planet is a botanical paradise. Clayborg's interested in plant evolution on a dying planet to see how the plants . . . er . . . solve certain problems. He recommends establishment of a permanent botanical experimental station on the planet—the Gaynor Research Institute. His suggestion, not mine."

"Maybe we *should* give Flora to the Russians," Berkeley remarked.

Gaynor ignored the remark. "I'm taking two members of my management team to Washington with me—you, Doctor Berkeley, because you can support me with the opinion of one who has been there; and you, Doctor Caron, because you weren't and can support my petition without planetary bias. Thus, you see, my advisory staff will be completely balanced, and you, Doctor Berkeley, might advance a few theories supporting the psychological benignity of Flora, as icing on the cake."

"What kind of theories do you want from me, Charles?" Doctor Berkeley grunted, and Freda noticed with horror that he had gone back to his crossword puzzle.

Gaynor looked at him, vexation flicking behind his composure. "You could shape the picture in a therapeutic direction, say—hit them with a few ideas from the mental-health angle."

"I'd have to take that suggestion under careful advisement. I'm not sure of my own reactions yet, and the reactions I've gotten from others point toward a few indices indicating earth alienation."

"Nonsense, Jim! If any member of Able Section has suffered at all, it's from a surfeit of honey. There are always a few malcontents in any administrative group. . . . What could you possibly object to?"

"The few malcontents who've tasted honey. I don't wish to sign any petition that might be construed later as an escape clause . . . from earth. How much time are you giving us to prepare an opinion?"

"Ten days is the most I can allow. I want to strike while the iron's hot, and send the Gaynor Station out with the Charlie Section."

"Ten days should be enough, one way or the other."

"One way or the other? Are you telling me, Jim, that I can't unequivocally count on a supporting opinion from your department?"

"Oh, you can get that. . . . Whatever I come up with, Doctor Youngblood is bound to come up with a dissenting opinion."

"Ah, yes," Gaynor said. "I've been favorably impressed by Doctor Youngblood. I think the lad's managerial timber."

From her course in management techniques, Freda knew that

Gaynor's remark was figuratively a knife against Berkeley's throat. Although she felt empathy for the Frommian, another thought had occurred to her: an experimental station included on its Table of Organization a maximum-care psychiatric ward. Although she did not for one minute think Paul aberrant, any man who even considered that orchids might be ambulatory had potentials. "Doctor Gaynor, I would be honored to condense and summarize the findings in favor of the Gaynor Station."

Without being dismissed, Doctor Berkeley arose and walked toward the door, grunting as he went, "Yep, beat the Russians!"

Doctor Gaynor shook his head sadly as the psychiatrist went through the door. "One would think he was presenting the petition. Sometimes I can't fathom Doctor Berkeley."

To that remark Freda breathed a silent "Amen."

In four days the mystery of the missing seeds solved itself. Two shoots sprang up from the base of the plant hanging from the rack—shoots with the unmistakable green of Flora. Freda had been so busy planting the seed boxes that the plants were three inches high before she discovered them. She was so excited that when she saw Hal waiting in a cafeteria line the next day she went to tell him.

He listened with a furrowed brow and said, "Doctor, the male plant was seven feet off the floor and twenty feet away."

"I know; that's why I didn't find the shoots until yesterday."

"You don't understand," he said, putting his empty tray down. "The female shot the seeds at the male plant. . . . Is your greenhouse locked?"

"Yes, but the seeds are glider seeds. They can sail twenty yards. It was an accident that they landed in the pot."

"No, ma'am," he said emphatically. "When a man makes two holes-in-one on a thirty-two-hole course, that's luck, yes. But at least you can figure the man was shooting for the green. . . . May I have your key?"

"What do you want the key for?"

"To stop a murder! When did you last see the shoots?"

"Yesterday afternoon. But if you think something's wrong, I'll go over with you."

"All you can do is unlock the door, but let's go."

As they cut across the lawn, she had to hurry to match his long stride. When she opened the door, he took the pot from its hook and brought it to the table by the doorway. Two tiny tulips with perfectly formed blooms had stood at the foot of the adult plant, and the female still stood. The male had fallen limply to the sod. Hal looked down and said, "Well, he got it."

"Paul told me the male root system drained the sod of chemicals necessary to other males," Freda said.

"Paul didn't want to upset you, but I'm not so sensitive. Look at this!"

He probed beneath the root system of the dead tulip with his finger. Cupping the bloom in his palm, he pulled the tiny stalk from the sod. Clinging to its roots was a tightly compressed nodule of extenders from the root system of the larger tulip that had destroyed the small male.

As if he were laying out the body of a dead child, Hal placed the tulip on the table and stood back, hands on hips, and said, "The big bull killed his competition early."

Sensing that he was emotionally shaken, she said, "Purely a behavioristic response to chemical stimuli in the root systems, Hal. The tulips can't think."

"Freda, you're choking on your own methodology," he said. "The big brute killed the baby. Of course it was a behavioristic response to chemical stimuli. What else *is* thinking?"

Silence was the better part of discretion, she reasoned, but she knew that disappointment had blunted his perception. Looking down at the tulip, burnished by the sunlight, she knew such beauty could never wantonly destroy other beauty.

"Maybe I am oversensitive," Hal said, "but I have a feeling for miniature plants. I'm going to Bakersfield Saturday to a bonsai exhibition. The tulip wasn't dwarfed. It was just a baby, but it would have caused a sensation."

He was coming out of his grief, and she offered, "You were right about the rare earths. Chemical analysis of the dead tulip showed an unusual rate of phosphorus, fluorine, and potassium, also. Of course, such analyses reveal nothing of the life-support system."

"Yes," he said. "When I feel egotistical I remind myself that I'm essentially nothing more than a bucket of water."

He rehung the tulips and locked the door for her, saying, "Doctor, you might be interested in the bonsai exhibit. Would you care to join me Saturday? I heard you were going to Washington. . . . If you're not committed to Doctor Gaynor's program, I've had second thoughts about Flora. I guess that was my real reason for wanting you to join me."

"I keep an open mind, of course. But so far, all the reports that I've summarized on the Planet of Flowers have been favorable."

"I know," he said. "The specialists can't see over the walls of their specialties. . . . And I'm only a poor druid priest."

Walking along beside him, she did not have to ask where he had gotten information on a trip that had not been announced officially. On checking the bulletin board in the ladies' lounge this morning, she had read the scrawled notation, "Charlie's going to do it to Freda, without love, when they get to Washington."

"Somehow or other," Hal said, "I've got the idea that Doctor Gaynor's experimental station may turn out to be a Siberia for Bureau employees who don't measure up to the doctor's standards of administrative excellence, and I'd resign from the profession before I'd go back."

Here was an attitude quite different from the earth alienation that Doctor Berkeley had feared. Freda alerted to an opportunity. "I would like to hear a dissenting opinion," she remarked, "particularly from a druid priest. Call me Friday. If I can get away, I'll go to Bakersfield with you."

If the choice of Bureau chief rested between her and Doctor Berkeley, she decided, she certainly merited the job over Berkeley. She had seen the writing on the wall, and the writing said Berkeley had an Oedipus fixation on all girls under sixteen and that he collected pornographic Rorschach inkblots.

43

Chapter Four

BECAUSE FIRST BLOOMS WERE BUDDING ON HER SEEDLINGS Saturday, Freda hated to leave for the bonsai exhibition in Bakersfield; even so, her outing would have been delightful if Hal had stayed sober.

The dwarfed plants were exhibited in a Japanese pavilion retained from some past World's Fair, and she was enthralled by a model railroad that ran among forests of live oaks, past corn and wheat fields, and whose trains pulled up at stations landscaped with live roses—all grown to HO scale. Looking down on the exhibit, arranged against a backdrop of painted scenery, she felt so much like some god of the twentieth century that she forgave such discrepancies as the Santa Fe Chief thundering past Fujiyama.

Afterward they took tea beneath wisteria in a garden overlooking a bamboo-framed lagoon arched by a stone bridge. A Japanese girl in kimono and obi clattered up on wooden clogs, bowed, and introduced herself as Haki. Haki announced, in the fluting intonations of Japan-learned English, that she was ready to pour ceremonial tea. Freda felt herself so much a part of Japan that she could virtually hear temple bells, until Hal ordered, "Pour the lady tea, Haki-san, but fix me a double martini."

"But, Hal," Freda protested, "this *is* the Orient."

"I hold no brief against the Orient, but I'm loyal to Martini, the greatest Italian since Marconi."

"Very well, but give me your negative report on Flora while you can still talk. Doctor Berkeley hinted that there might be side effects from a voyage to Flora, mental allergies, nostalgia, even earth-alienation."

"That headshrinker wouldn't have the faintest idea what's bothering me."

44

"Hal, at times you irritate me. You'll denigrate a whole field of study with one sweep."

"There is no field of plant psychiatry, and, I tell you, the plants of Flora are sane to a degree that makes them dangerous to beings on our level of sanity, as they are dangerous to each other."

"Doctor Hector," she reminded him, "said the plant life of Flora was noncompetitive."

"Superficially only. Soil conditions, drainage, prevalence of moisture, give a slight advantage to certain plants, but to seize on that advantage, they have to fight. There's not an inch of Flora not fought over. The soil is drenched with the sap of slaughtered flowers. As a druid priest, I tell you, the spirit of those plants, including my tree, is not benign."

"Are you telling me you've reevaluated your impression of a tree any jaybird would trust?"

"Yes," he said seriously. "I'm convinced the tree intended to kill me." His flat voice, sounding deep in his throat, alarmed her. Paranoia, she thought.

Haki clip-clopped to their table for the ceremonial tea-pouring, and Freda was grateful for the interruption as she watched the girl's movements, fluttering with a ceremonial charm which interpreted the briskness of tea. And Haki was versatile. She poured Hal's martini with motions that captured the sparkle of gin.

"What does Paul think of this?" Freda asked.

"Paul never commits himself," Hal said, sipping his drink, "but he's not fooled by appearances. You're proof of that."

Over her delicately poised teacup Freda asked, "Are you saying he doesn't find me attractive?"

"I'd be a maple-loving Florian to imply that!" He was beginning to gesticulate. "But a man doesn't marry a woman for the shape of her earlobes. Beauty vanishes, passion flees, and ardor can die within an hour. Give *me* fifteen minutes with Mona Lisa and she would be out the door, smile and shoes."

This boy was truly upset, she decided.

45

"A man likes to dip a spoon, now and then, into deep-dish apple pie," Hal continued, "but he marries for meat and potatoes."

"Are you complimenting me?"

"Yes, and Paul knows there's something rotten on Flora. He told me the blooms were originally to attract insects, but there are no insects. What happened to the insects? The flowers ate them!"

He paused, and his voice sank. "That tree was probing my weakness. It had found my libido. I would have died in that maple grove, a horrible death, in a way you can't imagine. . . . But they won't get Paul! They've found the wrong weakness—his pure, aseptic, scientific curiosity. They figure *that's* a weakness, so they aren't superplants. Yet, how many Paul Theastons are there compared to the Hal Polinos. Paul has no weakness."

Fascinated, Freda listened. Paul had said the orchids were concealing secrets. Hal's ideas were incoherent, but he was groping toward a theory which supported Paul. Paul had said that Hal was brilliant, but he wasn't too brilliant. She could certainly imagine what death awaited this semideranged lover in the maple grove.

He had finished his second martini and was waving for another. "Take animal life," he said. "All the substructure for an animal kingdom exists on Flora, particularly for herbivorous animals, and after the grass eaters come meat eaters. What happened to the meat eaters?"

He left the question unanswered, waving his glass. "There's a dolphin in the oceans of Flora, and the big fish eat the little fish. . . . But I can't be too optimistic, even there. If the sun doesn't die too soon, the seaweed will be eating the fish."

"Are you suggesting the plants are carnivores?"

"No, because the grass is cagey. It would poison grazing animals. When a seed falls in that grass, it just melts away. And the grass is right! Any plant on Flora is dangerous, because it has won all its evolutionary wars. Any plant you see on Flora is a victor, a hero, a champion killer."

He paused and cast a glance behind him. "I tell you, Freda, the plants are waiting. The flowers are watching. The trees are probing. Far back in their racial memories are recollections of a biped who swung from their limbs, ate their berries and nuts, pulled up their tender shoots. The memory of a biped whom they conquered once, and destroyed, and who has returned, is still with them, and they will strike again."

He paused over the remnants of his martini. "Yet, your chief and mine, the good Doctor Gaynor, ninety percent water and ten percent hot air, for the sake of perpetuating a meaningless name, wants to station human beings on that planet. That stupid ass! That administrator!"

He was teetering on the edge, and she snapped, "Polino, I can't permit you to discuss the chief of the Bureau in such terms, not in my presence."

Haki had come again with another martini. "Haki-san, do you know a pompous old ass by the name of Doctor Charles Gaynor who would low-bridge his grandmother for a political advantage?"

"He throw spit barrs, sir?"

"Right, Haki-san! He's the grandfather of all spit ballers."

"Hal, I insist! Pay the girl and let's go."

As submissive as a child, he struggled to his feet, totaled the check with one eye closed, and crumpled a handful of bills onto the table. He turned and held out his hand to Freda, who led him from the pavilion. When they reached the car, she took the driver's seat, and Hal spoke one sentence, sounding hollow in his throat, "Don't help Gaynor, Freda."

Freda had no intention of not helping Doctor Gaynor, and she likewise had no intention of not helping Hal Polino. Monday morning she arranged with Mrs. Weatherwax for an immediate appointment with Doctor Gaynor.

Although she deferred to him as Bureau Chief, she enjoyed talking to Doctor Gaynor. His manners that Hal had called pompous were courtly, almost majestic, and he, more than anyone else, was responsible for Freda's promotion to higher levels. He wrote her fitness reports. For that reason she dropped by his office less often than she would have liked, because some executives would grade an administrator down for currying favor.

However, Gaynor appreciated flattery insinuated unobtrusively into the conversation. Freda had detected his pleasure from his habit of blinking his eyes slowly and nodding slightly when a compliment was concealed in the conversation. Also, he was handsome, and he seemed to like her.

"How was your weekend?" he asked as a polite prelude when she entered.

"Interesting in more ways than one," she answered, "and that's why I called. I appreciate you working me into your busy schedule so promptly."

With an imperceptible nod and a slow blink, he said, "My door is always open."

"Saturday I visited a bonsai exhibit in Bakersfield in the company of Hal Polino, Paul's graduate-student assistant."

"Ah, I see." There was an implied rebuke in his remark. "You accompanied Mr. Polino?"

"Yes. He was basically my reason for going. As a student, I felt his interest would be stimulated by specific examples of applied plant science. But more, when Mr. Polino originally reported to me of Paul's progress on Tropica, I thought I detected in his remarks an attitude toward the Planet of Flowers quite different from the nostalgia of beginning earth-alienation which Doctor Berkeley mentioned."

"Ah, I see." Doctor Gaynor's eyes were beginning to glow. "Doctor Berkeley, I think, was overimpressed by a nostalgia that will pass, like the memory of a pleasant country we visited when we were young."

"Student Polino and I discussed the alienation effect, as Doctor Berkeley calls it, and as you just expressed more poetically and accurately." Freda was rewarded by another blink and nod. "But Mr. Polino's reaction was entirely different. He thinks the planet is malevolent, that there is evil beneath its beauty. He described it in terms which turned my concern away from the planet and toward him. He is so distraught that he considers the planet a menace to human life. I thought it might be advisable to place him under covert psychiatric observation, for the good of the Bureau as well as his own. If the Senate Committee were to conduct an in-depth investigation of your petition, a field interviewer might approach the young man. If he were under psychiatric observation, of course, any testimony given by him would be voided. Possibly a bonus vacation might be arranged."

"No. That would be too obvious. If I sent him off the base, and an in-depth investigation were held, he would be the first the field investigator would interview. . . . Polino, Hal. . . . Let me see."

He swiveled in his chair, his silver-gray smock rustling with starch, and pulled a file from his desk drawer. "Polino, Harold," he said again, looking at a file card he had selected. "Harold Michelangelo Polino, to be exact." He inserted the card into a computer typewriter, pressed a button, and the typewriter began to hum with the flick of its type ball. A sheet of paper slowly emerged from the typewriter.

Leaning sideways, intent on the record of Harold Michelangelo Polino, in his silver hair and his silver smock with his dead white face immobile, Doctor Gaynor reminded her of a bust cast from platinum as he scanned the record. Suddenly he looked over and smiled. "As you know, Doctor Caron, these reports are confidential, but since I repose special trust and confidence in you as a department head, and since this report was turned in by Paul Theaston, I will read you an excerpt: 'Subject student has wide-ranging imagination which permits him to observe phenomena from varying points of view. In pure research, this faculty might be valuable. Certainly it adds to his intrinsic interest as a person, but it detracts from his ability to focus on details. His responses are more weighted toward the emotional rather than the intellectual side of his nature—an artistic rather than scientific response. Barring difficulties of adjustment, he is over-qualified as a zoologist, although he would probably be more happy and stable in that branch of the plant sciences. In line with his present studies, I have recommended that he apply for a degree in cystology preparatory to a further degree in cell biology. His greatest handicap in this schedule would be his weakness in methodology. He is impatient with a step-by-step analysis of phenomena and reluctant to maintain precise records, but if his training could be extended to eliminate these tendencies, his potential contribution to the plant sciences is immeasurable.' "

"I'm somewhat confused," Freda admitted. "Is Paul damning him with faint praise, or praising him with faint damns."

"Basically, Paul's saying he's a brilliant student, if his nose can be kept to the grindstone. That he bears watching."

Gaynor turned and strummed his fingers across the polished top of his desk, lost for a moment in speculation. "Keeping his nose to the grindstone, I suspect, would anchor his flights of fancy. . . . Since I've taken you this far into my confidence, Doctor Caron, permit me to take you a little farther. You have met with favorable response in many circles because of your precise methodology. Your record-keeping is both precise and comprehensive."

Suddenly Freda Caron felt herself beneath an alpine overhang with a thaw setting in. Ominously, Doctor Gaynor continued. "You are concerned about the student, and your concern augments the official record. I commend your perspicacity. . . . Now, I see by your work projection for February that you intend to hand-pollinate the Caron tulips. This is a happy juxtaposition of events. I'm not infringing on your prerogatives as department head, but I couldn't think of a more painstaking and detailed task than the hand-pollinating of . . . er . . . sixty-three tulips, twice to the thirty-second power. Your student-rotation memorandum has been approved by the Suggestion Box Committee, and I'm going to assign Hal Polino to you, not only to maintain a covert psychiatric watch but also to apply the therapy of painstaking work to a student who needs training in methodology."

She was crushed by the avalanche triggered by her own memorandum: to save Paul, she had sacrificed herself. Polino was hers. One never objected to assignments given personally by Doctor Gaynor. On the contrary, one was supposed to show restrained enthusiasm.

"Why, Doctor, I hadn't thought of that," she said truthfully. "Hand-pollination will keep him so busy he won't have time to brood."

That, too, was a true statement. Hal Polino would not have time to focus his antagonisms on the planet Flora. They would all be focused on his taskmistress. The prophecy in graffiti had been prematurely fulfilled: they hadn't started for Washington, and Charlie had already "done it" to Freda.

Polino's reaction was precisely as she assumed it would be—chagrin and disappointment; but she had prepared a face to meet the glower that confronted her. "This was an administrative decision, Mr. Polino, and you have no choice but to follow through. I grant you it's tedious work, but it's necessary, and you'll be working alone for the next two weeks. All thirty seeds you picked from the floor, plus the thirty-two which Paul sent, are flourishing. The tulip I removed from the pot seems to accept outside conditions, so I'm confident you can transplant the seedlings outside within the next day or two. If they can adapt to earth conditions and temperature changes, your work within the next two weeks will be vastly increased but likewise more meaningful."

"Increased is absolutely correct, Doctor. I'll be overwhelmed."

"Your attitude is wrong!" she snapped. "You will be adding to the beauty of earth's flora if those plants adapt."

"Then, Doctor, you'd better correct my attitudes now." He was almost truculent. "If those beasts adapt, I won't have time to have any attitudes corrected."

"Number one, I want a log recording every fact relative to the Caron tulips, the time of each observation, and a record of barometric pressures, thermometer readings, or any climatic change that affects the flowers." He was gazing down on her with his hurt fawn eyes, and she relented slightly. "And I don't want the entries recorded in blank verse!"

He grinned at her sally and whirled away, singing:

> He's as busy as a bee!
> Who's as busy as a bee?
> That little old pollinator, me!

To handle him, she thought, would take firmness and authority. And she would not tolerate any familiarity from a student who had twice been drunk in her presence.

"One other item, Mr. Polino," she said, and he turned. "This telephone is for business use only."

"Aye, aye, ma'am."

Freda's visit to Washington began on a pleasant note, principally because Doctor Hans Clayborg joined the group at Bakersfield for the flight to Washington. He was a dynamic little man with a brain so charged with wit and ideas that his hair stuck out at right angles from the static electricity his brain generated. It was his Swedish-Watusi hairstyle, he told her, immediately after introductions, worn to distract attention from his beautiful teeth. When she commented on the perfection of his teeth, he took them out to give her a closer view. She was reassured and amused by his gesture: he wasn't stuffy, and he was too old to be a menace to her health and welfare.

She was pleased also that Doctor Berkeley had recanted from his previous position, despite the fact that he had filed only a neutral report on Flora's psychological effects on human beings. "I have reservations about the planet," he said to her during the flight, "but little stronger than my reservations about earth. Young Doctor Youngblood filed such an enthusiastic opinion in the other direction that he convinced me. Far from decrying the danger of earth-alienation on the planet, he said that the gorgeous scenery—his words, not mine—might straighten out the kinks in the necks of the stargazers. As a matter of fact, he recommended Flora as a sanatorium for neck-snappers. . . . I'll let you read his report."

Freda was surprised to find reporters waiting at the Washington airport, and they were bustled immediately to the Senate Hearings Chamber to meet the members of the committee, with the press in attendance. She was charmed by Senator Heyburn, Chairman of the Senate Committee on Planet Classification. "I would recommend that the young lady adviser for the Athenians be kept in the background," he told all present, who were mostly newspapermen, "because I function on this committee as the devil's advocate, and I fear my duties might be imperiled with an angel in the house."

Senator Heyburn exuded an aura of benignity. His large gentle eyes, his slow hand movements, his massive head with its lion's mane of hair, were fitting backdrops for his voice. She had never heard another voice quite like it: though low-pitched, it rolled with a gravelly resonance that filled the chamber. Afterward Doctor Clayborg said it reminded him of a foghorn sounding through velvet, but Berkeley said it sounded like he was talking with a mouthful of mush.

Press reaction startled Freda. Heyburn's remark about the Athenians insinuated that there were Spartans somewhere. The Spartans, she learned from the newspaper, were the southern senators on the committee who opposed opening any new planet to human colonization, since the manpower drain affected their section of the country more than others. Essentially, they were fighting to keep down the wages of their kitchen help, and Freda thought such a stand untenable; but the newspaper columnists were split down the middle. Some of them, even northerners, were supporters of the Spartans.

She had assumed that the petition hearing would be a gentlemanly get-together with Doctor Gaynor merely presenting his petition. Reports from Section Able had barely hit the newspapers, yet opposition was forming. On the first afternoon of the preliminary hearings, the attorney for the committee requested a four-day delay in order to assemble antipetition witnesses opposing a permanent scientific station on Flora. Freda asked Doctor Clayborg, who seemed to know politics, why anyone should oppose the station. "It sets a precedent," he explained, "which the UN usually follows, and the UN, from Russian pressure, would throw it wide open. Russia's unloading her Uzbek dissidents who're pushing for local self-determination."

In granting the delay, Heyburn made a rather long speech, Freda thought, giving as his reason "to further the continuing dialogue, pro and con, which makes this country great."

"He means monologue," Clayborg whispered to her. "Heyburn's cornered corn, and that ain't hay."

At the hotel, the Athenians lingered in the alcove reserved for them to discuss strategy. Doctor Gaynor—Freda never called him "Charles"—was disappointed by the delay. "I hoped to get my petition through before anyone could organize."

"Charlie," Clayborg snorted, "the battle lines were drawn before Flora was a gleam in Ramsbotham-Twatwetham's telescope."

"Maybe we ought to have a backup plea," Berkeley said, "that's not purely scientific, something to appeal to the bleeding hearts on the committee."

"What about Doctor Youngblood's idea," Freda suggested, "for using Flora as a sanatorium for the earth-alienated. At least, they wouldn't be falling down and breaking their kneecaps when they wander around at night."

"I'd hate to give the young sprout a swelled head," Doctor Berkeley said, "but, Charles, you mentioned you had confidence in him."

"As a potential administrator, Jim," Gaynor said. "I'm no judge of his professional know-how."

"If you use that approach," Clayborg interrupted, "I have a true ace in a real hole—Rosentiel. He's confined over at Saint Elizabeth's, and Rosie was Heyburn's fair-haired boy before he took up stargazing."

"Frankly, I wanted to avoid space madness," Gaynor said, "but what do you think, Jim?"

"It would have shock value. As I remember, he was an excellent speaker and popular with the press."

"That depends on which press you mean," Gaynor said thoughtfully. "He was controversial in the established press."

"But solid with the underground," Clayborg said, "which is the only press with power in Washington."

Suddenly Freda realized they were speaking of Henry Rosentiel, formerly Secretary of Space, confined these last five years to Saint Elizabeth's with the raptures of space. As Secretary, Rosentiel's perfectionism and sense of duty led him to ride the bridges of the space cruisers while awake, and there he had contracted that strange awe of distances called variously space madness, space rapture, and earth-alienation. In fact, he had attempted to defect from earth—an impossibility for one so prominent—and had been apprehended stowing away on a starship.

Unfortunately, the government bungled the affair. Even as the President's press secretary was announcing Rosentiel's resignation "for personal reasons," his picture was appearing in the underground press showing him emerging from the ship between two S.P.s, his head bent back in the characteristic neck-snap of a "night crawler." The photograph, taken from above him, had caught the wistfulness and hunger in his eyes with such poignancy that Freda remembered it to this day, remembered even the caption beneath it: "Like a Sick Eagle Looking at the Sky."

"What about Rosie's . . . er . . . oddity?" Gaynor asked Clayborg.

"He has control for extended periods," Clayborg answered, "particularly when no one mentions stars or the night. But Jim here can go to Saint Elizabeth's with me in the morning to vouch for his stability. If Rosie's willing, Jim agrees, and you give the go-ahead, you've got your Gaynor Station, and I have an entropist on its staff."

"Is it legal for a deranged person to testify?" Freda asked.

"It's not a legal hearing," Gaynor explained. "We're simply trying to persuade Heyburn. . . . Go ahead, Hans. But if Rosentiel agrees to testify, it must be stated plainly that his opinions do not reflect the official attitude of the Bureau."

"I should have brought my tulip along to testify," Freda said. "It could persuade Heyburn."

"Freda and her talking tulips," Gaynor said, patting the top of her hand with avuncular humor. By an act of will, Freda did not jerk her hand back but let him pat.

After the strategy conference she retired to her room to read, but her mind kept returning to Gaynor's pat and her distaste toward it. She awaited the inevitable tap on the door or the ring of her telephone as she might have awaited the in-swinging spikes of an Iron Mary. Once Gaynor started his maneuvers in private, it would be impossible to conceal her revulsion toward being touched. She tried to think of him as a Shasta daisy, but her mind rejected the subterfuge. She arose and paced the room. Once his hand touched her thigh, all that she had worked for, chairmanship of the Bureau, elevation to the Department, eventual Cabinet membership, would be lost in a shriek of horror that could not be disguised as delight.

She paced harder, thinking she was letting herself be driven mad by a scribble on a washroom wall. Gaynor was married with three children, and he flashed his platinum wedding band at the slightest opportunity—and those men were the worst kind! Well, she decided, she would simply tell him that she had contracted a case of leprosy.

Leprosy was such an absurd straw to cling to that she smiled, and temporarily relaxed. At the precise moment her smile was broadest, the telephone rang.

She jumped, then hopped and skipped toward the instrument, standing over it for a moment to let it ring a second time. At least she wanted him to know she wasn't eager.

She picked up the telephone and attempted a coo that ended in a croak, "Freda Caron speaking."

"Hi, Freda. This is Hans Clayborg. I'm interested in your tulip. How about dropping down to the Rendezvous Room for a nightcap?"

"Hans! You bet your sweet burro I will!"

"What do you want to drink? I'll order now."

"Whatever you're having, but make mine double."

Hans awaited her in a corner booth, and he said, "They tell me you've got a tulip that's out of this world."

"It used to be. It's near Fresno now."

He was fascinated by her description of the Caron tulips. By the second nightcap, she was telling the entire story of Paul and his orchids, Hal and his trees, and the conspiracy they both suspected on the planet. Wide-eyed and supercharged, Hans could only say, "Wonderful! . . . Incredible! . . . Superb!"

Hans was as confused as Paul about the orchid pollinators. "Paul's using the methodology I would use, and his deduction's the same as mine; through some illogical inconsistency, the facts aren't making themselves available. But your idea is good, too. Study the tulips and compute their solutions on a seven-foot level."

When she finished and they commenced their third nightcap, Hans in a spluttering spray of words told her how he had come to study entropy: "Because I lost so much reserve energy chasing women when I was young, I grew interested in energy as a thing in itself."

He tried to explain to her the reason for the past century's rash of exploding stars in relation to Goldberg's Law of Diminishing Entropy, but she could not share his horror at the death of stars. What if the life of the universe be shortened by forty billion years? As her psychiatrist would say, she couldn't relate to forty billion years. If a few thousand stars blinked out over the weekend, there were still millions left.

He surprised her more by agreeing with Hal that the plants of Flora might be more intelligent than men, but he almost tipped her with the suggestion that Paul's orchids were evolving away from—not toward—an ambulatory species. "That's my reason for wanting an entropist on Flora. Somebody has to plan for the day the sun dies, and the planning has fallen, by default, to entropists. Those plants know about their dying sun from the weakened quanta jump in their chlorophyll process, and they could be preparing their species to survive the long winter of dying and the heat of rebirth."

"You think like Hal Polino," she said.

"Yes. We use a lot of intuition at Santa Barbara," he said. "Human existence, as we know it, cannot survive the death and rebirth of universes; but we're working on the problem, even to burying capsules of stabilized amino acids five thousand feet below the Sahara Desert. Chances that one of those capsules will bob to the surface of an unborn ocean on a planet containing a fragment of this one to give evolution a head start on the next cycle of creation are impossible chances. But we deal in impossibles at Santa Barbara."

"So that's where the taxpayers' money goes," Freda snapped, "into a hole in the ground."

"Seeds might survive," he ruminated. "If we could contrive a kernel of human corn—"

"Now you sound like Paul Theaston!" she exclaimed, and, at Hans's insistence, she explained Paul's theory of orchid survival, slightly edited. "I thought he was a little wacky," she concluded, "but all wackiness is relative. Human corn, hah!"

"Speaking of corn," Hans said, "did you hear about the squaw who sold her favors for five dollars or a pint of corn seeds?"

"That sounds like a six-drink story," Freda said, "and I'm one over my quota with four. . . . It's two o'clock! Doctor Gaynor might make a bedcheck."

"If Gaynor makes a bedcheck at two A.M.," Hans said, rising, "Freda Caron had better be under the bed."

They supported each other to and in the elevator. Hans bade her good night at the elevator door before being wafted higher. Loss of entropy had claimed him for her own, he said. But she got the key in her door on the fourth pass and tacked toward her bed, musing over a strange discovery: after four cocktails, or four glasses of wine, she lost her aversion to being touched. She idly wondered what would happen after the fifth drink. An abreaction?

She awakened almost at noon and leaped from bed in revulsion at her laziness, until it occurred to her it was not yet eight o'clock in California. Nonetheless, she dressed hurriedly and took the express elevator to the main floor, sprinting across the lobby to the dining room. When she reached the alcove reserved for Athenians, all three men were present, but Doctor Gaynor was occupied with a reporter from the Washington *Post*, and Hans and Jim hardly nodded a glum greeting. She assumed from the air of gloom that Rosentiel either had suffered a remission or had refused to testify. That fear was put to rest when she heard Gaynor tell the reporter that they were overjoyed that the former Secretary of Space, Henry Rosentiel, had agreed to testify in favor of Flora as an open planet. But, Gaynor wished to reiterate, any opinion expressed by the Secretary was his own and in no way reflected the opinion of the Bureau of Exotic Plant Life.

When the *Post* reporter thanked Doctor Gaynor and left, Doctor Berkeley lifted a copy of the Washington *Posthole*, concealed on the seat beside him, and handed it to Freda. Spread across the front page of the crudely printed newspaper were the headlines: "Spartans Draft Navy for Fight Against Flora." Beneath the headlines was a three-column cut of Gaynor and his party descending from the plane—the photographer had caught her in a three-quarter profile, not her most flattering pose—and beneath was the caption: "Portrait of Four Lambs at Fleecing Time."

She scanned the story. None other than Admiral Creighton, Chief of Naval Discipline, had been summoned to testify against the opening of Flora to a permanent scientific station. His adviser, she read with astonishment, was Philip Barron, Commanding Officer, USSS *Botany*.

"Why, Captain Barron was enthralled by the planet!"

"That's what makes it tough," Clayborg said. "Barron's been there. If he never says a word—and he probably won't—his mere presence hurts us. He's in the position of a man testifying against his own wife, which means the lady is a tramp."

"If Rosentiel talks on the stand as he did to Hans and me,"

Doctor Berkeley said to Doctor Gaynor, "I advise you to stress the psychological factors, Charles. Hit the Navy where they can't hit back."

"Hans, how strong is that friendship that you spoke about between Rosentiel and Heyburn?" Gaynor asked suddenly.

"Rosie studied law under Heyburn at North Dakota," Hans said. "He was Heyburn's fair-haired boy, his campaign manager in the senatorial race. Heyburn recommended him for Space Secretary as a payoff."

"Sort of a father-son relationship?"

"That and more, Charlie. Heyburn feels responsible about Rosie—his space madness—because Heyburn practically sent him into the wild black yonder."

"Heyburn has another loyalty, it says here," Berkeley broke in. "The Navy. Without the Red River Repair Base and the Bismarck pad, North Dakota could fold up and go home."

"And there's the USSS *Heyburn*," Freda pointed out.

"The ship was named for his son," Berkeley said, "who was lost in the Andromeda swirl. . . . Say, let's swap queens! Why not match the Spartans' gold braid with Athenian pulchritude, Charles? Let Freda present our brief."

Gaynor whistled softly, "Jim, I play an aggressive game, but I can't see opening a bid with a singleton ace."

"To make metaphorical hash," Hans broke in, "I'm against leading with our right, because if our haymaker misses, we'll all be knocked on our collective prats, and Freda will be wanting a new front tooth."

"I don't like the idea of ordering Doctor Caron before that committee," Gaynor said. "Those southerners lose their chivalry when a dime's involved. . . . If we can persuade Heyburn, he'll find a way to swing their vote. I say, hit them in the fields of botany, psychiatry, entropy. . . . Bring in Doctor Youngblood's theory of an asylum. . . . Hit them with your ideas, Hans, about plant adaptation on a dying planet, how vital to us is the knowledge of the process. Of course, exposing Freda to a Senate Committee, the publicity . . ."

Freda, weighing matters quickly, finished Gaynor's dubious sentence. If she appeared before a Senate hearing, with the resulting publicity, she would certainly come to the attention of the Secretary of Agriculture, who would be interested in these hearings. If she acquitted herself well . . .

"Doctor Gaynor, anything worth believing in is worth fighting for. Since the Bureau is making this petition, I stand ready to assume any duty you gentlemen wish to assign me in the interest of Bureau policy."

"Good girl!" Berkeley exclaimed. "We could back her with Doctor Youngblood's therapeutic theory as our big guns and blast those Navy battlewagons out of space."

"There's a logic here," Gaynor admitted, "as long as our principal aim is to sway Heyburn emotionally. Anything that wins is right. If Freda doesn't mind the publicity, we'll try it. . . . Gentlemen, shall we order a round to toast our new Joan of Arc?"

"I'll take a bloody mary," Hans said, "to honor the decision."

Somehow, Clayborg's remark seemed sinister, and Freda resented the implication. It was as if Clayborg considered their cause lost because she had volunteered to present the Bureau's petition.

Chapter Five

FREDA DELIVERED THE BUREAU'S PETITION BEFORE THE COM-
mittee without stage fright and with enough composure to regret that she had to keep a three-quarter profile to the cameras.
At the end, the paraphernalia of national publicity—lights, cameras, and clicking steno pads—was less disconcerting than the
gaze fixed on her by the former Space Secretary. Rosentiel
made her wonder if only male nurses were employed at Saint
Elizabeth's.

Surprisingly, the devil's advocate, Senator Heyburn, was
merely dismissing her with the thanks of the committee when
the committee's attorney rose to a point of order. "Doctor Caron,"
he asked, "in reference to your allegation that Flora might
benefit night walkers, doesn't this conflict with the Stanford-
Hammersmith experiment on the raptures of space?"

"What's the Stanford-Hammersmith experiment?" she asked.

"Well, ma'am, if *you* don't know the answer, then I . . . er
. . . withdraw the question."

Before he finished stammering, the chamber was rippling with
laughter, and when he retreated to stumble back into his seat,
the ripples had grown to waves. Freda resumed her seat as Heyburn gaveled the room to order and whispered to Hans, seated
beside her, "What is the Stanford-Hammersmith experiment?"

"That question has a six-drink answer," he whispered back.

Admiral Creighton diverted attention from the lawyer's em-
barrassment. When called by the clerk, he advanced to the witness area, the line of gold stars down the outer seam of each leg
—insignia of the space pilot—glittering when he walked. He was
in full dress, with epaulets and in-looped gold cordon and the
gold stripes of a full admiral reaching from cuff to elbow. On a

little patch of blue above his left breast, the gold was nicely balanced by fourteen rows of ribbons denoting honors, from a good-conduct citation at the academy to the Order of the Southern Cross.

Hans had briefed her on Creighton before the hearing, and his record was formidable. Now Chief of Naval Discipline, he had been the first space sailor to "buckle the belt of Orion," which had won him the Israeli Order of Job. He had been first to rip the veil from Venus—for that, the "Pour le Mérite" of France—and he had felt the magnetic storms lashing between the Seven Sisters. All in all, he was a typical space admiral.

Speaking without notes, Creighton delivered the antipetition in a clipped voice, arguing that transport of civilians to Flora would incur problems of Navy discipline. He spoke of the two men who had jumped ship and of the peculiar biological qualities of the planet which made difficulties for search-and-seizure parties. "Fortunately, Captain Barron ransacked his boyhood memories and came up with a solution, which entails, however, the expense of sending bloodhounds to Flora."

Freda liked that! Captain Barron's memories, indeed!

"Flora invites lax discipline," the Admiral continued. "Blue jackets on liberty, once out of sight of the quarterdeck, removed all clothing. They were never reprimanded by officers on liberty because the officers, also, were out of uniform, completely. Captain Barron had to order decals of rank or rating applied to the bare skin; but this compulsion to strip, caused by the climate of Flora, has sounded a general alarm throughout world naval circles. Transportation of personnel to any permanent scientific station located on Flora would have to be accomplished without aid from the Royal Space Navy or the Greek Merchant Navy and at grave risk to the morale of our own."

From purely naval matters, Creighton diverted his attack to the challenge-and-response theory of motivation. "Flora is a huge San Diego," he said, pointing out that "goldbricking" in the Able Section of the Florian scientific expedition had hindered accumulation of hard-core information to the point where it was only ten percent of the median for other planets. "A fact that cost a dime on Ramsey 7 cost a dollar on Flora. We in the Navy are not generally concerned with budgetary matters, but patriotism forced us to call the Secretary of the Treasury's attention to this price tag."

Admiral Creighton nodded, wheeled, and glittered out, followed by Captain Barron, who would have some explaining to do, Freda promised herself, when he got back to the base.

Then the clerk called Henry Rosentiel to testify in favor of an open Flora.

Thin, intense, the former Space Secretary impressed Freda with his speaking ability and his sanity. Despite the cameras, the crowded chamber, and the whispering that greeted his name, he had such control of his mania that not a tic was apparent. His voice quivered, but only with the passion in his plea.

"If a man be mad with meekness, is it not fitting in the interests of a higher humanity that he be freed from surveillance? Is it not proper, taxwise, since the cost of his fetters is so much greater than the cost of his transport, that he be granted passage to a planet which might act as his sole warder until he yields, forever, to the pull of gravity?

"Why, then, are we held prisoners of earth? From some impulse in the hearts of men which says that he who rejects earth betrays a mother? From some ancient code which says that he who honors not his mother dishonors God? Eyes which have looked on the naked stars, tongues which have tasted wine-dark space, lips which have kissed the skirt hems of infinity, reject this mother no more, and no less, than one who said, ten score and two centuries agone, 'Woman, I know thee not!'"

Rosentiel was ready for Flora, Freda decided. He was talking like a fourth-generation Florian already. Still, listening, she was drawn to sympathy with the man.

"Few are the aeons remaining to Flora," Rosentiel continued. "When her last sunset fades, when her dark sun claims her and a nova flares across the Milky Way for our children's children's delight, I pray that a mote of the being which was I shall be

64

mingled in that glory. For I am done with an earth whose fruits are machines, where all Miltons are mute and a Cromwell would be a pleasant change from this unutterably inane. So, old friend and teacher"—here he turned toward Heyburn—"gentlemen of the committee, I plead for all who greet the dawns with sadness and evenings with delight. Grant us this sanctuary, where we may worship, in secret and alone, our mistress, the night."

Freda didn't share the former Secretary's disapproval of society and she didn't understand the reference to Milton and Cromwell, but she felt that Rosentiel's plea had been more effective than Creighton's. The Admiral had tightened the purse strings, while Rosentiel had tugged at the heartstrings, putting the choice squarely before the committee, money or the heart, cash or humanity.

Obviously Senator Heyburn had been touched. He was blowing his nose as he arose, and he gazed benignly down on his former student. "Yes, we have heard the bells at midnight, Cousin Shallow."

Clearing his throat, Heyburn turned to the audience and cameras. He thanked the petitioners and assured all parties that a fair and judicial atmosphere would prevail during the intracommittee debates on the petition, which would be held *in camera*. "When we discuss the stars, we discuss the future of mankind, and we on the committee are mindful of our trust to you, mindful, too, of the generations yet unborn for whom our universe is a heritage, and shall so remain, until this insubstantial pageant has faded."

Something he said must have aroused a memory, for the Senator's eyes went slightly out of focus, and the memory triggered an idea, which suggested a phrase, which prompted a sentence, and the chain reaction set his hands to moving in the ritual of oratory. "Yet, it is not in the stars, but in ourselves, that our ultimate destiny lies, for the lights in the skies are but beacons to lead us, onward and outward, beyond stars, beyond the cycles of motion, until we are masters of all stars. . . ."

Freda had been covertly studying Rosentiel because he had

65

been overtly studying her, and she saw his head twitch on the first "stars" Heyburn uttered. There was a pronounced pecking movement on the second "stars," and when the Senator said "lights in the skies," Rosentiel's head snapped back.

". . . until we, until . . ."

Heyburn's eyes fell on Rosentiel, and his voice trailed into silence. Seated beside his old friend and mentor, the former Secretary was gazing toward a zenith far beyond the roof of the chamber. His mania had claimed him, and, to Freda, he looked for all the world like a mute coyote howling at the moon. Clayborg beside her breathed softly, "Rosie's not listening, and we're shucked." (Freda heard him indistinctly, and she assumed that Hans Clayborg had said "shucked.")

With set features, Heyburn returned to his listeners. ". . . we bind the sweet influences of the Pleiades and loosen the belt of Orion. Class dismissed . . . er, session adjourned, thank you." Then, amid the hubbub of rising voices and squeaking chairs, Freda heard the mellifluent voice of Senator Heyburn calling a page boy, "Son, will you get this thing out of here?"

It was hard to assess the value of the day's events, Doctor Gaynor said as they were driven to the hotel, because of the complex factors involved in Rosentiel's moving speech and Heyburn's possible reactions to his former student's neck-snapping. His only comment on Freda's presentation was an implied rebuke: "Doctor, it might help if you read more widely outside your field."

She merely nodded, but Freda felt his remark unfair. By the time she had read and initialed Department Directives, Bureau Subdirectives, Executive Memoranda, Interoffice Memos, administrative-procedure pamphlets, and scientific papers he channeled to her, she hardly had time to wipe the ink from her fingers and scan the washroom bulletins, and she was a speed reader.

Berkeley rushed to her rescue, wielding a drawn blade. "That Stanford-Hammersmith foul-up was partly my fault, Charles. I shouldn't have let Freda see Doctor Youngblood's odd theory on environmental therapy. His logic was so full of holes that even a lawyer could spot them."

With a single sweep of his blade, Berkeley had nicked her Adam's apple and sliced Youngblood's jugular.

Gaynor asked Hans what their chances were for a favorable decision. "About fifty-fifty," he answered. "We'll know in a week or ten days."

"Heyburn said four days," Gaynor reminded him.

"I know, but Heyburn will call a recess."

At the hotel, Freda found a telegram: "Congratulate me. Am father of 2,016 babies. Within 8 days, if my little finger holds out, expect to be grandfather of 64,512. After that, what? Pollinator Polino."

Despite her gloom over the hearings, Freda was lifted by the telegram. Her exaltation carried over to dinnertime, when she was the only happy Athenian in the alcove. She explained her gaiety without showing the telegram; Hal's tone was too familiar for proper teacher-student relations.

Most of the unhappiness around the table was caused by a front-page photo in the Washington *Posthole*. Heyburn, hands waving in oratorical frenzy, was addressing the audience, while Rosentiel was gazing up and away. For the Senator, Freda knew the picture was worth one thousand insults, and, in Hal's phrase, as soon as he saw it he would "go ape."

After dinner she showered and put on the green frock Hal had liked and spent an extra five minutes on her makeup. She pleasantly anticipated meeting Hans, a pleasure at odds with her strategic position. Clayborg was no matinee idol, by one foot in height and by an additional six inches of flaring hair, but he attracted her like a vacuum cleaner, and his mind was a magic lantern.

While she watched the magic lantern cast shadows on the walls, the walls were closing in. If the petition failed, she knew she could expect a pleasant chat in Gaynor's office, with ceremonial tea, perhaps, and their discussion of Freda Caron's future would end with a guillotine-edged suggestion: "Freda, perhaps you'd be happier in pure research."

Once she had had a roommate in college, Freda recalled, a

Catholic girl of reckless nature who was always starting a novena about once every twenty-eight days, and . . .

The phone rang. Hans was waiting. "Standing by for six drinks and a discussion of the Stanford-Hammersmith experiment."

Downstairs she slid into their corner booth, saying, "I exaggerated last night. Four drinks is my limit."

"How'd you discover your limit?"

"I have a phobia against being touched. It leaves me after four drinks."

"Then your capacity hasn't been established empirically. What you've established is the number of drinks it takes to let you feel normal." He whipped a slide rule from his pocket and squinted at it in the pale glow from the table lamp. "Projecting the curve, your optimum feeling should occur somewhere in the area of five and three-fourths drinks. . . . Waiter, two double martinis!"

It was her first martini, and she liked the metallic tingle. "If this were a bell," she said, "it would strike a very clear note. . . . Tell me truly, Hans: what are our chances for getting the Gaynor Station on Flora?"

"Very slight."

"Oh, dear! If it fails, Doctor Gaynor will blame me."

"That's the name of his game," Hans said casually. "When the Navy moved in, Gaynor figured the petition would fail, so he set you up as a pigeon for the Navy's big guns. Now, you'll take the blame for the petition's failure."

"If you're my friend, Hans, why did you agree to let me present the petition?"

"I figured you saw a chance to get the personal attention of the Secretary of Agriculture, since he's watching, and I figured Rosie's eloquence plus your charm would give us a fair chance. So, I bet on you. Rosie's neck snap was the fickle finger of fate." He sipped his drink and said, "What I can't figure is how space madness got onto our agenda in the first place."

"James Berkeley steered it on," she said. "He and I are next in line for Bureau Chief, and he's cutting me out."

"Don't worry about Berkeley," Hans said. "You've got weapons to blast him out of any entrenchment, and I'll show you how to use them before the night's over. Anyway, in office politics, the methodology of the psychiatrist puts him at a disadvantage."

"Speaking of psychiatry," she said, "what's the Hammerford-Stansmith Experiment?"

"Stanford-Hammersmith," he corrected, eyeing her drink. "You're not ripe yet."

"You couldn't tell me anything more shocking than what you've already laid bare about office politics. I read the manual *Maneuvering for Promotion*. But it's one thing to read about knife fighting; It's quite another to feel a knife in your back."

"Shock lag between theory and practice," he said. "You're bloodied now. Sooner or later you'll learn to enjoy the thrust and parry, particularly the thrust."

He was talking on a high level, she knew, but, somehow, his language seemed slightly suggestive.

He leaned forward. "The first rule of office politics, Freda, is to form friendships in high places. At Santa Barbara, we're all given cabinet-minister status to spare us from intraoffice politics. Of course," he added cryptically, "we still practice extra-office politics, for our friends."

"Why, Hans Clayborg, you never told me you had cabinet rank."

"I thought you knew."

"I noticed Gaynor deferred to you, but I thought it was because of your political knowledge. I never thought pure-research people got . . ." She paused.

"So high," he finished for her, grinning. "Waiter, another round!"

Her first martini had made her bold. "Hans, why don't you get Gaynor transferred, and get me his job?"

"Gaynor's *my* pigeon," he grinned. "I need him to help me get

69

entropy experts on Flora. I may lose this battle, but the war goes on."

"You aroused his vanity so strongly with the Charles Gaynor Station that he's . . . willing to sacrifice me to get it."

"Well, I see your judgment's not impaired. Are you ready for the Hammersmith-Stanford theory?"

"Shoot, Luke," she said, using a Polino phrase and thinking that she sincerely liked this man with the wire hair and the rank of cabinet minister. She might very well make him her first friend in a high place.

He waited for the waiter to attend their drinks, then said, "Hammersmith and Stanford are two English experimental psychologists who set up an artificial tropical oasis near Loch Ewe, Scotland. In this garden, where dulcimers strummed through the warm and perfumed air, they placed maidens in various stages of dress. Into the garden they brought young spacemen whose profiles showed they had formerly possessed rampant libidos but who were now night walkers. The maidens cooed and sighed and beckoned, but to no avail. The spacemen kept their eyes on the stars.

"In particular, I remember one young leftenant, Ian Harris, whose fiancée awaited him in the garden. They had planned to be married after his shakedown cruise, but he had returned starstruck from his first voyage."

Hans paused, rolling his glass around the rim of its base, and Freda could have sworn his eyes moisted over. "Ian's beloved had volunteered to help him, and she was waiting in the garden when he entered, gazing up at the stars. She was not undraped in the academic sense, but she was tantalizingly clothed. When Ian entered, she said, 'Ian, this is your Suzanne, and I'm lonely.'

"For a fleeting second, his eyes dropped and he saw her. His responses were instantaneous, obvious, and normal. But his eyes went back to the stars, and in a voice trembling with passion he said, 'Suzanne, Sagittarius is so clear tonight, you can actually see the archer.'"

Hans finished his drink and ordered another round.

"What happened to the girl?" Freda asked.

70

"She married a swab jockey, better equipped for the rigors of space, who got into OCS through her father's pull—he was an admiral—and her husband's now commander in the Royal Space Navy."

"Why didn't they put her on a limb," Freda wondered aloud, "and put Ian underneath her tree?"

"I don't think that was the error," Hans said, "but there was an error. Currently I'm corresponding with the chief of the Psychiatric Department at Houston on this matter. I think the Hanford-Stammersmith theory takes a pratfall in the libidinal area."

"How so?"

"For the intellectual—and, mind you, only the most sensitive minds succumb to space rapture—the primary erogenic zone is the brain. Their libidos are not sublimated but coordinated. Intellectuals don't 'fall in love.' They form value judgments. For instance, if an architect is designing the Chartres Cathedral, a rape case strolling through his office couldn't draw his attention from the drawing board. Your boy Polino probably attracts you, but your libido, which is stronger than most, is focused on plant life. I contend that Hammerford-Stansmith offered libidinal lures without comcomitant values to be judged."

"If I have a strong libido, Hans, why do I resent being touched?"

"A defense mechanism, bars to keep the beast caged, levees to keep the flood channeled for socially useful purposes." Again he whipped out his slide rule, squinting at it in the dim light. "You've had three doubles; according to my calculations, your thalamus should be in balance with your cerebrum. Let's try a game of 'feelies.' Here, give me your right hand."

He took her right hand with his left hand and ran his fingers up and down her bare upper arm. "Any reaction?"

"Goose pimples!"

"Normal. You're slightly ticklish. Now, through my coat, squeeze my right arm with your left hand. What does it feel like?"

"Hard. You're very muscular."

"I play handball with that arm. . . . Now, Freda, close your eyes and place your right hand, palm up, on the table. I'm placing my index and second finger of my right hand into the groove formed by the index and second finger of my left hand and placing the four fingers in your palm. Now, grip the four fingers lightly. Good! Any repulsion?"

"None whatsoever!"

"Very good. Now, here. What do you feel?"

"I feel like another round. Order us one while I go to read the scoop, but send them to my room. That bartender's getting mighty curious!"

On her way to the pill dispenser for the first time in her life, she felt weirdly buoyant and free. Something was wrong with gravity!

Part of her airiness came from the certain knowledge that Hans Clayborg was the best ally in a high place any woman administrator could possibly have. This man was an authentic genius. He could read her mind. He could manipulate bureau chiefs over telephones. He could explain the Goldberg theory to a botanist and write directives to a neuropsychiatric chief denouncing the Hammerstand-Smithford theory. He had promised to teach her how to blast out an entrenched foe. She would feel safe around him even with a dying sun. He could figure out a way to relight the lamp. He had taught her, with a flick of the fingers, that her life-dominating obsession was merely a childish aversion, even if he didn't guess the right reason. She didn't have the slightest doubt that this boy would come up, sooner or later, with a handful of human corn seeds.

She returned to find him standing to meet her, fighting his own battle with gravity, and he said, "I've rechecked my figures by the bar lamp, and I think you've gone over the optimum. Besides, I don't want room service coming in. My first reaction would be to jump out of the window, and sixteen stories is a long, long drop."

"Come along, then, little man. But there's one house rule in my room. . . . No teeth! You take them out. How'd you lose them anyway, Hans?"

Always the gentleman, he retrieved her purse from the table and slipped his teeth into the bag, explaining, "I was trapped in a vulnerable position."

It was a strange interlude, without apprehension, without even expectation or curiosity. Somewhere near the ceiling Doctor Caron floated and observed with clinical detachment the crab which scuttled toward Freda, sounding like a seal strangling a bark. But to Freda it was a turtle, and she giggled. "What are you giggling about?" he asked.

"I remind myself of a beach," she said, "and you're a turtle digging in the sand to lay an egg. But why doesn't your shell clack?"

"I could clack my teeth if you prefer clacks, but you took them."

Later, he said, "Oh, boy," as he dragged her to the shower, "you *are* different."

Courteous as always, Hans turned on the cold water as she sat in the corner of the stall. Leaning above her, grinning his toothless grin, he said, "Now, Freda, once more, with Gaynor. He'll give you the Bureau, send Berkeley to Tucson, and throw in the experimental farm as a bonus."

Suddenly his enthusiasm changed to gentleness. He bent beneath the pelting drops, kissed her tenderly on the cheek, and said, "Good night, sweet princess, and bands of angels lull thee to thy rest."

His gentleness touched her, and as he softly closed the shower-stall door, she began to weep. Poor Paul! One girl's defloration was another's efflorescence, Polino had said; but, here, on a night that should have marked her entry into womanhood, she had felt nothing but a whimsical merriment, thought of nothing but crustaceans.

Her analyst was right. Condemned forever to psychic virginity, she was as frigid as the water pelting back and sides. *Caronous sireni pseudodos!* Frozen Freda! Paul, her beloved, was

73

getting nothing but an empty package. Her warm tears merged with the cold shower and she slept.

At almost five o'clock she awakened with nausea, and turning off the shower, she went to the toilet and was sick. The pill, she thought. She was allergic to those quick-action pills. Considering the matter objectively, a momentary nausea was far, far better than coming to her wedding, gowned in white, and five months advanced into pregnancy.

She dried her cherry-red body and calmed her chattering teeth, checked to see that Hans had not forgotten his teeth, and crawled into her mussed bed.

Strangely at peace with herself, she joined the Athenians for breakfast. There was an air of subdued elation in the alcove, though Hans greeted her with his ordinary cordiality, no whit the more, no whit the less, and handed her the reason for their happiness.

A columnist in the *Posthole*, the Eavesdropper, reported that the debate in the committee was splitting along party lines, which meant that if Heyburn went with his party, Flora would be admitted to earth's colonial system.

"What do you think now, Hans?" Gaynor asked.

"Things are brightening up," Hans said.

Gaynor beamed at her. "If this goes through, and the Gaynor Station's established, we'll owe it all to our Department of Cystology."

As Freda ordered ham and eggs with a stack and a sausage patty, plus a large orange juice and a bloody mary, she read Clayborg's mind. He did not figure for a moment that the petition would be granted. He was giving her this last opportunity to bask in official sunshine.

Tonight she would begin that novena, she decided. She could get a third of the way through. She was not particularly religious, but any little thing that could help should be tried. Anything to prevent her from using her big guns on Charles Gaynor.

Food and the bloody mary helped realign her focus on the world, and Freda spent most of the day in the Library of Con-

74

gress reading in a field outside of her field. She skipped lunch and dinner with the Athenians, but she welcomed the eleven-o'clock call from the bar. "Don't wear that green dress," Hans said to her. "Or I'll keep my teeth."

Dressed in blue serge, she entered, and Hans went straight to the point, over sloe-gin fizzes. "I knew you knew what I was doing when I sounded optimistic this morning. You and I are in rapport. The Navy's going to work Heyburn over from stem to stern. Speaking of framework, I apologize for last night. My calculations were off. When we reached the sensitive area, I couldn't see the slide rule. I was blinded by your green dress and golden hair. Barring a few idiosyncrasies, you're the most potent combination of beauty and brains I've met, but there's no true beauty without some strangeness of proportion. Please, dear lady, never wear green again. You need Santa Barbara. Santa Barbara needs me, and you throw me off my game. Always wear navy blue to our rendezvous. It's safer, since I'm allergic to the Navy."

His plea was jocular, but there was intensity in his eyes and rigidity to his hair that belied his humor. Gently she reached over and took his hand. "Hans, you've taught me great truths, and I'm grateful. I enjoy our nightly sessions, and I don't wish to throw you off your game. I promise you, I'll never wear green, never drink over four drinks, and never ask you to remove your teeth again."

Hans's incredible ability at offhand predictions proved correct when, after three days' deliberations, Heyburn was wafted to North Dakota as a guest of the Space Navy to dedicate the Senator Heyburn Training Pad for student pilots. The committee went into recess pending his return.

Freda was grateful for the time. She was involved at the Library of Congress, but her reading was done on the premises, and no book was checked out in her name.

Frigidity in the female was a battlefield, she found, which had been fought over since the reign of Queen Victoria. It was a field littered with the misspent efforts of psychologists, psychiatrists, gynecologists, and French woman novelists. As a speed reader, she covered forty volumes in six days. Books by psychiatrists were legal briefs beginning with an assumption supported by quotations from other books to prove the validity of the assumption, and the other books quoted the subject book to support their assumptions. This was how "schools" of psychology were born, she discovered, and each had its guru. Brushing aside the drones to get to the queen bee, she found two well-documented opinions: (1) Frigidity in females did not exist organically. (2) Orgasms in females could not occur organically. On the seventh day, she rested and tossed a coin—heads "yes," tails "no," but by now her platonic friendship with Hans had progressed to the point where she could discuss anything with him, and with freedom. She tossed the problem to Hans.

He clapped an astonished hand to his forehead. "Child, you *are* naïve. I told you it was a slide-rule error."

"But you were only figuring my optimum drinking capacity."

"Not your drinking optimum," he assured her, "but your feeling optimum. I was calculating the point at which your desire to be loved balanced your fear of being touched. Because I was too drunk to read the scale correctly, I took you beyond the point of no return. Your cerebral impulses had correctly ceased to function, but your thalamus was too dead also. When you giggled, I knew I had lost. I could have waited in the shower with you until your sensitivity came back, but, frankly, I couldn't take the cold water for an hour or two."

He shook his head slowly, "Don't let your life be wrecked by my physical cowardice. On your wedding night, carefully measure out and drink four and one-quarter martinis, then pray for the safety of Paul Theaston."

She appreciated his reassurance, but she knew, sadly, that he was her friend now. He wouldn't hesitate to lie to her. Anyway, her problem was as bad as ever. Paul strongly disapproved of drinking, and he would think it suspicious indeed if his supposedly innocent bride carefully measured out and drank four and one-quarter martinis on their wedding night in order to prime herself for their nuptial couch.

Chapter Six

ACCORDING TO FREDA'S ACQUAINTANCES WHO WERE INFORMED on such matters, a novena was a devotion stretched over a week and two days. If she had started prayers on the first night, forgoing the fornication and intoxication, she might have finished her devotion with a day to spare, but her faith in prayer might have suffered a setback. Heyburn gave the Flora plea a flat turndown.

Findings were announced Saturday at two P.M., two days after Heyburn's seven-day revel amid the fleshpots of Bismarck and Mandan had ended. It was a blustery, snowy day outside, but Freda had to admit he looked chipper and cherubic after his all-expense-paid tour. In a crowded chamber, at one minute after two, Eastern Standard Time, the Senator rose to face the red "action" lights of the cameras, rapped his gavel three times, and announced:

"Comes now the findings of the Senate Committee on Planetary Selection. To all present, the President of the United States sends greetings. Be it known that his committee, by a vote of five to four, finds that the planet known variously as Flora, the Flower Planet, and the Planet of Flowers, coordinates 121.63 degrees horizontal, 3.187 degrees vertical and down, 14.383 parsecs out from Galactic Center, on the wheel of the Milky Way, is hereby designated a pariah planet. To his beloved constituents, the Citizens in Good Standing of the United States, on earth or in high heavens, he does declare said planet now, and forever more, unsuitable for their habitation, unless this decree be revoked by the UN Planetary Council in subsequent session assembled. This decree, issued on the eleventh day of February, 2237, does in no way revoke the terms and privi-

77

leges of scientific expeditions currently employed or in process of being employed upon said planet until the third day of November, 2237.

"Many cogent and well-phrased, even attractive arguments—" here he focused a smile on Freda, who almost reeled from its impact—"have been presented to this committee, but the President, in his wisdom, finds the weight of his considerations in favor of the nay-sayers.

"Gentle petitioners, I am charged to express the President's high appreciation for your concern in matters pertinent. Hearings are over. Petitioners dismissed."

Once only he rapped his gavel, and the sound rolled through the chamber with the hollowness of trapped thunder.

To Freda the sound was a knell. On this spot, on this day, her career was ended on the lower levels of administration. She had let herself be shamefully outmaneuvered by Berkeley and shamelessly sacrificed by Charles Gaynor. Never would her guns be trained on Berkeley, for Gaynor would have to pull the trigger, and Charles Gaynor would never pull her trigger. Sadly she knew her resolution to be academic. In a symbolic sense, the oracle of the ladies' lounge had prophesied truly: Charles had already done it to Freda, without love, in Washington.

Freda arose to leave, when Hans restrained her, saying, "Wait."

Heyburn still stood before the lectern, looking up at the cameras as if to check that all lights were out. He licked his lips avidly, and the spectators seemed to lean toward him. Watching, she saw the cherubim die behind his pancake, saw the grease-paint wrinkle as his jowls slackened. Even the color of his eyes seemed to change from pale blue to steely gray, and his lower lip extended a full quarter inch from beneath his upper. Before her very eyes, the devil's advocate was assuming the form of his client.

"O.K., boys," he growled, "this is off the record."

Reporters near Freda, who had folded their pads and laid their

78

pencils down, drew steno machines from their coats, and she knew an underground press conference was about to begin.

"Dear friends and dearer enemies"—Heyburn opened with an oratorical roll, but the honey had gone from his voice—"when this motley concord of bleeding hearts, Easter eggheads, and Southern California ballyhoo artists, including a starlet with the bumpers of a lavender Cadillac, swished into this chamber, the place began to reek with undue influence on a Senate committee."

"How much did the Navy pay for your vote, Heyburn?" someone shouted.

"Thank you, dear enemy, for the inspiration of rage. But that's for me to know and Internal Revenue to find out."

He paused, took a sip from a glass beside the lectern, and bowed his head in appreciation of the jeers and cat-calls. But when he raised his hand for silence, silence was immediately granted.

"While the honored petitioners paraded their wide-eyed ingenue and an emotional cripple before us—that hound dog baying at a midday moon—the motto of the great state of Kansas kept rolling in majesty through my mind, *Ad Astra per Aspera*, to the stars, the hard way."

It was an off-the-record speech and would be honored as such by the home-circulated newspapers, but the clicks of the steno machines were rising and falling with the pace of Heyburn's words.

"*Ad Astra per Aspera*," he repeated, and paused for sad effect. "A motto inscribed on the grave of a dream where rots the moral fiber of our Republic, destroyed by the four horsemen of civilization: ease, order, intellect, enlightenment. Dear friends and dearer enemies, there is no moral equivalent of war, no progress without pain, no color without conflict, no vitality without violence. I oppose all Tahitis in space. I close all cul-de-sacs of flowers. Sound for me the iron ring of the deadly planets, and I will raise my hand in blessing, saying, 'Go. Meet and overcome the challenge.' But I will sound forever 'Nay!' to the lotus eaters, the lovers of ease, the oglers of nonfunctional beauty."

"Hate! Hate!" a heckler shouted.

"There is no progress in paradise," the Senator continued. "Man could not have walked so splendid in the sunlight had he not been cast from Eden. But the circle of fate which led from the apple has brought us back again to applesauce. When Adam went east from Eden, he moved in the vicious logic of the circle. The farther from Eden he walked to eastward, the closer to Eden he came from the west. Even now my nostrils scent the effluvium of that oasis which will prove the grave of our spirit."

"Die! Die!"

"Dear enemy, die I shall; but I shall die standing on the legs of a man, hurling curses at the dying sun, and not as a vegetable succumbing silently to the first nips of frost. And I shall die blaspheming the name of the Great Circle, God, as a circle that ever returneth in to the self-same spot, with little of sadness and less of sin and compassion the soul of the plot."

"Heresy! Blasphemer!"

Suddenly Freda noticed that members of the audience were throwing their shoulders in feints, pecking their heads, putting body-English on his words in the manner of vicarious participants at a prizefight.

"Honored petitioners"—he turned toward the Athenians—"you have received the thanks of the President. Now, accept my little contribution. To the Hollywood ingenue with more up front than on top, hail and farewell. To the platinum-colored egghead, hail and farewell. To the bush-league couch climber, hail and farewell. God grant you a turbulent flight back to your irrigated geraniums!"

Freda was appalled by his discourtesy uttered with such venom and accuracy, but the crowd was hushed and waiting. As the Senator took another sip of his liquid, she heard the sough-sough of breathing around her. Heyburn had named but three of the Athenians, and she, too, leaned forward, waiting.

"And you, O antenna-headed Daedulus, master fabricator, I fear your Icarian messengers have flown too close to this sun—"

"Of a bitch!" Someone yelled, and the audience tittered.

"The wings you built had a malfunction in the cooling system. Your Icarus has taken another pratfall. Return, O puppet master, to your Santa Barbara rehearsal rooms with your strings and your puppets and your hurdy-gurdy tunes. You have rolled snake eyes once more. Your dice game is over. There'll be none of your craps on Flora."

He drank again, keeping a steady eye on Clayborg. When he spoke again, he seemed to petition the petitioner. "Clayborg, I've asked you before, and I ask you again—quit playing by the rules! When the outermost stars have faded and the outermost planets fall, when the great galaxies collapse, give us a head start on the next cycle. You know the path before you. Take it! Break the Great Circle and let us mold its contours to our own design. Cheat God! Cheat the Great Cheater!"

A contagion swept the audience, which began to chant, "Cheat, Clayborg, cheat! Cheat, Clayborg, cheat!"

Hans stood and raised his hands for a silence granted. "Ladies and gentlemen, I'm not gifted with the Senator's eloquence, so I'll not harangue you. Let me say simply: there's a divinity that ends our shapes. . . . True, there is no moral equivalent of war. But there is no warlike equivalent to morality. To cheat God, to short-circuit evolution, would demand a long journey, and who would we send on that journey? Our liver-lipped Senator from North Dakota?"

Clayborg let the shouts of "No! No!" die a slow death.

"But he would have to go, as a bribe for his cooperation."

"Let us all die," someone shouted.

Clayborg raised his hand. "So, you see, a choice would be difficult. I have met few in my life whom I would send beyond the worlds' end. This lady, so grossly maligned by the gentleman from North Dakota"—here he laid his hand atop Freda's head, and she felt as if she had received a benediction, although this was a purely intuitive feeling, since she had no previous experi-

81

ence with blessings—"is one of the few I might select for such a journey. From personal knowledge, I can attest that she has more on top than up front."

She would have to take that remark under advisement, Freda thought, as Hans removed his hand and continued. "But I have accepted the Law of Morality, and I will not cheat. We have been given the cycles of creation, and we will work within those cycles. We will defeat God at His own game, playing the game by His rules, but we will defeat Him as men, to join with Him as men. Despite the Senator's proposal, I do not choose to be Lucifer by popular acclamation. I do not choose to be Prince of Darkness by senatorial appointment. I certainly do not choose to be Beelzebub to yonder Satan."

He paused briefly for cheers of approval.

"Once we take arms against God in open warfare, there can be no victory, there can be no armistice, and there'll be no discharge from the war. I am not proposing passive acquiescence to fate. I am a militant. I shall not cease from mortal strife, nor shall my sword sleep in my hand, till we have built our New Jerusalem; but, by God's grace, gentlemen, we'll build His city with mortal fingers. . . . I thank you."

There was a reverent pause. Nothing more could be said, and the crowd began to file from the chamber. Freda noticed that most of the men were sweating profusely.

Berkeley and Gaynor left promptly, but Freda stayed behind with Hans to receive the handshakes and backslaps of the right-thinking listeners, while the others went to congratulate Heyburn. In her opinion, Clayborg had definitely won the confrontation. She was not positive what the confrontation was all about, but it had been thrilling. When she finally got Hans away from the group and they were walking down the corridor to the taxi stand, she asked him what it was all about.

"Oh," he dismissed the incident, "Heyburn was simply provoking the moral equivalent of a street riot. You have to give the crowd its bread and circuses. Stripped of rhetoric, Heyburn knew that I was behind the Flora petition, and he would have known it if I had been in South Africa during the hearings. . . . I liked that 'Easter egghead' he tagged on Charlie. . . . Of course, I'm sorry you were involved. I should have suspected Gaynor was up to something when I met you in Bakersfield, but, hell, I can't worry about anybody's plots but my own."

He held the taxi door for her, and as he slid into the seat beside her, she asked, "What was the argument about cheating God and breaking the circle?"

"Some more barnyard oratory. The universe collapses and explodes, in and out, like this." He moved his hands like an accordion player's. "And he wants me to rev up a starship to a velocity that will send it out of space and out of time. In that condition, you are nothing and no longer subject to natural laws—beyond God, in Heyburn's language.

"It would be a simple matter, according to Goldberg's Law of Diminishing Entropy, to figure when the next explosion will occur and make a round trip into nothingness with preset controls to come back during the next cycle with fully evolved human beings, their technology microfilmed and ready. But I can't buy it—lurking outside the law, waiting to pounce on a virgin universe.

"We'd control evolution, and then what would the next cycle produce? More Heyburns? Who among us is qualified to twist the helix?"

"Surely there must be some worthy persons. You even mentioned me."

"Would you like to go?" he asked seriously.

"Certainly not! I'd be a very defective specimen."

"Your answer qualifies you for the voyage and proves my point. At Santa Barbara, we call it Catch-69. Those who are qualified to go won't go. Only predators, the greedy and power hungry, would be willing to wait outside the law and pounce on a virgin universe. They would have absolute power over the wellsprings of creation. Since absolute power corrupts absolutely, who wants a totally corrupt God? No, Freda, my ship won't carry no fakers, marihuana smokers, or acid-trip takers."

For a moment he paused, then added, "So, I'm sending no ship."

"What about your seeds?" she asked.

"Seeds? Oh, they conform to law."

When she and Hans got back to the hotel, there was another telegram from Hal: "Am getting assistance from unexpected source. God bless the grass of Flora! Soon, tulips will be in Bakersfield; tomorrow, the world! Strumming a dissonant guitar in Old Town. Having a wonderful wish. Time you were here."

Both vexed and amused by his language, she noticed the dateline was Friday night and that it had been sent from Fresno. She handed the telegram to Hans, who was checking out at the desk, and said, "Interpret this."

Hans glanced at it. "The tulips are adapting to earth so fast they need controls. 'Tomorrow, the world' was the slogan of twentieth-century Nazis, who set out to conquer the world. Since he's been freed of stoop labor by some undesignated pollinator, he's playing a guitar in a jazz joint."

"Do you think he was drunk when he wrote it?"

"No," Hans said, "His spoonerism is too apt. The boy has a man-sized crush on you."

"Oh, Hans." She blushed. "He knows I'm engaged."

"Which only makes you more of a challenge. . . . Keep in touch with me about those tulips, Freda, but don't feel hurt if I don't answer your letters. When I'm solving impossible problems, I tend to get absentminded."

Because of the blizzard, there was a two-hour delay in the takeoff for the land of irrigated geraniums. As Gaynor and Berkeley dozed in the seats ahead, Freda and Hans enjoyed their last double martini together on the one-cocktail flight. Between them lay the bittersweetness of parting for two, Freda thought, who had loved not wisely and not too well.

Hans tended more toward the bitter. "I feel guilty about you, Freda," he complained, "because you reflect on my chess playing. I tried to sacrifice a pawn, Gaynor, but Heyburn jumped him to capture the queen, you."

"Gaynor was responsible for the sacrifice."

"Yeah, he got in the game. But the game's still in progress. Clayborg hasn't lost."

"Caron has," she said.

"If life were played by chess rules, yes," Clayborg admitted. "Heyburn's unofficial reprimand hurt you. As time passes and his august reputation grows and senility hardens his dislikes, he might block your appointment to the bureaucracy—if you can get by Gaynor."

"I'm a realist, Hans. Gaynor will assign me to pure research, and I'll end my days puttering around among potted plants."

"There's another way to go—my way," he said. "If you can come up with an authentic contribution to the plant sciences, you can win an appointment to one of the Think Factories— Princeton, Santa Monica, or Santa Barbara—which will make you the peer of the chief executive."

"I doubt my capabilities," she said.

"I don't! Listen, Freda. I have a hunch about those tulips. They may be your key out of the administrative cellar. Here's the crux of my suggestion. Observe those flowers from every possible angle. Assume, for instance, that they evolved from field mice, and look for facts to prove the theory."

"You sound like a psychiatrist."

"Maybe," he admitted. "But it's not enough to 'see life steady and see it whole.' You have binocular vision, and to use it you have to keep shifting your head. A student of mine in Australia has created a successful methodology merely by attributing impossible causes to phenomena.

"You *must* practice the suspension of disbelief, for the universe is illogical, and you yourself are a mathematical impossibility. You were a million-to-one shot on the night you were conceived—project those odds back through the generations!"

Freda pinched herself. She was there.

"Here's my suggestion," he continued. "If you find anything

85

about the tulips which merits a monograph, write the treatise and send it through channels. The channels will protect your authorship even though every bureaucrat who reads it will add a dissenting opinion to show he's thought about the subject in even greater depth.

"Now, this is important: send a copy of your dissertation to me. The Institute for Advanced Studies will rule on the validity of your theorems without the handicap of forty-eight different negative endorsements. I'll see to that. You know I'm a manipulator, and you have no reason to trust me; but you do, don't you?"

"For some reason, Hans, I do."

"I could verbalize your reasons." He grinned. "But I won't."

Freda let him have his moment of self-indulgent triumph, but she knew very well why she trusted him. With or without his false teeth, he loved her; and, she could have added truthfully, in an abstract, impersonal, and highly sanitary manner, she returned his love.

After a farewell dinner for Clayborg in Bakersfield, Gaynor's group returned to the base in the Bureau's helicab. In the cabin, with the friendship and protection of Hans gone, she could feel the beginning chill of Gaynor's estrangement. He had apologized at the dinner, but his apology had been a reprimand. "I'm sorry, Freda. I should have turned the pleading over to a more experienced administrator."

"Oh, no, Doctor," she said. "You made no administrative error in giving me the assignment. Our cause was lost as soon as the Navy moved against us."

Now, leaning back, gazing idly down on the Coastal Range, she could feel the beginning chill of his estrangement, and she could plot its course from the textbooks. He was opening with polite hauteur, known in some circles as *Sic Semper Illegitami*. Feeling herself apart from the competition now, she could watch Berkeley's maneuvering with cynical amusement. Gaynor said little, but what he said was quickly seconded by the psychiatrist. He smoked little, but the cigarettes were quickly lighted by

Berkeley with a movement called by some "the brown-fingered flick."

As the helicab hovered over the Bureau Chief's garage, Freda noticed the parking lot was empty; obviously, memories of their old love were gone from Section Able. As the helicab descended, she glanced eastward. Through the deepening twilight over the San Joaquin Valley she could see the lights of Fresno twinkling on. South of those towers, she mused, it was promenade time in Old Town.

Suddenly her mind was flooded with longings. Literally, she could hear the heel clicks of senoritas on the cobbled plaza, the fading diphthongs of Spanish, the half-suppressed laughter from under lace mantillas. She could feel the sway of their hips in her hips as they strolled, clockwise, around the fountain, ogled by lean-flanked boys in sequined trousers strolling counterclockwise in the outer circle. She could see the sun-pinked solidity of adobe walls and smell the musky mealiness of cooking tortillas. She could hear the strumming of guitars through the oaken half-doors of cantinas as musicians readied their rhythms for Saturday night in Old Town. Overwhelmed by the imagery, she achieved a hauteur of her own as she bade the two men good night after the helicab had landed. Walking alone down the mall to her quarters, she found her footfalls gliding into the one-two-THREE (½), one-two-THREE (½) syncopations of a dissonant tango.

No power of analysis Freda could summon explained this surge of joy and sadness which pulsed through her like a current from an anode in search of a cathode. Perhaps, she mused, something more than nothing had occurred in her hotel room in Washington and this was a delayed reaction. Perhaps, subconsciously, she was bidding farewell to her dream of a career. Or, perhaps, her feeling was the conscious knowledge that she was coming to her tulips.

Sunday morning, after breakfast, she took only time enough to stop by the ladies' lounge to check the bulletin board before hurrying over to the greenhouse, but she was so shaken by what she found, that she was delayed longer than she had planned. Scribbled in that now familiar handwriting, she read: "Charlie did it to Freda in Washington, without love. Hans couldn't do it, with love. Hal's closing fast. Who'll beat Paul to the wire?"

She was so irked by the scrawl that she ripped the February sheet from the wall, tore it to bits, and flushed it toward the Paso Robles outfall.

Her act was not good form, she knew. Graffiti sheets eased social tensions as gossip surrogate, but whoever wrote those squibs about her was taking unfair advantage. Obviously the scribbler was a reporter on the underground press and had picked up the snoop from the UP wire service. Freda sat fuming in the lounge until her boil dropped to a low simmer, trying to force all negative thoughts from her mind before greeting her tulips.

To a degree, she succeeded, and the walk across the lawn in the warm sunlight, with the green grass underfoot, helped restore her further.

As she rounded the corner of the greenhouse, she was brought to a dead stop by the shimmer of gold and green which greeted her, the colors and the magnitude. Four beds wide and six beds deep, the tulips stretched a quarter of the distance to the fence, and the first twelve beds were blooming.

Hal had separated the beds with strips of canvas, four feet wide, to catch the seeds, which would have fallen on the footpaths, but inside the beds he had planted each tulip with care, almost precisely six inches apart. Whatever sins Hal Polino might commit in his thinking, his practical procedures had been as carefully planned as the moves of a three-dimensional chess champion. Her garden radiated beauty.

She walked slowly toward the center of the plots, watching the golden spokes revolve to the motion of her eyes, listening to the soft murmur arising in the air chambers, caused by the slight turbulence of her passing. She could feel the radiations infuse her cells and corpuscles with quanta of joy from the shimmering greens, the singing, and the gold. The sound was a fluttering purr, but more sibilant, like the slithering of silk from the falling raiment of a vestal.

Suddenly a breeze stirred in the garden, and she had to lift her eyes from the flowers to focus her senses on the sound. She stood, head up, ears alert, as the eddy passed through the blossoms, and the tulips sang.

They sang an oratorio to gods of gentler climes, Jupiters without lightning, Thors without thunder, ungibbeted Galileans. Not until their diapasons had swelled around her and died across the garden did she dare lower her eyes to their beauty. Adoration in their singing had touched her with a Sabbath awe, giving new dimensions to—

"They never sang to me like that!" Hal Polino was calling. He stood by the corner of the greenhouse, sun-burned, shirtless, wearing Bermuda shorts, with a coil of electric line wrapped over his shoulder and some object in his hand.

"Hal Polino, they're just gorgeous!" she called. "Go away! Go inside! Let me commune with them alone."

"I'll give you five minutes to commune with the little beasts, then I'm setting up for some controlled music." He went into the greenhouse and closed the door.

She was alone again. On a whim, she bent to her knees and sang, "I come to the garden alone . . ."

Her voice activated the closer tulips with a rustling echo of her words. With both knees on the canvas, her arms spread in the manner of a choir leader, she conducted them, three notes at a time, "While the dew . . . is still on . . . the roses. And the voice . . . I hear . . . falling on . . . my ear . . . the Son of God . . . discloses."

She laughed with happiness, her laughter rippling through the tulips. She had scored a first in the history of humankind. She had led a choir of flowers.

"Try a waltz." Hal stuck his head from the doorway. "They really swing to a four-beat measure."

"Back in your hole, mole!" she shouted.

89

She still had the first hymn-singing of flowers on record, she felt, looking at the tulips from knee level along the farthest expanse of the flowerbeds. She raised and lowered her head to get the best possible angle of vision, making new arrangements of green and gold. By raising her head and looking down, she could crop the distant brown trunks of the eucalyptus out of her vision. From this position, her line of sight downward and focused in close, she spotted a flaw that horrified her with its implications. Not three feet from her, the lower-interior petals of a female were spotted with purple. Against the iridescence of the gold, the purple canker was loathsome. Rising, Freda looked around her. Over there was another. Here, another. If a blight had struck these tulips, and if Hal Polino was making no attempt to control it, she would see to it that he'd be strumming his dissonant guitar in the cantinas of Mars.

She turned and strode toward the greenhouse, eyes blazing, jaw set. As she started to swing open the door and open the questioning, she saw a purple smudge on the white paint of the glass near the door. Her fear subsided, but a residual kickback of anger remained at the sight of the smudge. Somebody had wiped his pollinating finger near the door.

Hal opened the door. "Welcome back, Doctor."

"Hal, what are those horrid purple stains on the tulips?"

"Plant dye."

"You used dye on my tulips, when you know it kills them?"

"I figured they were vulnerable only from the root system, so I took a chance."

"Took a chance?" she flared. "What kind of procedure is that?"

"It worked." He shrugged. "If I'd killed a few, what difference would it make? We have thousands of the brutes, and we may have to exterminate them all."

"Over my dead body! You wait here. I want to look at the log."

"May I remind Doctor Caron that this is Sunday, my day off," he said, stooping to plug in the electric lead line.

"As of right now, it isn't! Please remain in the area until I've checked your records."

"Yes, ma'am. I intend to," he said, almost insolently, backing toward the beds and uncoiling the line. "But all you'll find in the log are observations. The deductions are up here." He tapped his brow with his fingers, slowly, ominously, as he stooped to pick up a small, battery-powered electric fan.

He turned and walked away, dragging the heavy extension cord down the canvas path. Under the tension of his effort, she noticed, the muscles of his back were long and striated, like the muscles of a distance swimmer. It was almost indecent the way his torso rippled when he bent and swayed, and she made a mental note to post a notice on the greenhouse bulletin board that all personnel must be properly clothed while working in the seed beds.

Chapter Seven

AT FIRST POLINO'S LOG WAS METICULOUS, EVEN TO HIS PENMAN-ship. After Tuesday, January 24, two days after she had left for Washington, his penmanship faltered. Since his first seed harvest occurred that day, she could forgive his subsequent haste. He had been busy pollinating. For the twenty-seventh she noticed an entry: "Detected sugar in nectar. No sugar before. Tulips must be aware bees are pollinators, and sugar attracts bees. How did they find out?"

On January 30 Polino had made another entry relative to sugar content of nectar: "Lab analysis shows sugar content of nectar now 22%. The bees are coming."

Then the entries grew interesting from several points of view: as scientific observations and nonscientific observations, errors in record keeping, faulty use of nomenclature, and flights of fancy. This ingenue, Freda thought, is reading her first movie scenario.

February 2: Bees won't do! Four honeybees got their heads crushed by the calyptra of female tulips.

February 4: A wasp laid an egg in a calyx.

February 5: More wasps arriving. They might serve. Found four wasps dead. Identified wasps as *Masaridae,* or Mexican ground wasps—the only species of wasps that feeds its larvae on honey and pollen.

February 6: Stained abdomen of a wasp purple. Stain showed on oviduct of 68 tulips before wasp died of fatigue.

Caron tulips are conning wasps into *thinking* that they are laying eggs.

February 8: No wasp fatalities today. Stained another wasp green. Only ten stains showed on tulip oviducts. Tulips have learned not to work wasps to death.

February 10: More wasps arriving (From Mexico?) A beds germinating, B beds pollinated. C beds blooming. D beds growing. Preparing E and F beds for planting.

Freda closed the logbook with a thump and stalked into the garden. Polino was sprawled on the canvas between the blooming C beds and the green shoots of the D row. He had set up the portable fan to blow in the hundred-degree arc onto the blooms, and he was adjusting dials on the black box. As the fan blew against the tulips, they fluted and sang.

"What's that?" Freda asked.

"A high-fidelity, stereophonic recorder," he answered. "I tape their music and splice it into illogical progressions, and play the notes until I get disharmonies I like. I write them down and play them on Friday and Saturday nights at the Mexicali Café. These babies have turned me into the top guitar soloist in Fresno. Aficionados of dissonant jazz come from as far away as Madera and Dinuba to hear me play."

"How interesting," she snapped. "I must attend one of your recitals. . . . At the moment, Mr. Hal Polino, there's a matter of record keeping I'd like to discuss."

"Doctor," he said, rising, "I can tell from your expression it's not something I want recorded. You might damage my equipment."

"Come to the office!"

She turned and strode back to the greenhouse. When she entered, went to her desk, and opened the logbook, she turned to him and tapped the entry for February 6. "Flowers do not 'con' insects into 'thinking.' A manual of scientific observations

93

is not a journal of wild speculations in the dialect of another century. Young man, you were assigned to me for one principle reason: to improve your methodology. Not only is this slipshod record keeping, it reveals a cavalier attitude toward scientific nomenclature and complete indifference to precision. I want you to understand that this logbook is an official record. It is signed by me and forwarded to the Department of Agriculture archives. All I want in this book are observed facts. Leave the synthesis of those facts to the computers, which are far better qualified to relate them to the existing body of knowledge than you or I. I want these pages rewritten Monday, without any references to plants indoctrinating insects or other theories, hypotheses, pipe dreams, or fantasies. Is that clear?"

"Yes, ma'am."

"Now, what's this mumbo-jumbo about wasps? Sit down."

He sat, uneasily. "I don't know how to tell you, without using conjecture. . . ."

"Polino, you're talking off the record to me. Say what you please. I can discount it as you go along."

"All right, I'll tell you straight! For the first three days, after I moved the seedlings outside, I pollinated them, as you instructed, with a medical swab. But I found my little finger was more efficient, since cotton stuck in the plants. Inadvertently, I licked my finger, which didn't matter. But one day I thought I tasted sugar, so I took some of the pollen nectar over and had it analyzed. The lab tests are entered."

"That's a reasonable observation," she conceded, "and it was handled correctly."

"Working with the plants all day, naturally I kept them under close observation. Doctor, you can take it or leave it, but *they* were experimenting, not me. One day, after the nectar turned sweet, I saw a hummingbird hovering over a bloom. Now, I'm not allowed to enter into the log what doesn't happen, and that hummingbird didn't touch the bloom. The tulip didn't like the looks of the sharp-pointed spear, and, zap, the hummingbird

94

took off. It didn't come back. What's more," he added emphatically, "no hummingbird ever will."

Freda restrained a smile at his emphasis and asked, "What's your theory for that?"

"The air chamber of the tulip is sort of a Helmholtz resonator with a high pass filter. The tulip bopped the bird in the head with a high-frequency soundwave when it saw that needle point probing at its stigma."

"Saw?" she asked.

"Sensed," he corrected. "They emit their sounds from their calyx, and their petals could be echo detectors."

This boy was mad, she decided. He was approaching the tulips from a perfectly irrational point of view. . . . The same point of view, she suddenly recalled, that Hans Clayborg had suggested she adopt. Perhaps Polino might be of value to her, after all.

"There's a possibility," she agreed, "that an echo-ranging mechanism might be employed by the tulips, though purely as reactive behavior. Sunflowers are light-ranging devices, but I've never met a 'thinking' sunflower. What about the bees?"

"They worked all right with the males, but their hairs irritated the oviducts of the females. So out went the bees."

"And in came the wasps," Freda said.

"Yes, ma'am. When I first noticed the wasps, one was crawling up the stem and backing into the oviduct. I couldn't figure out why it wasn't flying. I had seen a few flying around. So I took it over to 'Bugs' and had them identify it. When the wasp rested up a little while, it flew back to the tulip beds. So, I stained one, and found the tulips were working them to death."

"Hal, quit personifying plants. All that happened is that the wasps found an ideal cell for laying their eggs."

"Doctor," he protested. "These tulips are intelligent. They found the only species of wasp on earth that could do them any good. Through some understanding of the ovulation processes of wasps, they've hypnotized the insects into believing that they are laying eggs. They lay some eggs, and the tulips let them

95

hatch, but the wasps keep right on backing into the tulips long after they've quit laying. The tulips know more about the wasps than I do, so they're smarter than I am. What's more, those wasps have been laying their eggs in the ground for thousands of years. In less than a week, the tulips changed behavior patterns which took aeons to evolve, so they've pulled a trick beyond the power of human intelligence. I'm not a methodologist, and I'll admit it, but I'll bet you Paul Theaston knows these plants think. And I'll bet that when Paul gets back, he'll be bringing seeds of the damndest orchid this planet has ever seen."

Freda couldn't repress a smile, and Polino relaxed slightly. "I'm convinced he's right, ma'am. Those orchids walk at night to do their own courting."

"Hal, there's not one item you've touched on here which cannot be explained logically. . . . Have you discussed these tulips with anyone but me?"

"Certainly not, Doctor."

"Why the 'certainly'?"

"I don't want a one-way trip to Houston. And I'm getting credit for their musical compositions. I like the money and the glory."

"You mentioned your fear that these plants will have to be exterminated."

"I think they're dangerous. They've learned to adapt, and to those babies out there, the earth is an easy mark. . . . They could eliminate the birds, the earthworms, and all the insects they don't need."

"But that would take hundreds of years."

"They don't care."

"But they couldn't eliminate us."

"No, ma'am," he said. "I don't think they could hurt us. . . . Unless Paul brings the orchids, and the orchids and tulips form an alliance. Then, watch out! The orchids could kill men with ease."

"Are you telling me Paul's life is in danger?"

"Absolutely not, Doctor. The orchids wouldn't raise a tendril against Paul."

"Why are you so confident, Hal?"

"Thanks for calling me 'Hal,' Doctor." He grinned, visibly relieved. "The orchids would save Paul because he's the only specimen they have, and they want to study him."

Hal's conversation on Sunday began a week of change for Freda, as Gaynor's frostiness became publicly apparent. In the executive dining room he spent shorter and shorter periods of greeting at her table, busying himself with other department heads. Her stock went down two points because of his shortened greetings. When, by Thursday, he had not invited her into the Bureau Chief's alcove to lunch at his table, other administrators were beginning to notice, and her stock dropped another three points.

Thursday was a particularly bad day. Hal had forecast a second crop of seeds from the A beds, but they didn't materialize. Friday he was still worried, but Freda's stock readings improved slightly. Captain Barron returned from Washington, and he and Commodore Minor joined her at lunch. Up four points!

"Captain Barron," she said archly, "I was certainly surprised to learn of your boyhood among the bloodhounds of Arkansas."

"Admiral Creighton sends you his apologies, Freda. His aide briefed him wrong. . . . But I was surprised, also, that you presented the petition after you found my name on the list."

"Doctor Gaynor thought my costume jewelry might help off-set navy gold braid. We matched a foil against a broadsword."

"Commodore," Captain Barron said suddenly, "did you ever land on Carston 6?"

"Ah, yes," the Commodore nodded. "The slugs."

"Come, now, gentlemen," Freda said, "what are the slugs on Carston 6?"

"Huge snails without shells. They travel through the dense foliage of the planet's tropics," Minor said, "by eating every-thing that gets in their way."

Neither of the officers had indulged in gossip. They had not mentioned a name, but Freda knew she had allies. She belonged to another jurisdiction, and she was being rejected by her peer group; yet she had an anodyne for her hurt in the tulip beds. The A beds, heavy with seeds, had little time for music now, but the B group still sang lustily, and she found herself hurrying from lunch to spread an air mattress near the tulips and listen to their melodies while she looked up at the clouds.

Hal spent most of the week rolling out strips of canvas to catch the seeds and preparing the E and F beds for planting. He would lean over the A beds to point to his distant squares of spaded loam. "There's your target, girls. Now, hit it. I don't want to be cleaning up after you. And keep those seeds six inches apart. I don't want to spend a week thinning the shoots."

According to his calculation, the second crop from the A row, closest to the greenhouse, was overdue. The seeds should have been ejected from the pods on Thursday. When noon came Friday, Freda was tempted to pluck a pregnant female and dissect the ova pod, but Hal protested. "No, ma'am. I planted them in geometrical alignment. You could destroy my pattern. They'll come along. The temperatures this week have averaged about four degrees less than the week before, and they're sensitive to temperature."

"About four degrees!" Freda exclaimed. "A detail as important as this shouldn't be left to speculation. . . . Give me the exact figures."

Shaking his head ruefully, Polino went to the greenhouse to prepare a graph of the temperatures. The week ending on Thursday, February 9, showed a mean temperature 3.8 degrees higher than on the week following. On Friday, no seeds were ejected.

Saturday was Hal's day off; but she found him, lithe and bare-torsoed, marking off with whitewash the next beds for Mr. Hokada to spade on Monday. She went inside to prepare notes for her monograph, and when she emerged she saw him, his tasks completed, pacing the canvas path downwind from the A row and anxiously trying to spot the first airborne seeds. His harassed face made her smile.

"Hal Polino," she called, "you're the picture of an expectant father!"

"Father, hell," he exploded. "I'm having labor pains. No wasp appreciates what a man goes through to deliver his child. What was the temperature, Doctor?"

"Seventy-six."

"Come on, get up. Get up!" he yelled to the temperature, walking down the path, his hands folded behind his back, bent forward, peering truculently at the tulips. He was suddenly an old young man.

"Where are the wasps?" she called as she unfolded her air mattress.

"The tulips have a few standing by, probably to give homing signals to the rest of the wasp fleet cruising around the neighborhood somewhere. The tulips don't need them at this stage of the game. Besides, they might get hit by a seed. But nothing's happening. I can't even find a bloom in my C row."

A wind stirred in the garden, and the B row fluted musically. "They're trying to tell you to cheer up, Hal."

"Liars, sluggards, goldbrickers," he snarled at the A beds, swaying back and forth with their heavy pods.

By two P.M. the temperature had dropped a degree, and a cold, moist air front was moving in from the ocean. "There'll be no deliveries today, Hal," she called, "unless I perform a Caesarean."

"You're no obstetrician," he called. "Besides, they deliver eight at a time, in four rows."

"But remember the dying tulip. She delivered them herself."

He walked over and looked down at her. "Give them another day," he said.

"Polino, you claimed she shot those seeds at the pot. Here's an opportunity to demonstrate pragmatic empiricism. I'm pulling one up. We can replant a seedling in her spot to preserve your precious geometry."

"Doctor, you're sap-thirsty. You'd murder little girls in the interest of science."

"Come, now, Hal. You're supposed to detest the brutes."

"Doctor, I don't care for them as a group, but I like them as individuals."

"Then concentrate on your bigotry and pull one up."

"Pull it yourself," he said flatly. "You're the scientist."

"Chicken." She hurled one of his twentieth-century epithets at him as she reached over and plucked a tulip from the edge of the bed. As she pulled it up, she heard, definitely this time, a soft explosive sigh from its air chamber, the same sound she heard the night she cut the leaf from the tulip that died. Suddenly she was glad he was out of earshot, standing, dramatically posed, his hand over his eyes. Polino would have written a thesis on that sound, weaving from it all sorts of airy theories and dreamy hypotheses to prove that the plants could feel.

"It's done," she said. "You can look now."

"Murder, most foul," he exclaimed, walking over to stoop down by the tulip she had laid out on the canvas. Its swollen seed pod was cracked on one of the vents to show a row of eight tiny capulins, but the pod was completely inert. With her thumbnails, she pried the vent open. "They're fully as mature as the other premature seeds were, and those lived."

"But she isn't ejecting them in her death throes," he complained.

"The other plant died slowly," she said.

"You're right," he agreed, "and it knew it was dying. This one didn't expect death. She trusted you."

"I'm sure that once the stalk has dried, the seeds will pop out."

He thought for a moment. "When I thinned out the beds and threw the shoots into the bin, they didn't dry. . . . Listen!"

A slight breeze stirred the garden, triggering air chambers of the tulips with faint rustlings which returned the echo of the dying tulip's sigh. Sounding in unison, the air chambers produced a sound as loud as a moan, tinged with regret and sorrow. Each tulip passed the sound to its neighbor, and the sigh rose and fell in ululations of sorrow and grief. Freda looked up bewildered, as Hal said, slowly, with no intention of profanity but only of regret, "Jesus!"

The wind had died, but the sound was rising.

It had become a sobbing, and Freda felt herself pervaded by a sadness from out of her childhood and its agony under the elms, a distillation of grief and regret, acute and personal, yet poignant and general, as if she were feeling the sadness of all children. She felt her spirit drawn down corridors that led to a void where nothingness waited, not life or death or joy or pain, but only an emptiness eternal. Still, the sound was rising, keening and throbbing, scaling heights of anguish, and the void was opening. "Stop them, Hal!"

He was on his knees, shouting to the tulips, "She didn't know. Stop it! She didn't know!"

And the sound was gone.

Freda was slumped on the canvas, her torso twisted, her head dropping, leaning on her arms. Echoes of the anguish still sounded in her memory, as Hal bent beside her. "I felt like I did the night my mother died," he said. "They were keening for the dead."

He laid his arm across her shoulder. It was a spontaneous gesture of brotherhood and humanity, and she appreciated it. Squatting beside her, he said nothing for long moments, then, taking her by the waist, he said, "Come, Freda," and he led her back to the office. She was aware that his arm encircled her, and she welcomed his touch. Out of the voids of space and time had come a grief that touched her, a mourning for the death of universes, and her concerns were lost in the vastness of the sorrow.

He helped her to her chair before the desk, and she heard him move behind her to his own desk, and she knew, vaguely, that he was making an entry in the log; then she heard the logbook close, heard the rustle of waxed paper. As the sorrow withdrew from her mind, as she emerged from the grief of the tulips, she heard him chant softly some twentieth-century lament for the dead, chant softly but clearly, and she caught every word:

The chambers in the temple of my heart,
In every one whereof your image dwells,
Are black with grief eternal for your sake.

His lament, so appropriate and so profound, drew her gaze
to him. She saw he had brought the tulip in and laid it on a
piece of florists' paper, which he was folding, tucking in the
edges, enclosing the tulip. As she watched, he took the flower
in both hands and bore it reverently through the door, into sunlight whose colors it would no longer reflect, into air where it
would sing no more. The song and its singer were done. At her
desk, and alone now, Freda dropped her head and wept uncon-
trollably. She was glad Hal had not invited her to the burial.

In fifteen minutes he returned, and she had dried her eyes
and made her face. He sat down at his desk, slumped in his chair,
and swiveled toward her. "You mustn't grieve, Doctor Caron.
What's done is done and cannot be undone."

"Call me 'Freda,' Hal," she said.

"They were talking to us, Freda."

"They communicated with us. Grief is universal, as two times
two is four, anywhere in the universe."

"True. But they communicated. I would like your permission
to send some of my tapes to the Bureau of Linguistics to have
them anaylzed for repetitions or recurrent patterns."

"To determine if the tulips communicate with each other?"
she asked.

"Between us, yes. 'It's my wish,' I would phrase the letter, 'to
have the enclosed tapes analyzed for musical dissonance.' I think
I could get that much accomplished without getting us both sent
to Houston."

"Hal, you're being naïve. I saw your purpose immediately.
By the time your request passed through channels to Agriculture,
over to Health, Education and Welfare, and down to Linguistics,
you and I would both be notorious and our Bureau would be
the laughingstock of all departments. Our careers would be
ruined, our reputations smirched, our honor stained."

"The only honor I honor is honor," he said, "and the one sure way I can dishonor myself is by worrying about my reputation. If a thing's worth believing in, it's worth fighting for."

"Ah, yes," she nodded, "and I was spitted on that spear in Washington."

"If you refer to the Gaynor Station, all you were fighting for was a monument to Gaynor; if you *believed* in that," he added bitterly, "then you were born without honor."

"I agreed with the administration's policy and volunteered to enter that petition," she flared. "But I don't wish to discuss administrative matters."

"I'm not going to," he said, "but if the truth is our goal, it doesn't matter whether we win or lose the approval of the apparatus. If we are right, we are right for eternity, and let the administrators be damned. In my considered opinion," he flared, "those puke-lickers— But, I don't wish to discuss administrators. All I want is information from the linguistic-computer banks. If you approve the letter, they're required to honor it. If Linguistics detect a pattern, I'll buy a secondhand copy of *Crypto-Analytics* and decipher the pattern myself. . . . If I find what I think I'll find, no bureaucrat in the world will be able to challenge or demean or suppress the Caron-Polino theory of plant communication."

He had invaded her temple and whipped her priests as money changers, and she more than half-agreed with him. He had made her ambition seem shameful, and she felt shamed. He had linked her name with his in a coupling as ridiculous as an *Einstein-Valentino Theory of Relative Ardor,* yet his idea might be the key to a Cabinet post for her.

His idea also held dangers, and for the moment she was most concerned with the dangers. No matter how valid this boy's contempt for the power structure, it still had the power. And ridicule was bureaucracy's deadliest weapon.

"I'll not permit you to send the letter. We haven't a shred of evidence to support such a theory, and there's no place for intuition in an exact science. It's not enough to 'have a hunch' that the tulips communicate: it must be shown how they communicate."

"But, I'm seeking evidence only. . . ."

"Based on sheer intuition," she snapped. "You would need evidence to justify the man-hours Linguistics would have to spend analyzing the tapes. I'll forward your request only when it's backed by evidence."

"Yes, ma'am."

"You've been under a strain, Hal, pacing the delivery-room floor. Get out, and go play your guitar."

"You're under a strain too." He grinned. "Why don't you drop by the Mexicali tonight and relax to the dissonant rhythms of El Toro Polino?"

"Is that what the senoritas call you?"

"That's my bandstand name. I'm playing my new composition tonight. 'The Caron Can-Can.' I'm too cowardly to admit that the tulips composed it, but I can dedicate it to them in the title."

"Polish it up," she said. "Maybe someday you can play it for me, but never in Old Town."

She did not know what hours he kept on Saturday night, but he was in the tulip beds before her Sunday morning, in shirtless informality. Sunday had dawned clear and warm, and she came to the beds early to find him pacing the paths, cursing the "brutes" and "beasts." "I've got a feeling about today. Last night I played to standing room only at the Mexicali, and 'The Caron Can-Can' had the *olés* shaking the cantina. A promoter hit me up to make a recording."

"Oh, won't it be lovely," she said, "when in all the low dives of the world, lissome legs are being flung to 'The Caron Can-Can.'"

"Oh, it's not a French can-can," he explained. "It's sort of a four-and-a-half-beat Spanish can-can with a boogie-woogie bounce."

"With a little chili pepper added, no doubt," she said.

"Freda, you don't know good music. You should come by some Saturday. I'll play it special for you."

"Perhaps I may," she said.

"Just let me know in advance," he warned seriously, "so I can make table reservations."

Oh, what a sly one, she thought, as she unrolled her air mattress. He wanted to make arrangements, all right, this el toro, Polino, but there were going to be no four and one-quarter martinis drunk by Freda Caron to the four-and-one-half-beat measure of a Spanish can-can in the Mexicali Café, Old Town, Fresno, California. Stretching out in her navy-blue slacks with the gold sweater to dampen enthusiasms, she relaxed to the pleasant sounds emitting from row B.

Hal had said that the tulips were more musical during their pollinating period, and he was correct. She was beginning to have more confidence in his record keeping: he could probably draw her a graph of the decibel levels from his tapes, and this morning the flutings were almost all from row B. In the beds of row A, there was an ominous silence. Lying and listening, she heard a distinct "plop" sound from row A, like the sound of a crushed maypop, and she raised to one elbow to look. Four beds down the row, Hal sang out, "Thar she blows!"

He was crouching, facing her, looking to his left, seeking the source of the sound, when she heard one nearer, followed by a plop-plop-plop and a whirring sound that made the B beds rustle. Suddenly Hal was on his hands and knees, crawling toward her, under a blurred and darkening archway of flying seeds. And she was crawling to meet him.

On her right, the ova sacs in the A beds were popping, like popcorn in a popper, and the B beds were singing to the whirr of seeds. She and Hal met halfway, their inner tensions breaking with seedpods, and sat cross-legged, kneecap to kneecap, slapping shoulders, laughing and crying, under a bridge of flying seeds.

Hal was shouting in near-hysteria, "Talk about communicating! Freda, the little bastards are doing just what I told them to do. The A beds are shooting at the E and F rows. The A buds are *aiming* at the E and F plots. Now I've got pragmatic damned, empirical damned, statistical damned proof in my secret damned logbook." He pounded the canvas in his glee.

"Have you been keeping secret papers?" she shouted over the whirring and singing and plopping.

"Reams of them," he yelled.

"Why did you keep them secret from me?"

"You weren't ready yet," he shouted, and Freda fell backward to the canvas, tears of happiness and joy rolling toward her earlobes. Hal Polino had earned a four-and-one-quarter-martini weekend. He had been forging in secret the key to unlock her administrative basement. The Caron-Polino experiment would knock the scientific world into a cocked hat; and the black arch above her, graying now with the diminishing plops from the pods, were proof, written in the sky, that the Caron tulip would survive on earth.

Chapter Eight

IT TOOK THEM FOUR DAYS TO GET HAL'S NOTES IN ORDER, BUT he wrote the first draft of the letter all by himself, and he read it aloud to her in the office with gestures:

From: Director of Cystology, Bureau of Exotic Plants. Department of Agriculture.

To: Chief of the Bureau of Linguistics, Department of Health, Education and Welfare.

Subject: Student request for cryptographic-sound analysis. Forwarded without comment.

Reference: Administrative Directive 38753-42, Office of the President of the United States.

It is requested that enclosed tapes of sounds made by the exotic plant, *Tulipa caronus*, habitat Flora, be analyzed for phrase repetitions, dissonance patterns, or coherent frequency changes. This request is made to establish the validity of interplant communication based on the nonrandom ejection of seed from seedpods and from the plant's control of the pollinating agent. Pertinent copies of log sheets enclosed.

"Does it have the roll of thunder which heralds a new discovery," he asked, "or, more to the point, is it sufficiently non-sensational?"

Freda shook her head. "When you drop a firecracker in the middle of an old ladies' sewing circle, it matters little whether you toss it gently or lay it down. It's going to cause an explosion.

. . . But put in 'selective control' instead of merely 'control.' The tulips don't make the wasps dance."

"Yes, I see." He made a notation on the sheet.

"Another discrepancy—nonrandom discharges of seeds implies visual control. Are you saying that the tulips can see?"

"Statistics point that way," he admitted, "but I hope they'll slur over that."

"They won't," she said emphatically. "Here's the fluoro print of the vein system. Enclose it with this log sheet. Those white strands are nerve fibers, so add this paragraph: 'Strands of nerve fibers converging to a nexus beneath the air chamber indicate a rudimentary system for control of the air chamber and ova. These fibers diverge in a fanlike system onto the upper leaf system and connect with areas rich in fluoride and phosphide compounds of rare earths.'"

He whistled. "You've agreed with me all along."

"Not necessarily," she said. "When I was in Washington, I was taken by psychiatrists who wrote books: they first advance the theory and then find the facts to back it up."

"Freda, that ganglion would be a brain, those spots eyes. Are you sure you want to send this?"

"Yes," she answered, "but I wish to make another change. Delete 'Forwarded without comment' and insert 'Forwarded with approval and addenda.'"

"Freda, I didn't ask this," he protested. "I'm willing to put *my* future on the line, but my ante isn't worth much. I'm not asking you to commit professional suicide."

She looked at him and smiled with mock sadness. "Hal, you're risking a great career."

She rose and walked to the door, looking out. The first three rows were blooming now, with the C row singing its children's songs. Mr. Hokada and two helpers were spading the G and H beds, and the wasps were out in force over the A and C beds, ignoring the pollinated B beds.

"As Doctor Caron," she said, not looking at him, "I would still advise you not to send the letter. You are sending yourself with it, through a maze more devious than any you imagine, with every Bureau subassistant and departmental junior executive adding an endorsement, slashing at you to prove his own wit and worth by drawing your blood."

"I'm aware of that," he said.

"Doctor Caron would say 'no,'" she continued, "but Freda will go with you into the labyrinth to protect you with her body from their knives. Then, maybe you'll survive, or we'll bleed to death together. . . . Take the draft over to steno and get three extra copies, one on onionskin, for my files, before I weaken and refuse to sign."

Going out of the door, he said, "You must come and hear 'The Caron Can-Can,' Freda. It wasn't really named for the tulips."

Small chance, she thought, turning back to the desk. She was done with tacos and tangos, flamencos and frijoles, rumbas and "Carambas." She selected from the innermost recess of her lowest drawer a box of personalized stationery, colored lavender and reeking with *Eau de Chat Château* that some misled sophomore had given her in college. She began to write:

Dear Hans,

We have graffiti boards for scurrilous gossip, an underground press for all the news not fit to print, but with this note I lay the groundwork for an infrastructure of science.

My impetuous student, Hal Polino, your spiritual godson if you ever had one, sparked the letter to Linguistics, copy enclosed, which I felt it my duty to approve and supplement. If his idea is valid, and my experiments support his hypothesis, it will be invaluable to the thesis I am writing on the possibility of intelligent plant life, "An Inquiry into Plant Communication."

My rump still pains me from the Icarian pratfall, but it only hurts when I rumba or when Gaynor sticks pins into the voodoo doll made in my image which he has hanging by a noose in his office. After this letter reaches "channels" administratively, I'll be a corpse with a sore sacroiliac.

I'm sending the onionskin of Hal's letter in my most flagrantly fragrant and lushest lavender envelope in order to render it inconspicuous amid your incoming mail.

Almost yours,
Freda

She had barely finished the note and hidden the stationery when Hal returned and laid the typed letter before her to sign.

"Freda," he said, putting a hand on her shoulder, which did not offend her, "sign this and you become a pioneer of science. My name will be linked to yours long after you've lost yours to Paul Theaston."

"*If* there are coherent patterns to the sounds," she reminded him.

"I feel in my bones that the patterns are there," he said.

"Yes, but you are pattern-happy and find cause to give to dissonance rhythms," she paraphrased Shakespeare to shock him. "Now, get thee to the tulip beds."

He was gone, but the memory of his touch on her shoulder lingered like a fragrance. He was a strange boy. Unbeknownst to him, he had kept her awake last night, speedreading Shakespeare; but she would have to shun him more in the future. In his direction lay her ancestral madness, though the problem was strictly her own. Hal Polino would never know why he attracted her so strongly, for she would never tell him that he smelled like elm trees.

She took one of the green shoots Hal had thinned from the new bed, slid it under the electron microscope, and back-lighted it. The plants were coming along fast, she thought, and the observation reminded her of the latest prophecy she had read this morning from the washroom sibyl: "Coming down the homestretch, Hal's ahead of Paul and gaining."

She smiled to herself. The underground press had wires to Washington, but there were no wires to the future.

She put the letter "in channels" on Thursday afternoon. The next day, for the first time in a week, Gaynor stopped by her table. "Doctor Caron, I forwarded your request to the Secretary without approval."

Freda flashed a radiant smile. "Thank you, Doctor. I'm so happy you did. I wouldn't want my request to reflect on the efficiency of your team."

As a reflex, he smiled, nodded, and walked away, leaving around her, she was gleefully aware, a confused group of power speculators who had seen the smiles without hearing the words. Her stock this Friday would shake the market with rumors.

In a beginning flurry of excitement and seeds from the C beds to the G and H plots, the week passed swiftly to a climax on Thursday, when the oldest flowers in the A beds shot a long-range barrage toward the newest plots, the J, K, and L beds, sending seventy percent of their discharge over a range of forty yards.

"Whooee!" Hal said as he gathered the undershot seeds from the canvas. "In another month, we'd better start thinking of a canvas wall along the Land Company's fence, or they'll be picking talking cotton, come August."

On Tuesday of the week following, a mystery developed. Hal came into her office wearing a quizzical expression. "Freda, the new shoots are showing. To me, it seems impossible that some of the undershots didn't land in the E beds, but not a single new shoot has sprung up, and the geometry is perfect."

"Perhaps all the undershots landed on the divider, at least," she suggested.

"Could be, but I'm suspicious of these brutes. Bed A waited for a favoring wind before shooting its broadside, but even so, such accuracy means either that each tulip is a mathematical wizard or that there's a central fire-control plotting station somewhere in the bed.

"That's an incredible thought, but my other thought's even worse. If each tulip plotted its own trajectory when it shot its seeds, that means their average intelligence is greater than mine.

I don't mind bowing to a genius, now and then, but I hate to think they've *all* got more brains than me. . . . And they even spot the males in their harems when they shoot those seeds."

"Male placement is random shooting," Freda said. "Females outnumber the males thirty-two to two."

"I'll buy that theory," he said, "but I'm beginning to sense something wrong. Look, Freda, did you see this?"

He had stood by her desk, thumbing through the mail, and he pulled out an "Action" pouch.

She opened it. Gaynor had read it, and forwarded it by routine mail, a deviation from procedure denoting either lack of urgency or contempt. Inside the pouch were the four tapes and a letter from the Chief of Linguistics, which, stripped of its gobbledygook, said: "Madame: Careful analysis of the enclosed tapes show no significant repetition of sound patterns."

She handed the letter to Hal, who read it and sat down, slumped with such abject dejection that she walked over and laid her hand on his shoulder. He looked up, smiled wanly, hugged her briefly around the waist, clapped his hands together, and stood up. Walking to the door, he said, "Don't worry, Freda. Truth crushed to earth shall rise again as a nonisometric polyhedron."

Looking at the tulips, he had dismissed the letter. "There's something wrong out there. That bed is a brain, each tulip a cell, and the larger it grows, the smarter it gets—a great amoral beast who would smite us for its sport."

His words suggested ideas she should think about, but his embrace had opened areas of feeling she had never felt before. Warm and humid, a sirocco blew in from the Saharas of her being to strum soundless pizzicati down her spine, plucking the low notes last. She heard her voice, vibrating with an alien resonance, say, "Hal, did the girls in Old Town give you the name 'El Toro'?"

He cocked his head at her non sequitur, then nodded. "In contempt. I haven't made a veronica since you kissed me."

"Was I that effective?"

"From your kiss, 'The Caron Can-Can' was born."

"I thought the tulips composed it."

"That floral computer contributed four notes only, one morning when you walked by. Your song is all mine, and you've never heard it."

Her voice coiled around him and drew him toward her with its beckonings. "I've been inconsiderate, Hal."

She paused, then softly added, "Play it, and I'll come to you, my lad, when twilight tints adobe walls with pink. And if your song has half the grace of you, I'll dance a Caron can-can to your tune. Next Saturday, at the Mexicali."

"Of all Saturdays!" He was genuinely crushed. "I leave for L.A. Friday to make the recording, and I canceled at the cantina. My dad needs the money, but I'll break the contract."

"No, you won't," she said. "We'll make it the following Saturday, the eighteenth. Here, I'll mark it on the calendar. Now, begone."

Freda returned to her desk after he left and sat musing.

For a moment they had stood naked before each other, stripped of pretense, each aware of the other's membership in some secret order of depravity, and their eyes had signed an agreement with all clauses understood. She squirmed in her seat, conscious of thighs grown heavy, liquid, and warm with intimations of a four-and-one-quarter-martini tryst.

Ebbing, the surge left her stranded on drier ground. There had been no contract pledged; what she had seen in the boy as perception of her soul's hunger had been, if anything at all, an animal's awareness of her femality. She could never expend her spirit in a waste of shame. She had taken Polino to spare Paul, and it would be madness to let herself be spitted upon a staff of dissonant music. And she would not be. There was more to life than dancing, and she rallied her resolve around one certitude—it took two to tango.

Their turndown and her passion came at noon, Monday, March 6, a date she would later think of as "the morning of the first day." Tuesday morning she went about her lab work, and her responses to Hal were normal. She gave him orders with crispness and precision, which he fulfilled promptly in a ripple of muscles. There was no familiarity in his manner, and his smile resembled an ogle no more than a mist resembled rain. By noon the Mexicali Café incident had assumed proper proportions in her mind: she had merely hinted she was willing to attend his musicale, and he had extended an invitation.

When she hurried back to the tulip beds after lunch, to what she and Hal jokingly referred to as her "conversations with the tulips," she went into the greenhouse to get her air mattress. Engrossed in a manual on radar which he was currently studying in hopes of relating the principles to tulip communication, Hal failed to notice her entrance. Bent over the book, he was singing to himself an old song, "An Apple for My Teacher," but he was singing the word "apple" in the plural, and he changed the case of the objective phrase to the genitive.

Irked by the Heyburnian connotations of his song, she slammed her locker door to signify her presence and stalked out with her deflated mattress. Unrolling and inflating her mattress helped ease her indignation, but when she stretched out, her ears close to the D-row tulips, the sirocco blew in, and she swayed once more in the winds of her desire.

In her madness she retained her methodology, carefully noting that the attack commenced at one-fifteen. Here was empirical proof that the boy neither knew nor shared her longings. He was in the greenhouse, and she was in the garden.

Listening to the tulips hum, chatter, and gurgle around her, the pangs subsided, and in her thoughts she could consider Hal Polino with a widening field of vision. Basically, there was little wrong with the boy apart from his ancestry. Latin volatility took the weights from his mind and made it difficult for him to concentrate on his chosen field. Socially, this defect was partly an asset, since it permitted him a range of conversation that could be engrossing and even charming. (Charm was another of his defects.) He could shift from Byzantine art to the mathematics of music and point relationships between the rococo paintings of Rubens and the poetry of John Dryden. In a way, he was a latter-day Leonardo da Vinci; but in the modern world of specialists there was simply no market for a generalist.

It was as a generalist—she tried to be frank with herself—that he offended her most. As a teacher, it was her axiom and policy to read ahead of her students; one should always be prepared to answer a student's questions promptly and accurately. Vis-à-vis Hal, she had zipped through Shakespeare to footnote her student's frequent quotes, but Shakespeare had a charm. Hefner, McLuhan, and Leary frankly repelled her. To read ahead of Polino demanded first a knowledge of the direction he was taking, and the agility to leap ahead of him in that direction, the speed of a sprint reader and the endurance of a long-distance reader. He ate books like slugs on Carston 6 ate foliage, and he pounced on ideas like a sex maniac.

On Wednesday the sirocco struck at two-thirty, and she fled to the library to get completely outside Hal's influence. Once safe, she constructed a graph of her emotions and found, to her alarm, that on the morning of March 19 she would peak at one-forty-five A.M. Her date with Hal was on the evening of the eighteenth. Bars in Southern California closed at one A.M. Allowing half an hour to finish drinks and stow musical instruments, she and Hal would be leaving the Mexicali at one-thirty A.M., fifteen minutes before her wave crested. Morning discount rates at Fresno motels went into effect at two A.M. At her period of highest receptivity, Hal would have her trapped between closing time and motel time.

Looking down at the graph paper, Freda felt tiny and alone. Once she had thought Paul needed her on Flora; now she knew she needed Paul on earth. There was no one she could turn to. With her father dead and her mother in Tijuana, only Hans Clayborg could have helped; but Hans was in Santa Barbara, too busy solving God's problems to work on hers. There was one other man whose sympathy and support she could count on to help her through this crisis, but he was Hal Polino, who *was* the problem.

She had known from childhood, with a knowledge since reinforced by analysts, that she was emotionally unstable, a woman living on the edge of a volcano. Hal Polino was less the cause than the catalyst of the cataclysm which threatened her, but as such he could still be catastrophic. With a Paul Theaston to steady her, she could walk the thin edge for a lifetime. But a Mexican hat dance with Hal Polino around the volcano's rim could be a one-and-a-two-and-a catapult into the chasm.

She couldn't keep moving Polino around like a pawn, particularly since she had cosigned the Linguistics letter, which was evidence she trusted his judgment. Her other alternative was to move herself.

Suddenly, with the clarity of religious revelation, her problem was solved.

Personnel of the Charlie Section went in quarantine preparatory to hibernation in early April, readying for the May liftoff for Flora. Paul had asked her to relieve him on Tropica. All she had to do was to put her name on the list. As department head, her request would be honored automatically.

She had until the morning of the nineteenth before her test with Hal. If she failed, she thought, what she learned from Polino, she could teach Paul. Distaste for the idea convinced her the winds were northerly, and she returned to the greenhouse.

Doctor Gaynor was unable to see her on Thursday morning, but his secretary arranged a consultation for six minutes between 3:38 and 3:44 P.M. Mrs. Weatherwax spoke so curtly that Freda told her that three minutes would be all the time she needed, that Doctor Gaynor could have three minutes back.

Freda made a point of arriving promptly at 3:37½.

She regretted that she had to make even a routine request from the Executive. She had taught Polino methodology, but he had taught her attitudes. His vile but apt term for administrators stuck in her mind. He *was* subversive. If she had let him remain with Paul, he would have inveigled her fiancé to join him in some cantina of Old Town.

Doctor Gaynor was bland and affable when he rose to greet her, waving her to a seat before the desk—a straight-backed, armless chair. The upholstered chairs were exiled to far corners of the room.

As briefly and as clearly as she had delivered the petition to the Heyburn Committee, she entered her request for space duty, citing Paul's need for a cystologist on Tropica, the apparent traces of hemoglobin in the sap of the orchids, and the mystery of the invisible pollinators. "Paul sent the tulips," she added, "to give me working specimens on earth in order to formulate a hypothesis on the methods of pollination used by the orchids."

"Ah, I see. So, that must account for your, er, rather unusual correspondence with Linguistics. By the way, how's the psychiatric watch coming on young Polino? Any remission, or further disintegration?"

She had completely forgotten the "cover" she was to put on Hal, but she said, conversationally, "It was discontinued because he did such a splendid job while we were in Washington presenting your petition. His methodology is so improved that he can continue the Caron-tulip culture alone during my absence."

"I'm having trouble with Finance," he said. "Your petition for the botanical station made waves. Navy gave those 'facts-for-a-buck' figures on Flora to Finance, and Finance chewed out Agriculture. Ag passed word for me not to rock the boat, finance-wise, so I'm lopping Tropica from Flora's Charlie Section as part of my overall economy drive. I ran a tab on Paul's facts, and his fact returns are three dollars per unit on the Able briefing. Of course, Paul's an excellent research man, and I expect him to lower that average on the Baker briefing."

"Need I point out, Doctor Gaynor, that some facts are worth more than others. Besides, my research would not be restricted to Tropica. If I can detect hemoglobin, or an equivalent in sap, my discovery would be of paramount importance to Doctor Clayborg."

"Oh, him. I was under the impression that he was more concerned with energy reserves in the overall universe."

"Hemoglobin is a form of that reserve, sir," Freda said, thinking that if Gaynor were considered with detachment and objectivity, he would emerge as an idiot. Was there such a thing as a "special" universe?

"Oh, yes. Of course. . . . Doctor Caron, if you go to Flora, Budget might consider it an act of defiance on my part. Senate might think I was sending you to Siberia because your petition failed, which is an admission on the part of an administrator that he can't season his own managerial timber."

"This is a *research* project, Doctor."

"Yes, that's correct." He nodded sagely. "Personally I have confidence in your professional abilities, Doctor Caron, particularly in research, but, frankly"—he smiled—"you've become controversial. We'd better let that ninth wave pass, and try our surfboards in calmer water."

"To the extent I'm controversial, Doctor Gaynor, you and Doctor Berkeley share in the controversy. I was not alone before the Senate Committee."

He tilted back in the swivel chair, tilted his head further still, folded his hands across his chest, blinked his eyes three times, and said, "Rather I had in mind, Doctor Caron, your odd request to the Linguistics Bureau."

"Oh, fiddlesticks!" she exploded. "That was pure research into possibilities."

"Still, I thought you might have become, er, emotionally—is that the word?—involved with the flowers, and, perhaps, had worked with undue dedication to the point of nervous strain."

"Absolutely not! On the contrary . . ." A covert glance at her watch showed 3:44, one minute to sirocco time, and Freda felt a stab of panic. Even if she could stomach the platinumed fop, this was neither the place nor the time for unethical persuasion. ". . . my conversations with the tulips are tranquilizing."

Gaynor's eyebrows seemed to leap a full quarter inch above his eyesockets. "Perhaps, Doctor Caron, you really *do* need a vacation."

She was rising, and the wind was rising. "Oh, don't take me

literally, take me physically, I mean figuratively. Good morning, Doctor Gaynor."

"Good afternoon, Doctor Caron."

Freda virtually sprinted to the ladies' lounge and sat down to gather her wits in man-free privacy, where the winds might blow freely. She had truly muffed the request. When the sirocco had blown past, she rose and from habit checked the bulletin: "If Francine didn't quit, she'd be run over by an automobile, chasing it. . . . Doctor Hector was levering Suzuki over the final exams so skillfully that the Japanese girl had completely lost her bias to Caucasians." The ordinary chitchat, witty, allusive, and highly informative. She was almost turning away when her eyes fell on a familiar scrawl at the foot of the sheet, in handwriting so small she had to stoop to read: "Freda, beware the ides of March . . . A Friend."

This time the oracle had erred with her prophecy! Violating the cardinal rule of prophets, she had been too specific. It wasn't the fifteenth of March Freda feared; it was 1:45 A.M., Sunday, March 19.

On Friday she was deliberately so peevish and irritable with Hal Polino that he left early for his recording date in Los Angeles. She got him out of the greenhouse before five, before the sirocco blew in.

Saturday was clear and warm. With Hal and the gardeners off the base, Freda gathered her air mattress, sun lotion, and eyeshade and went to the tulip beds after lunch. Bikinied to the sunlight, she lay on the mat and listened to the flowers coo and whistle contentedly in the dry heat. Serenity lay all around her. There was even a quietness inside her, for she was resigned to her fate now. Yet, something seemed missing. With no Hal Polino around hurling curses at the "little brutes," the "floral computer," the "yellow peril," the peace lacked punch.

Perhaps, she mused, her glandular reaction was prompted by a fondness for the boy, not her fondness by her glandular reaction. He could never approach Paul in precision of thinking or selectivity of emotional response—she had never heard Paul sing a Christmas carol—but she didn't have to rob Polino to praise Paul. The two men were merely different but equal, allowing for Hal's lower place. Paul was a bridge-of-the-battleship man. Hal was a stern-of-the-canoe man. Paul would be best for the long haul, the sustained effort; Hal would be good for the short stroke, the explosive effort.

It was harder to keep one's distance from a man in a canoe. Her position and age meant little to Hal. He was not impressed by one's status, and he wasn't that much younger. In worldly matters, he was doubtless an octogenarian in contrast to both Paul and her. Probably he was masterful, considerate, and mature enough to be gentle with his strength. Italians were supposed to have a delicate touch in those areas. That sign on the washroom wall, "Latins are lousy lovers," had been nothing more than a female trick to divert the other girls from a find.

Freda adjusted the shade more firmly to her eyes and turned her midriff to the sun, arching her spine away from the heat of the exposed mattress to squirm back to her cool spot. She enjoyed the sensuality of her own rippling muscles as she tensed her buttocks and spread-eagled, yielding her inner thighs to the sun. Nearby, tulips clucked disapprovingly, and she smiled to herself at their modesty.

She had been unkind to Hal yesterday. Henceforward she resolved to be less shrewish with the lad. Sins of one's mother should not be visited onto other mother's sons. It was more than unkindness, it was an injustice for her to continue to punish a young man because a little girl, whom Freda could hardly remember, had once heard her father say to her mother, "You Mexican whore!"

Chapter Nine

"DOCTOR CARON, MAY I INTRODUCE MR. PETER HENLEY?"

Freda flicked her sunshade to her forehead, snapped her knees together, and propped to a sitting position in one motion. Hal and a stranger stood almost over her. No doubt they had been admiring her gymnastics. "I thought you were in Los Angeles!"

"I finished the session this morning. Mr. Henley's from Australia—on a fellowship to the Bureau of Linguistics."

"Don't stand there gaping, Hal! Bring me my smock."

"But, Freda, on some beaches you'd be well dressed."

"I'm not on a beach, and get my smock!"

Hal turned and fled to the greenhouse, leaving the strange young man to leer. Peter Henley looked like something from Australia, she thought—from the Outback. Tall and slender, his blond hair flared at the sides and lay flat on the top. A sharp chin gave his head the outline of a V broken by a flap of ears. His nose was pointed, tilted, and balanced by eyes so large and blue they could have been borrowed from some Antipodean marsupial cut off from the mainstream of evolution. His Adam's apple was bobbing slowly up and down as he kept swallowing, and Freda thought, even his neck is ogling me. "I'm sorry, Mr. Henley," she said, "but I thought I was alone in the garden. I must have embarrassed you."

"No, ma'am. On the beaches of Sweden, the girls wear nothing. Even so, I dare say they can't quite compare with Fresno."

"What may I do for you?" she snapped, and somehow his appearance made her question seem suggestive.

"I came from the Bureau of Linguistics, though in no official capacity. I'm on my vac."

"Your vac?"

"Vacation, ma'am."

Hal was back, holding her smock, which she eased into quickly and buttoned rapidly, trying to maintain polite conversation. "Fresno in March is a strange place for a vacation. It's like Dubuque in August."

"Doctor Caron, Peter's got some interesting information."

"About those tapes, ma'am. The ones you and Hal sent."

"What about the tapes, sir?"

"They were merely given a four-B analysis, ma'am." His "ma'am" sounded like "mum." "Which is a courtesy analysis to honor an official request. It's thorough enough, mind you, a four-B is, but I felt . . . Well, ma'am, I felt that they hadn't been handled correctly. There were some smudges atop the spectrogram—"

"Did you call the attention of your departmental superior to this discrepancy?"

"Well, ma'am. You know department heads. Begging your pardon, ma'am. If your idea turns out well, it's their idea; but if it doesn't, you get your bloody teeth kicked in."

Yes, she was familiar with such department heads, she thought, and she was also familiar with assistants such as Peter Henley, the ones who rose not by tearing down others but by bootlegging information on the sly to spring it on their superiors in the presence of their superior's superiors later, at the right tactical moment. Peter Henley was known in some circles as an interdepartmental rat.

"Go on," Freda said.

"I was thinking, ma'am, since the smudges occur at fairly regular intervals, they might be the lower nodes of higher-pitched sounds that Hal's equipment didn't pick up."

"You think the tulips might be sounding at a pitch we can't hear."

"No, ma'am," Henley said. "I don't think so, because I have no evidence, officially. Unofficially, I have a piece of tape I pulled out of the boss's wastebasket, but it just gave me a hunch."

A veritable jackal, she thought. "May I see your visitor's pass, Mr. Henley?"

His pass checked out. Hal had certified it. "Let's continue this conversation in the office," she said.

Hal had gathered her sunbathing gear, and he fell in beside her on the way to the greenhouse. "Peter's from the University of Sydney. He's in the States on a fellowship, and he's one of Professor Grant's students."

Freda knew from Hal's tone that she was supposed to know all about Professor Grant, but she didn't. "Who's Professor Grant?" she asked.

"He teaches a rather unique methodology. Tell her about it, Peter."

"Doctor Grant's theory is that no investigating procedure should use logic, because the basic elements of the universe are irrational. Doctor Grant says, take the bloody standard procedure and throw it in the bloody wastebasket."

"He reminds me of a friend of mine," Freda said, "Hans Clayborg."

"Grant studied under Clayborg," the Australian said.

"Yes, I remember now," Freda said, highly pleased by her first attempt at name-dropping, "and Hans thinks highly of him."

"Doctor Caron, here's my evidence, for whatever it might be worth." He pulled a roll of spectrograph tape from his pocket, snapped off its rubber band, and spread it on her desk. "This is the sound you hear," he said, pointing to a jumbled pattern of wave lines. "But up here, you'll notice, there are smudges on the tape."

She would not have noticed them had he not pointed them out to her. They were so faint, they were hardly visible, and seemed discolorations of the paper. "I know so little about sounds, Mr. Henley, but couldn't those be shadows from an overtone?"

"Logically, they would be, at first glance. Standard procedure calls for checking overtone shadows, and S.O.P. says they're there. But these look a little pregnant to the left and then swing over to a right-hand pregnancy, which could mean an undertone shadow from a higher pitch, falling a little out of sync."

"Couldn't they be smudges from a soiled gripper on the spectra machine?" Methodologically speaking, she had feinted with her right and connected with her left.

Peter Henley flicked her haymaker aside. "I clean the machine with carbon tet containing dilute aniline. My smudges are all blue."

"Very well, Mr. Henley," she said wearily. "We concede they are suspicious smudges. What is the next step in this Bloody-Grant-Clayborg method?"

"Throw away the old tapes, and start over again, using a more sophisticated detector on a higher frequency. Why higher instead of lower? Because if the bloody tulips are trying to fool us, we'd logically figure they're whispering low."

She thought for a moment. Doctor Gaynor would never permit, and rightly so, the use of unauthorized personnel on the base, particularly if the request originated from her. Security measures had to be maintained. Moreover, Peter Henley had seen her virtually in the nude, and he knew what lay beneath her smock. One sirocco at a time was all she could handle. A hot wind blowing from the Outback would be too much. "I can't permit you on the base, Mr. Henley."

"I neither need to be nor wish to be," Henley said. "I don't want Gaynor to even know I'm in Fresno. Hal can plant the tapes for me, this afternoon, bring them to me, and I can analyze them from my diggings in Fresno."

"Very well," Freda said, "you have my unofficial blessing. Show Mr. Henley our tulips, Hal, but make it snappy."

"First let me show you the A plot, Peter," Hal said, ushering him through the door. "We expect another crop of seeds Monday, and I have a bet with Freda that the tulips can clear a toss of fifty yards. . . ."

As their voices drifted out of earshot, Freda turned to stow her gear in the locker, wondering why all the young men from the English Confederation were named "Peter."

Freda's collision course with Saturday night and Sunday morning commenced on a sinister note before breakfast Monday morning. She had barely finished her orange juice when the waitress in the executive dining room brought her a cryptic note in Hal's handwriting: "Get to the beds quick. Something's gone haywire."

Freda gulped her coffee, grabbed her coat to ward off the early-morning chill, and left her order of ham and eggs to be served to an empty chair.

Hal had come early to the beds, no doubt to change the tapes, and she noticed, as she rounded the corner of the greenhouse, the wasps were swarming in the A beds, and she called to him, "What's wrong?"

"Look at the A beds," he called.

She looked. The seedpods had burst.

"Were you in the tulips Sunday?" he called.

"No, I went to a concert in Bakersfield."

"I was in Fresno with Peter, but it looks like I've won my bet on that distance throw by the A beds. They must have put the seeds in orbit."

"Aren't there any on the canvas?"

"None. Nary a seed, anywhere."

She stepped back and looked onto the roof of the greenhouse. "Could they have shot them west, over the greenhouse?"

"I've been here only ten minutes, but I checked that. None in the grass on the other side." He had come near her now, and his face wore an expression of concern and mystification. "This can be serious, Freda. I calculate we've got about seventy-two thousand seeds we can't account for, minus a few from unexploded pods. If we've got runaway seed production here, our goose is cooked."

"Perhaps the third harvest is barren. I know nothing about the life cycle of these plants."

"Well," he said, scratching his head, "that's illogical enough for us to consider. But I can find out very quickly. Cover your ears, girl, for here comes that sound again."

Moving carefully through the flowers, Hal reached over and pulled up a female tulip whose pod was unopened. She braced herself for the lament for the dead, but the tulips stood mute.

"Maybe no one liked this one," he said, holding the limp stalk in his hand and prying a vane apart with his thumbnail. Before it opened, she could see the row of eight tiny seeds inside.

"It would have borne seeds," she said, "as soon as the temperature had risen."

"That's why they're not chanting their death chant," he said. "It's too cold. Do you have a motion-activated camera in the store room?"

"No. I have to requisition them from photo, and they're not open."

"Then I'll make a side-door requisition," he said, peering among the tulips for another unopened pod. "Keep an eye on this old girl, Freda, while I get the camera."

He was back with the camera in less time than it would have taken after the stockroom was opened. "I used my I.D. card on the door latch," he explained, "an old burglar's trick. Any movement?"

"None at all."

He focused the camera on the unopened seed sac and set the motion activator with a zoom attachment. When he had completed preparations, he stooped to pick up the dead plant and held it before her. "Look, Freda, cavity but no seeds."

"The wasps!" she exclaimed.

"You're right," and to her surprise his face was flooded with relief. "And I'll wager that within five days we'll find shoots growing in H and I patches, exactly six inches apart." He opened the remaining vanes and laid the plant down so the wasps could reach the seeds. "I don't mind assisting in a Caesarean," he said, "but I'm no abortionist. Since I'm convinced you've won your bet, Freda, I'll buy your coffee and doughnuts at the canteen."

It was not proper for teachers to fraternize with students; it hurt the teacher's standing in the eyes of Gaynor. Since she was perfectly sure she had no standing with Gaynor, the consideration had become academic. Happily she accepted and strolled over several lawns with Hal to the canteen.

"What makes you so confident the seeds will be placed in the right beds?"

"The tulips know that the soil has been primed with rare earths. They're not ready to try their wings yet. But I had better put a twenty-foot tarp up next Monday, as a temporary policy of containment. We should start a long-range policy, here and now. If those brutes get out of hand, it could be very serious."

"But, Hal, they're so fragile and delicate and small and beautiful."

"So are you, Freda, but they're females, and, like you, they can be dangerous. If Old Pete can learn to talk to the boys, maybe we can reason with the males, learn to coexist."

Once her strangely scheduled disturbances around Hal had passed beyond the working hours, working in the beds became, once more, enjoyable. The movies of the wasp transport carrying seeds to the H and I beds turned out exceptionally well, to the vast relief of both, who had feared a random expansion, and to their gratification, since the movies added valuable documentation to their monograph on the plants.

For a ground wasp to lay an egg in a flower which resembled a wasp cell presented a phenomenon, however unusual, which reflected the adaptability capabilities of ground wasps only. For the same wasp to transport a tulip seed and bury it in a wasp cell in the ground, laid out according to a pattern favoring the plants, would create questions in the mind of any scientist. Once the Caron-Polino theories were published, Freda knew, they would gain a wide hearing in scientific circles.

Of course, the entomologists and behaviorist psychologists would swoop down on their thesis and tear it to bits in defense of the modified behavior of social insects, but she and Hal would be able to count on the support of plant scientists and free-will psychologists. Ecologists would probably be split down the middle, but both sides would be fascinated by the symbiosis.

Hal pointed out a curious ramification when they were assessing potential supporters. Without a shadow of a doubt, the powerful florists' lobby would be on their side. "Freda, I can see the headlines now: 'Own a Flower Pet—Buy a Caron Tulip.'"

Despite their fun and games, once on the job Hal obeyed her promptly, never questioned her decisions, and even cut down on his profanity. Only once did he question her judgment. Immediately after they viewed the film of the wasp carriers in action, she commented, "You see, Hal, how wrong you were! The tulips are cooperating with me because they know I love them. They want to show their appreciation by being obedient."

"Wrong," he snorted. "They know if they get out of line, I'll whip hell out of them." In the darkness of the projection room, she giggled. She and Hal were behaving like a mother and father discussing the rearing of children.

Beyond their skylarking, and in a great measure responsible for it, lay the invisible, to her, and godlike figure of Peter Henley; and Hal was fast developing into the god's first representative on the botanical station. Officially, or unofficially, Henley represented Linguistics, which had once spurned them, and he definitely represented a cloud on the veto Linguistics had issued. They used the code name 'Old Pete' when discussing him at the canteen, an ideal cover name, since no one would think of referring to the real Peter Henley as "Pete."

Hal was so enthusiastic about the man that Freda felt a beginning resentment toward the paragon of the irrational approach. "This man is an authentic genius, Freda," Hal said. "The other night, we were out having a couple of brews, and he gave his interpretation of the United Nations Council in an emergency session, speaking in twelve different languages, including Swahili, and interpreting into English in an undertone. At the end, when they all started yelling at each other at once, the poor interpreter almost cracked up, and everyone at our table was fractured, completely fractured."

"Who was at the table with you?" she asked, her voice suddenly harsh and suspicious.

"Oh, no one from the base," he said, misinterpreting her anxiety. "Just a bunch of truck drivers on the L.A.-to-Frisco run."

Nevertheless, she felt she would rest easier once Peter Henley was out of town and Hal was out from under his influence. As a footloose young bachelor with an Australian accent who had lain on nude Swedish beaches, he couldn't be entirely innocent. Hal was weak around women anyway, and she didn't trust Peter Henley. She remembered how his Adam's apple had bobbed up and down at the sight of her bikini.

"How long will it take Old Pete to finish analyzing the tapes?" she asked.

"He figures on wrapping them up by the end of the week and going on to Dubuque. He wants to see what he can find among the Iowa cornstalks."

"Oh," she said, "I see your boy is a wit. Are you inviting him to join us Saturday night?"

"Absolutely not," Hal explained. "He's a wit, a raconteur, a genius, but I don't want anybody entertaining Freda Caron Saturday night but Hal Polino."

Freda had experienced a sudden hope that the man from Linguistics might be her salvation—she wanted Peter Saturday night—and at the moment she was disappointed in Hal's too emphatic answer. Later in the evening, after she had stretched out to relax, the sirocco blew in with gale force, and she felt differently.

She would face her evening with Hal, and she wanted no assistance in overcoming the darker angels of her nature. She would fight her battle alone against the Prince of Darkness, and by opposing, end him.

Contrary to the dire prophecies of the sibyl, the ides of March passed in a flurry of pleasant excitement, when the first crop from the D beds blew in with the conventional trajectories and landed precisely in the K and L beds. The tulips were halfway to the fence now, and on Monday Hal was preparing to rig the tarp to prevent the seeds from encroaching onto the freshly plowed field of the San Joaquin Land Company.

Thursday morning—Freda was ticking off the days now, to the moment of confrontation—Hal came to work with a large carrying case. He told her, "Peter's winding up his phase of the experiment today. It looks like a good day for action. The forecast calls for eighty-two degrees at one-thirty, clear and bright. . . . What's on the agenda?"

"I want you to collect some wasp larvae for me this morning. I'm making a comparative study of tulip-born wasps and cell-born wasps to see if there's been any mutation."

"Peter came up with a beautiful theory about the wasps, if you have no faith in our golden horde. He thinks the little Huns direct the wasp by focusing high-frequency sound cones that they have to travel in or suffer the consequences. I'd like to talk to Paul about that."

"What's wrong with my knowledge?" she snapped.

He caught the hurt in her voice, and standing behind her, he tapped her head. "Nothing. But my question takes a morphologist. I want to know if they could focus their sound without bending their heads. You know, Freda, we have a time-focus camera on the blossoms. If one petal folds down, however slightly, that might indicate—"

"You get so lost in sound theories," she said, reaching into her drawer, "you overlook the unsound areas. Here are your photos."

One photo showed all petals cupped. Another shot of the same tulip, five minutes later, showed the tip of a petal turned slightly. She had noticed the changed conformation a week before, when taking stills for her album. At the time, she had attributed no significance to the change. Now she handed him the photos condescendingly, and the look of awe he gave her was worth the deception.

"This would indicate that they can and do," he said after studying the pictures. "After lunch I want to wrap it up for Old Pete, and I wanted you to clear the tulip beds when I do. Pete says he gets an aberrant reaction when you walk through the beds, because the tulips think you're their mother."

"Then he's getting a pattern?"

"It seems so. He gave me this high-frequency howler to jam their frequency, to see how it affects their jabber. My mikes will pick up their reaction to the jamming. Which bed do you want the larvae from?"

"The C bed."

"May I delay long enough to transcribe a few notes, Freda?"

"Certainly."

Over a hamburger-and-coffee lunch at the canteen—Freda had not lunched in the executive dining room all week—Hal made one of his rare confessions of sentimentality. "I'm getting ambivalent about the tulips. They seem willing to cooperate. Maybe we can coexist. The first human reaction to anything strange is hostility, but the tulips seem to get to me."

"We may not have to erect the tarp," she said between bites, "if you'll just put your foot down and be firm with them. You're the father figure. The children will obey you."

"Someone has to balance the overindulgence of their mother," he said.

Hal and she were children, she thought, playing mama and papa, and Hal never smelled more like elm trees.

After lunch she went with him to the slight knoll on the southeast corner of the plot and watched as he set up his howler. His hands moved with a surgeon's deftness, and, shirtless in the sunlight, his corded muscles rippled and flowed. Michelangelo, she recalled, was his middle name, and standing, looking down over the garden, he reminded her of the statue carved by his namesake. His dark hair lay in ringlets, and if he had taken off his dark glasses and put on a fig leaf, he would have been the model of Michelangelo's *David*.

"Stretch out on the grass," he said. "Relax and enjoy the view. But keep an eye on the howler. The children might get annoyed and strike back."

He unrolled a lead line from the howler to clear himself of

the machine and stretched out on the grass beside her, cuddling his head on an elbow and looking down over the tulips. "I'm setting it to sweep a thirty-degree arc, three times, over the bed."

"It won't injure the tulips, will it?"

"No, it won't injure them, but it might be a little painful. If you were a dog down there, it would make you howl. All the little ones will pick up, if anything, will be a sound on their frequency which they can't understand. Old Pete wants to hear how they react to a strange voice. Whatever their reaction is, it'll be picked up by the mikes. If we can decipher the sounds, we can talk to them on their frequency, maybe."

"Oh, Hal, you've had it! You've gone wild."

"I'm starting the howler now."

"They aren't paying any attention."

"They don't seem to be. Maybe it's a wolf whistle. They have heard that sound before. Don't they glitter from up here?"

"They are beautiful," she agreed, looking down over the scene. Obviously they were not responding to the sound, but they were certainly responding to the sunlight. They shimmered in waves of color. "You know, Hal, you spoke the truth when you said we humans might err in thinking everything hostile. Don't you think we throw up our defenses unnecessarily, like cavemen, constantly overmobilizing for defense? Probably the universe is neither hostile nor friendly, and we might serve ourselves better by assuming that it's friendly, don't you think?"

She cast a glance in his direction, but he was entranced by the tulips, a devilish half-grin playing over his smile.

"I think you and I should sign a mutual-delusion pact, Hal, and agree to accept all things as friendly until proven differently. Papa used to say that he treated all women as ladies, until after he got married. Of course, he was joking. . . . Hal!"

His face still reflected the same sardonic enchantment, and she leaned over and removed his dark glasses. Behind the glasses, his eyes were not focused on the garden, or anything at all. She had been chatting happily to a dead man.

Freda took the extension cord from his hand, rolled it, and

hooked it to the howler. She would have to smuggle the howler back to Peter somehow, for it was doubtlessly a valuable piece of equipment. Historically, it had become the most valuable specimen of scientific machinery in the world, for the howler had established, beyond a doubt, that the flowers communicated; but the howler's historical value would never be recognized, because Hal's death had complicated matters.

If the tulips were found guilty, they would be destroyed as hostile to an earth environment. The Crusades had been fought over religious relics. Down through the ages men had sacrificed their lives, for sculpture, painting, monuments, for all things of beauty, and Hal Polino was born of a nationality which had, perhaps, suffered the most to protect things of beauty. She would not deny him a place in the tradition of his people.

She folded the tripod around the howler and scuffed the grass where it had rested. She took one final glance at the boy who sat gazing at the flowers he had loved, and walked down the hill, carrying the equipment.

Looking out over the tulip fields, more beautiful than ever, she knew that she could never let them be adjudged hostile to earth. Who among earth's inhabitants would be capable of sending a high-frequency sound wave ripping through those blooms? Who would have reason to? And no one would ever hear her testify that Hal had done so. She could never permit the Caron tulips to be executed without even the dignity of a trial.

Back at her office, she dialed the coroner's detail and told the duty officer, "This is Doctor Caron speaking. I have a dead man at greenhouse five, Hal Polino, a student."

"We'll be right over, Doctor."

She put the howler back into its carrying case and noticed the slots for tapes. She started to place the case on Hal's desk, when she noticed an envelope lying there: "To Freda—Personal." She opened it and read:

Dear Freda,
    If I don't come down from the hill with you, take the

tapes from the garden and put them in the case with the howler, and call dispatch. Ask for Fred. Tell him the package is ready.

Don't blame the tulips too harshly. The howler did not injure them, but it pained them terribly. Besides, I owe much to the tulips. They were the golden band which wedded my spirit to yours.

You see, I loved you. Deep inside your austere and methodist exterior is a very warm and catholic woman. Deeper yet, I saw a little girl, lost and wandering, whom I longed to take by the hand and lead back to her elm grove. If you are reading this, sticks and stones may break my bones without hurting me, so I make bold to confess my love without fear of your lecturing tongue.

Dearly beloved, God grant you, always, elm trees.

Hal

Gently she folded the letter and returned it to the envelope, which she placed in the pocket of her smock. She arose and went into the garden and collected the microtapes. Returning to the office, she put the microtapes into the packing case and called Fred at dispatch.

Fred came before the coroner's men and took the package. As the men went to pick up Hal's body, Freda answered the few questions the coroner's chief asked her, establishing the time of the death and asking if there had been any erratic or unusual behavior on the part of the dead man prior to his death. She answered all questions truthfully but volunteered nothing.

In twenty minutes Freda was alone again.

She walked to the doorway and looked out. Her tulips seemed to beckon her, and she walked among them. Bending down over the most active patch, she whispered, "He loved you."

Rippling away from her, the tiny voices answered, "He loved you."

"He loved us," she said, getting to her knees.

"He loved us."

"We loved him."

"We loved him . . . loved him . . . him."

"I'll never betray you."

"I'll never betray you . . . betray you . . . you."

"I loved him!"

"I loved him . . . loved him . . . loved him . . . him."

Only two persons on earth had come to love the tulips, and, knowingly and unknowingly, they had come to love each other, till death did them part. Tulips had forged the golden band, and the band would not be broken, though now there were two persons on earth who knew the tulips could kill. Peter Henley's knowledge would be suppressed by the very administrative processes he had sought to subvert, and the tulips would live forever, her secret tribute to the boy she loved in secret.

"Dearly beloved, God grant you, always, elm trees," Freda murmured, and her iron controls vanished. She threw herself to the canvas, and cradling her head in her arms, she wept as she had wept as a child beneath the elms. Around her the tulips were weeping.

Chapter Ten

ALTHOUGH FREDA KNEW THAT THE DYNAMO HAD TO KEEP PURR-ing, she would have liked it better if the pulsations had wavered slightly when such a saintly discard as Hal Polino was tossed into the scrap bin. On her way to her Friday-morning lecture in cystology, she paused to check the official bulletin board in the administration building. Gaynor's economy drive was in full force, she noticed. With characteristic originality, he had posted a typeset notice: ATTENTION—ALL PERSONNEL—ECONOMY MEAS-URES MUST BE IMPLEMENTED AT EVERY OPPORTUNITY. A SHEET OF CARBON SAVED IS TEN CENTS EARNED. HASTE MAKES WASTE. THE MANAGEMENT.

Among the memoranda and trivia, she noticed thumbtacked on the lower-left corner a simple card trimmed in black:

In Memoriam
Harold Michelangelo Polino. Born, March 22, 2216.
Passed to his eternal reward, March 16, 2237. Funeral Mass,
10:30 A.M., Saturday, March 18, at Cathedral of the Sacred
Heart, Fresno.
Arrangements by Hanarihan Mortuaries, 470 Sutter
Street, Fresno. Fine Funerals Since 2218.

She was surprised to find that Hal Polino had been religious. Not that she disapproved. She herself occasionally attended non-denominational services at the chapel on the base, but her attendance was more a matter of form than conviction. Religion was outside her field of study.

Now she was grateful that Hal had been a Catholic, since his denomination was permitted ground burial in soluble coffins. Somehow she gained comfort from the knowledge that Hal's upright skeleton would nestle awhile in the loins of earth. His bones would be his monument, and as long as Freda Caron lived, some of his spirit would survive. Winter hills would be a little greener for her, the mountains more majestic, her tulips more golden because Hal Polino had walked the earth. A tightening of the throat as she paused before the board was evidence that she had been touched by the poet, and she breathed aloud one of Hal's own lines, plucked from her memory: "Now, boast thee, death, in thy possession lies a lad unparalleled."

As she hurried onward, a thought occurred to her: the prophecy on the washroom wall had named the ides of March as a day of foreboding. On that day, the plans had been laid which had led to his death on the sixteenth. The oracle of the ladies' lounge had not erred!

It was unseasonably warm Saturday morning. A Santa Ana was blowing off the Mojave, and Freda chose light clothing for the funeral. She donned a black skirt and a white blouse with a wide collar that overlapped a black shoulder cape trimmed with narrow bands of white and secured at the front by two large white buttons. She chose a white pillbox bonnet with black-lace netting to simulate a veil, and matching gloves of white lace. Whirling before her mirror, she could almost hear Hal say, "Fetching, Freda. Very fetching." He would have loved her in mourning.

Deliberately she was one of the last to arrive at the cathedral. Funerals were arenas for emotions, and emotionalism depressed her, especially at funerals for those who had died young. Once inside, she felt embarrassingly blond and out of place among the snifflers; her greatest consolation was that Old Platinum Head, in official attendance, must have felt even more conspicuous than she. Understandably, though not to her, the ceremony was conducted in Latin, and it was delivered briefly, with restraint.

Freda had hardly adjusted her ears to the flow of words when the priest, gorgeously robed, was rattling a mace over the coffin and sprinkling it with sand out of deference to the high solubility of the compressed nitrate of soda from which the coffin was molded. Then the mourners knelt, said a prayer, counted a few beads, and the rites were over.

She waited for Doctor Gaynor to clear the aisle before she arose and left, to stand for a moment atop the cathedral steps looking out over the grass and newly leafing trees. Tonight was the night for their date at the Mexicali Café, but she could not quibble over her Hal's excuse for breaking the date.

One benefit she gained from his death was the right to wear white to her wedding with Paul, she thought. True, there had been the encounter with Clayborg, but she didn't count Clayborg. Although she was not well informed legally on such matters, Freda felt that a woman should not be held accountable for a liaison during which she had felt nothing. Pragmatically, she wasn't even sure there had been a liaison. She had been too drunk to remember anything but Hans's gentleness in dropping her under the shower, and there should be something more to a tryst than mere tenderness, unless that Frenchwoman in the Library of Congress had been right.

"Very fetching, Doctor Caron," a voice said behind her. "Black becomes you."

She turned to Peter Henley, ears aflop and Adam's apple abob, standing behind her and to her right. No doubt, while she stood lost in thought, he had circled around her rear.

"Good morning, Mr. Henley."

"Too bad about Hal," he said.

"Death comes to us all," she consoled him, "sooner or later."

"In ninety-nine deaths out of a hundred, that's a comforting thought," Henley said, "but not with this death. Hal had something to give."

"You bet your sweet burro he did," Freda said, "and something to get!"

Peter looked out over the greenery and shook his head. "He

138

would have a go at it, against my advice. He seemed to be trying to rush the experiments, to get me out of town; but the bloody little beggars did him in. Haste makes waste."

"The coroner said he died of natural causes, a brain hemorrhage," Freda said.

"He died of a brain hemorrhage," Peter said, "caused by high-frequency sound waves focused on his thalamus."

"Are you accusing the tulips of his murder?" Freda feigned surprise.

"Of course not!" He looked at her in amazement. "How would I bring murder charges against a bloody bed of tulips?"

"You don't," she agreed, "particularly when you're carrying out an unauthorized investigation at a Government Research Center without a security clearance."

"I wasn't sent here to prove anything in court, fortunately," he said. "My assignment calls for me to prove it only to you."

"You were assigned! By whom?"

"Clayborg."

"Hans?"

"Yes."

"Why all this sudden consideration from a man who won't even acknowledge my correspondence?"

"Clayborg's a thinker . . . not a writer."

"You say you have proof?"

"In my diggings, five blocks north of here. But I'm afoot."

"Is this some Bloody-Grant-Clayborg procedure," she asked haughtily, "for getting a woman into your apartment?"

"Nothing of the sort!" he snapped. "Your virtue's safe in that apartment."

His horizontal fins had stabilized, she noticed, and his Adam's apple was at rest. Either he was calm or this was part of the famed illogical methodology. Two months ago she would have gone to his apartment without a thought, but Hal had told her there was a woman inside her—she already knew about the little girl—and with Hal gone, she wanted to reserve the woman for Paul. Still, if Clayborg was involved, she wanted to get any evidence against the tulips before Clayborg saw it. "Very well," she said, "I'll drive you down."

Easing into the seat beside her, he commenced what she was almost certain was an approach. "Hal was quite smitten with you, though I'm sure you knew that."

"I gathered it, not so much from his words as his gestures."

"He thought your sense of humor was exceptional."

"Is that all he thought exceptional?"

"That's all I'm discussing in mixed company."

"My sense of humor is a shield," she said. "My wit is my rapier, so let's not discuss personalities, Mr. Henley. You're vulnerable."

There were other areas that rendered him vulnerable, she thought, as she steered the car to his directions. His ears stuck out too far. If he tried a direct assault, she would grab him by his ears.

Henley's quarters were on the tenth floor of a rooming house entered through a lobby containing a chained sofa and decorated with a lithograph of a desert scene in a plastic frame. Beside the entrance was an artificial aspidistra in a styrofoam tub painted to resemble terra-cotta. He conducted her across the lobby and pushed the button of an elevator, whose shaft moaned and shook until the door wheezed open. They crowded in with the odor of a disinfectant, as Henley apologized obliquely. "Winos," he said.

Their lift-up led to a trek down a tunnel to a three-room apartment whose street-front exposure must have cost the Australian fifty cents extra a month. The three rooms were ingeniously disordered. Henley had unfolded a card table above his coffee table to store electronic equipment on three decks, counting the floor. Actually, he had been defeated in his struggle for storage space: Freda considered it a violation of the rules to store tubes on the divan and put coiled wires on the chairs. All the electric outlets had plugs plugged into plugs with a Medusa-like sprouting of electric cords from the top of his only floor lamp. Despite the evidence, she assumed he was very sparing with electricity, since he flicked on a forty-watt overhead light when they entered.

She waited while her host removed a dismantled speaker assembly on his single upholstered chair and flicked the cushion in a grand manner with his pocket handkerchief. She took the hand he offered to aid her cakewalk to the chair over the coiled lines. When she turned and lowered herself into the chair, she saw into his bedroom, where crates were piled on his bed. She relaxed. As he had said, there would be no seduction in this apartment, unless he hung her from wall hooks.

"I see why you call these your diggings," she said. "You dig your way in and dig your way out."

"It's a mess, but I'm pulling out Monday."

"Literally and figuratively," she agreed, thinking of all the wires in all the sockets. "So, you've found incontrovertible evidence that the tulips talk to each other?"

"No evidence is incontrovertible, ma'am. A man throwing a brick through a jeweler's window at four in the morning could be a baseball pitcher warming up for tomorrow's game." He was tiptoeing to pull the drapes as he spoke, leaving illumination of the room to the single bulb. "I have edited and spliced the tapes you'll hear. That box beside the telly converts its picture tube to a spectrograph, so you can watch the tapes as you listen through the telly's speaker. My formulae are figured from the spectrograph. I'll mail them to you Monday, to attach to the Caron-Polino theory. Your acoustics department can check them out. . . . Now, listen!"

He turned on the television set, and the viewing screen lighted as a recorder atop the set began to play the tape. Sounds came from the speaker, and a black line zigzagged across the screen. "I've lowered the pitch and slowed the frequency so you can hear the sound as you watch it."

Both sight and sound were repetitive. The sound came in lilting whangs, which reminded her of someone flexing the blade of a handsaw.

"Sounds Greek to me," she said.

"More like Mandarin," he corrected. "The grammatical structure resembles Chinese. But listen."

Suddenly the lines wavered in a variation on the pattern. Her own voice issued from the speaker, saying, "Hal Polino."

"The mikes picked up my voice!"

"Not at these frequencies, ma'am," he said. Suddenly the Mandarin coming from the speaker began to click and jabber, like Swahili.

As the Swahili began merging back into Mandarin, he said, "The tulips used your name for Hal, even your tone of voice. When he walked into the garden, a tulip gave warning. The stepped-up frequency, the agitation, signifies fear or alarm even in rabbit language. Now, listen."

Gradually the staccato died and the singsong recommenced. Again the pattern changed, and suddenly, clearly, she heard a feminine version of Hal's voice say, "Freda."

Her name was not followed by the clicking jabber. Instead, the tulips' singsong slowed, grew more rhythmical.

"Your presence calms them," Peter said. "You're their blooming mother. You couldn't hear their sounds, but you could pick up sympathetic vibrations in sensitive areas of your body."

They listened, while the tape ran out and the flickering died on the screen.

"This tape was taken Tuesday, at the beginning of the experiment," Peter said as he removed the reels. "By Tuesday last, the tulips were calming down in Hal's presence, accepting him as a father figure. That's when he started to feel safe.

"But he wasn't safe," Peter added, putting a new reel onto the recorder. "The next sounds were recorded from individual tulips—you'll be able to tell male from female. Mind you, Doctor, what's taking seconds to play back was recorded in microseconds. . . . This tape was spliced from those you sent me Thursday morning and are the most interesting from a linguistic point of view, because they were taken just before Hal died."

He clicked on the machine, and the now familiar singsong came from the speaker; the darting lines showed on the screen.

Suddenly the sound changed to a high whine, soaring, to peak and decline. At the peak, the darting lines on the screen narrowed, became no wider than a heavy pencil mark, and then spread again as the sound died. "The first sweep of the howler," Peter commented. "Now, listen to the tulips react."

As if attempting to match the howler, the tulips were talking with a chittering buzz that narrowed visibly on the tube. Several times, blurred but distinguishable, she heard, "Hal Polino . . . Freda." Then the sound died into the whine, which peaked again and fell back into sudden silence. "I'm picking up a single male tulip following the second sweep," Peter said, speaking rapidly.

Very distinctly, and surprisingly baritone, she heard her voice say, "Hal Polino." There was a finality in the voice that made her shudder, and it helped little when Peter commented, with Australian *sang froid,* "He's making a choice. If he had said 'Freda,' Hal and I would be discussing this tape. . . . Third sweep commencing."

Again the high whine peaked and fell into silence. Peter said, "I'm picking up everything on the tape now. Listen."

At first there was silence. Then, over the stereophonic tape, she heard a male to her right say, "Hal Polino," and far to her left another male echoed, "Hal Polino."

Now the silence seemed as sinister as that which precedes the second creak of an opening door at dead of night, and she was an awakened sleeper, waiting, with a scream gathering in her throat. On the screen there was only whiteness. She waited.

Suddenly, with the quick rasp of a striking match, a streak darted across the screen. The rest was whiteness and silence, and Freda sat shaken by this almost subliminal vision of sudden death.

"In a rather ironic sense," Peter said as he clicked off the machine and began his ballet toward the drapes, "what you heard was a bunch of flowers picking a human. Hal would have been safe if he had stopped after the second sweep. When he came back with the third sweep, the tulips didn't know when it would end. Two males on the outer edge of the howler's traverse triangulated on him, using sight, X rays, heat perception—some form of detection—and the tulips zapped him."

He pulled the drapes, wheeled, and toe-danced back, saying, "Their silence before the zap was to store up energy. Their silence afterward was to recoup. Most important, from a linguistic point of view, was their agitation and argument after the first sweep. Since I know what they plan, I can fairly well figure their language, though only mathematically, but that's all you'll need for the thesis. When I send the formulae Monday, I'll send along Hal's request that the tulips be eradicated."

"But Hal loved those tulips!"

"I know. But I wouldn't give him the howler until he signed a recommendation. They were seducing him through his paternal feelings, just as they pranged you. Given another week, they might have had you two in front of an altar, playing 'mama and papa' for keeps. Hal couldn't see this because he wasn't that sort of a thinker, but I'm sure you must have felt it."

Indeed she had, she thought, with regularity and increasing gusto. But she said, "When will you tell this to Clayborg?"

"I report to you, Doctor Caron. Nobody tells Hans Clayborg anything. They only listen. And don't be misled by his setback in the Senate. He'll get representatives on Flora if he has to bootleg an expedition via the Jordanian Space Navy."

He put the two tapes into a mailing container he pulled from beneath a woofer and handed them to her. "Send your request for a reevaluation of these through channels. Linguistics will comply, and H.E.W. will ask questions, like—why weren't the bloody tapes evaluated correctly the first time? Then I'll catch hell."

"Will this hurt your career?"

"What's my bloody career when the earth's ecology is at stake? Anyway, when the Chief eats me out, he'll be wondering if I have friends in high places, if I'm setting him up for a kangaroo kick, as we say Down Under."

"What's a kangaroo kick?"

"A bash in the head you give a former superior when you hop

over him to higher levels in the organization. . . . Let me help you out of the coils, Doctor. I don't want to hurry you, but Hal's funeral set me back, and I've work to do."

"Will you report Hal's murder?"

Henley seemed taken aback by her question. "My field's linguistics, not homicide detection. I'll have my hands full deciphering their code. If you're thinking of preferring charges, forget it. Spliced tapes can't be used in a felony case, though they could get Hal's parents a handsome settlement for damages in a civil suit.

"Anyway," he added, as she stood clear of the coils, "it wasn't murder. As Hal guessed, the tulips are individual intelligences which operate as a unit. You can't try an army for the death of a single enemy, particularly when the army smites in anger and not in malice. . . . I'll see you to the street. Women aren't safe in buildings anymore."

On their way down, she asked, "Do you think Hal was a genius?"

He considered for a moment. "No. His methodology was too weak. You might be a genius. I might be a genius. Hans Clayborg is certainly a genius."

Still thinking as they crossed the lobby, Henley added a postscript to his thoughts. "Hal was something better. He was the last Renaissance man."

Freda lunched in Fresno, dawdling over a meal she couldn't taste to avoid the midday heat and regaining her sense of reality from the gaily voiced vacuities of housewives and clubwomen in the tearoom. She was suffering retroactive jitters from the sounds she had heard in the darkened room and chills from the ice-mind of an Australian who considered a boy's life less important than the linguistic clues his death revealed. She was choking on empirical pragmatism.

It was two-thirty before she left the air-conditioned room to face ninety-eight degrees of heat, and the thermometer was not dropping. It was the hottest March 18 on record, the announcer said over her car radio as she pulled into the base parking lot. She fled to the greenhouse to assemble Hal's final notes on *An Inquiry into Plant Communication.*

She was putting the monograph into the office safe when an explosion shook the greenhouse, staggering her, and she heard the tinkle of falling glass. She first thought the tulips had attacked, but a rush of hot air drew her attention to the corner of the greenhouse, where a hole gaped in the corner of the roof. Beneath it, the wheeze and click of the air-conditioner, working against impossible odds, restored her faith in normalcy. It also drew her gaze to the air-conditioner, which had heretofore been silent.

The sound damper over the condenser had disappeared, through the roof, carrying a goodly portion of the roof glass with it.

Freda reacted to the crisis with the same calm with which she had reacted to Hal's death. She walked to the phone and called Maintenance. "This is Doctor Caron in greenhouse number five. The noise damper on my air-conditioner has blown through the roof."

"Oh, hell," a tired voice said at the other end of the line. "Very well, Doctor Caron. I'll have a crew over to repair the roof, but I'm refusing to put the damper back on the condenser. Some fool came up with that bright idea in January. . . . Very well, Doctor, I'll get a crew over, but stay away from the other greenhouses."

With a sinking heart, Freda recalled her double triumph at the Suggestion Box in January, student rotation and noise dampers on the air-conditioners. She walked to the doorway. Far down the slope, she heard what must have been greenhouse number ten blow. She couldn't determine exactly if it had been ten or eleven. It was hard to place the explosion exactly. In a few minutes, it didn't matter. There was a rolling barrage up and down the line as condensers blew dampers through rooftops. She actually saw number six blow. The heavy, asbestos-lined box sailed through the roof, cleared the building by twenty feet, and fell back through another section of the roof.

Freda turned and walked slowly inside. Figuring $228.00 per pane, and averaging a pane and a half per greenhouse to take into consideration the dampers which fell back through the roofs, she estimated the cost at $5,010, exclusive of labor. Her two suggestions had cost the Bureau $5,010 in breakage, and one promising graduate student. Perhaps Doctor Gaynor had been correct in assuming she was inexperienced as an administrator. Her future did not look too promising.

She smiled grimly to herself. Humor was a wonderful defense against adversity, but it got bloody tiring, this snickering behind grave clothes.

Her greenhouse was untenable in the heat, though none of the plants was in danger, and Freda returned to her room to work on her portion of the monograph. Except for the addenda to be added by Henley, she finished the actual composition of *An Inquiry into Plant Communications* that evening, concluding it with a paragraph: "It is with reported and extreme regret that the coauthor of this treatise, Harold Michelangelo Polino, graduate student in zoological botany, passed away on the eve of its publication."

She was almost obsessed with the urge to add, "killed in the line of duty." She would love to see Papa Polino retired to a comfortable old age, but not at the expense of the Caron tulips.

Human needs were fleeting. Beauty was forever.

Monday at breakfast Doctor Gaynor stopped by her table for the first time in two weeks to wish her good morning. "Well, Doctor Caron, it looks like our noise dampers didn't work out quite as we expected. Glass breakage alone came to over ten thousand dollars over the weekend, and right at the height of my economy drive. . . . Well, we live and learn, Doctor."

He moved away chuckling, and she commented to herself that this was the first time she had one of his trite expressions muttered with such full-bodied satisfaction and deep-down delight, and without the filter of administrative urbanity. Somehow he had managed to get a sinister quality into a chuckle.

Freda was late to the greenhouse Monday. She had to stop by the secretarial pool to select a temporary office helper until a new student assistant was assigned to her. Out of four she interviewed, she chose a dark-haired girl by the name of Jacqueline Manetti, whose brown eyes reminded her of Hal's and who could take dictation at a "fantastic" rate, according to the pool supervisor.

She had another stop to make—at the ladies' lounge, driven there by the inscrutable smile on the face of Doctor Charles Gaynor. And her sibyl had not failed her. Across the top of the wall sheet was written in a large, spidery scrawl, "Freda, Beyond this place of wrath and fears looms but the Horror of Big H . . . A Friend."

Big H was the slang term for Houston, Texas, and the Horror was the neuropsychiatric institute for mental ailments. Though the institute was nominally reserved for space-incurred aberrations, NASA extended its custodial facilities as a courtesy to employees engaged in extraterrestrial projects peripheral to the Space Agency.

Gaynor was planning a sanity hearing for her, and, oh, what a sly trick. For him to dismiss Freda outright would be an admission that he erred in placing her in a supervisory capacity in the first place. And the first rule of the administrator was to shift the blame for an error. Gaynor was trying to shift the blame to a malfunction in Freda's own psyche.

At the greenhouse she found the repairs had been made and the air-conditioner shamelessly and nakedly whirring away against the third full day of the Santa Ana. She walked into the tulip field to check on the B patch, noticing the activity of the wasps as she walked, to find that the patch had blown prematurely, no doubt because of the heat. But the wasps were active over the D patch and E patch. Curious, she went to investigate. D and E had also blown, and delivery beds had been prepared only for B. The heat had proven a tremendous stimulant to the germinating process in the plants, she realized, but whither had gone the seeds?

A quick investigation of the prepared beds, which had been designed as the K and L patch to take the B seeds, showed the shoots already an inch high and planted in geometrical harmony by the wasps. Not only germination but growth had been stimulated. Freda became concerned for the seeds from D and E patch. No doubt the wasps had moved them into the grass, where the earth had not been treated to accept them. She walked out onto the grass and was rewarded by spotting the shimmering green shoots of Flora among the drabber greens of earth. Raising her eyes to the gray, freshly plowed loam of the San Joaquin Land Company, she saw a shimmer of green spreading like an alluvial delta beyond the Cyclone fence. The Caron tulips had encroached onto the Land Company's property.

Freda returned to the office and called Ground Keeping and asked for Mr. Hokada. It took him several moments to get to the phone, and she knew a fan-tan game was in progress in the nurseryman's shack. "Mr. Hokada, as soon as possible, take a disc plow outside the fence and bring it up to five. The tulips exploded over the weekend and have encroached on the Land Company's property. They haven't planted yet, have they?"

"No, ma'am."

"Thank heaven for small favors! . . . Get hopping, Mr. Hokada, and plow those shoots under. All I need now is a complaint from the San Joaquin people."

She went back to the office to search through the papers stuck on Hal's spindle to see if he had jotted down a sketch of the tarpaulin wall he had planned, but she could find nothing.

Hal's poor methodology was returning to haunt her, she thought, as she sat down at her desk and began to figure out the materials she would need. As the figures slowly emerged, Freda felt a pang of sympathy for administrators. Just at the height of Gaynor's economy wave, when he was exhorting the base to save on toilet tissue, fifteen greenhouse roofs had been wrecked and the erstwhile favorite member of his team was putting in a requisition for two thousand square yards of canvas and twenty eight-by-eight poles at least thirty feet in height, she figured, to allow for a third of the depth to be sunk into the ground, forty sacks of cement, and two hundred seven-inch nails.

Calculating as she wrote, she was finishing the requisition form and getting it ready for the arrival of the typist when she heard the putt-putt of Mr. Hokada's approaching disc plow coming up the hill from the north gate. She laid a note on the requisition instructing Miss Manetti to type it immediately and send it to Supply.

Through the doorway she could see the Japanese, wizened, shirtless, and wearing a flapping straw hat, driving the plow up the grade toward the peninsula of green jutting beyond the fence. She moved out to direct him, thinking that at his angle he might not detect all of the wispy green she wished plowed under. He could plow the area outside the fence, first to get rid of the evidence, and then plow the inside at his leisure, unless the Santa Ana continued to blow.

Apparently he could see well enough. He lowered the discs in front of the plow to approach the eastern, or outer, rim of the encroachment. She was thinking that it must be terribly hot for him, mounted atop all that steel, when almost in response to her thought he removed his hat and started to fan himself as he steered the plow. He was using some peculiar Oriental method of fanning, because he was fanning away from himself. But as his movements grew more rapid, as he swung the straw hat in wider and wider arcs, she ran toward the fence, shouting, "Mr. Hokada, drive away from the shoots. Turn back, Mr. Hokada!"

Obviously he did not hear her. He leaped from the seat to the ground, whirling, as the machine moved on toward the shoots. In the bright sunlight, his figure grew more and more indistinct in the gray fog growing around him. "Run north, Mr. Hokada! Don't fight them. Run!"

He did not hear her. By the time she reached the fence, the gray fog was rising from his lifeless body. It was doubtful, she knew, if he had ever heard her calling to him above the swarm of angry wasps that were stinging him to death.

Gripping the fence, Freda watched as the tractor continued to head south, swinging eastward from the slope of the hill and heading downward toward a concrete drainage ditch. She watched as it rolled to the lip of the ditch, and from two hundred yards away she heard the sound of the impact as it demolished itself against the floor of the ditch. Vaguely she was aware that those tractors cost in the area of seventeen thousand dollars, give or take a few thousand; but she was more interested in a phenomenon she had observed: not a wasp had neared the tractor as it cut a swath through the eastern edge of the seedlings. The tulips had not been acquainted with Mr. Hokada. Theoretically, they didn't know him from a plow. Obviously, the tulips knew their enemy on sight, and their enemy was man.

Freda turned and trudged toward the office, seeing Miss Manetti emerge around the corner and enter the office. She paused at the B beds, looking down at the blossoms dancing in the sunlight. The flowers were mothers who had protected their children as any mother would have done; but the maternal feelings they had aroused in her foreshadowed future conflicts of interest. Mr. Hokada's death had created a present conflict of interests. If NASA agents found her protecting exotic plants hostile to the welfare of man, she would be charged with a felony.

She could not conceal Mr. Hokada's death.

Still, she let her hands play over the blooms as she walked, feeling the sadness of farewell. All that she could do for the flowers, now, she would do: she would grant them a peaceful death.

Miss Manetti was typing away at the requisition when Freda entered and went to the phone to dial the coroner. "This is Doctor Caron. I have a dead man at greenhouse number five, Ralph Hokada, a gardener."

"Didn't we pick up a body there Thursday, Doctor?"

"Yes, but bring a stile for this one. It's lying outside the fence."

She called Equipment to tell them where to find the wreckage of the plow, and then called Base Security and asked for Commodore Minor.

"To what do I owe this pleasure, Freda?"

"Havoc and destruction, Commodore. My tulips are running amok. If you and Captain Barron care to join me for lunch, I'll give you the details."

"Affirmative."

"However, at the moment I need a spray plane with five hundred gallons of Formula 256 plant dye to spray my yard and a small area outside the fence. And I need the plane quickly, Commodore."

"Generally a plane takes two or three hours; they're flown by civilians under Navy contract. But I think I can have one over your yard by thirteen-thirty. There's a cold front from the northwest due to hit here around fourteen hundred, and the coming turbulence might help shake the lead out of the pilot's pants. I'll go ahead on the order, but send along the req sheets, Freda."

Formula 256, Freda remembered as she hung up, was $2.80 a gallon. Fourteen hundred dollars would buy a lot of carbon paper. She hoped Gaynor's economy drive was successful, because she was going to need every dime he could save.

As she wrote out the requisition for the typist, Freda recalled that Peter Henley had said the tulips had manipulated her through her maternal instincts. Her mama-and-papa games with Hal had been an outgrowth of that manipulation. Hokada's death confirmed to her that the flowers were polarized along a germinal-maternal axis. But their scheme had boomeranged. Only by informing on the tulips could she get to Flora and rescue Paul Theaston from the orchids.

Hal had said that the orchids could not attack Paul's weaknesses because he had none. Hal was wrong. The orchids would attack Paul's weakest point, his unaroused libido.

Within her, a synthesis of intuition and analysis had occurred, and she knew with certainty that unless she went there and presented Paul with a counterattraction, he would vanish on Flora forever as the two Navy men had vanished.

Paul had not invited Hal Polino back into the orchid groves because he did not want some other man fooling around with his women. The orchids had aroused his libidinal drives, and he would wander among them, as love-smitten as an overhormoned sixteen-year-old, until his hands grew too palsied with age to draw the blossoms down to him and gaze at them with the ardor she remembered from the film.

It mattered little to Freda how the orchids pollinated. She had lost her scientific curiosity in the aroused femininity of a woman whose maternal drives were in danger of being thwarted. Paul's libido belonged to her, and she was in danger of losing her lover to flowers polarized along a carnality-romance axis.

Gaynor had denied her passage to Flora for economy reasons. He was threatening her with a sanity hearing, which she had already taken steps to thwart. Armed with the Bloody-Grant-Clayborg methodology, she would kangaroo-hop Gaynor and bash his platinum head in with her hind paw as she hopped. She was going to Flora with the Charlie Section, despite the fact that it was already in quarantine and being prepared for hibernation. She would manipulate the manipulator.

Freda turned and handed the requisitions to the typist, saying, "Miss Manetti, would you agree to work overtime this evening, if I gave you the remainder of the week off?"

"Certainly, Doctor!"

Chapter Eleven

DINING WITH OLD SPACE DOGS WOULD BE A BOON TO WEIGHT-watchers, Freda decided at lunch. The appetite was ruined. Commodore Minor and Captain Barron were blasé about *An Inquiry into Plant Communication.* "I've never heard of plants communicating," Minor admitted, "but plants thinking. . . . Say, Phil, were you ever on Gorki 3?"

"Ah, yes," Captain Barron nodded. "The noose vines. Remarkable plants."

"What were the noose plants of Gorki 3?" Freda asked.

"A tree-growing liana," Minor explained, "with hollow thorns —bloodsuckers. They would let a line of men pass along a jungle trail below; but let there be one Chinese in the line, he would be lassoed, hoisted, and emptied of body fluids. Chinese were excluded from the second expedition, but the noose vines claimed one victim, a Caucasian. We ran a check on his file card and found that he had been a vegetarian and an inordinate rice eater. Some vitamin deficiency caused by eating polished rice attracted the noose vines."

By the grins, she knew they practiced Navy humor, but the events of the past few days had dulled the edge of Freda's appreciation. However, they were happy to provide the deposition she sought. Seated at the table, Minor wrote in longhand: "I hereby depose that on or about 12:00, January 17, 2237, in the presence of Doctor Freda Caron and Captain Philip Barron, USSN, I did sing 'Anchors Aweigh' in a duet with a Caron tulip. John A. Minor, Commodore, USSN."

"I hereby depose that I did join in the chorus with Commodore Minor and the Caron tulip. Philip R. Barron, Capt., USSN."

"This will help acquit you," the Commodore remarked. "It's good to be tried and acquitted. It's best to have never been tried. The whole purpose of this farce, of course, is to get the entry on your record."

Freda knew the purpose of the hearing, but she was confident it would never be entered on her record.

Commodore Minor was on hand at thirteen hundred with a sailor in a communications jeep. Freda outlined her wishes to the Commodore and suggested that they park the jeep under the tool shed to avoid the spray. "I can hose down the greenhouse after he makes his pass."

Minor contacted the plane at its base, where the pilot was standing by to take off, and it was a relief to hear the Commodore's terse orders, impersonal and objective. He kept her mind off the tulips, bending in the hot gusts of the Santa Ana's east wind.

"Hello, angel, this is base. Do you hear me? Over."

"Hello, base, this is angel. I hear you five by five. Over."

"Angel, I propose to drop a purple flare. When you see it, approach the flare on a course two hundred and seventy-three degrees true, altitude one hundred feet. Commence spray one hundred yards east of wire fence and cut spray when dead over greenhouse. Circle south and fly north along eastern edge of wire fence, commencing spray fifty yards south of former spray's line when water tower is abeam. Cease spraying fifty yards north of spray line. Over."

"Roger. Wilco. Am taking off. Out."

"It will be about ten minutes, Freda," the Commodore said, and turned to the enlisted man to direct him where to plant the flare. Freda, as rapt as a nun, hardly heard him; she was holding her last communion with the flowers.

She knew they had manipulated her by her maternal instinct, but human children were capable of pulling the same deceit, so who could blame tulips? Mother love was the mother's responsibility. Children were children the universe over. These tulips were particularly delightful children. Had they been able to control their homicidal impulses, they might have supplanted cats in the affections of old maids.

If Hal had only been content to remain a firm but loving father, this beauty would not have perished from the earth. But he had insisted on rushing the experiment to get Peter out of town before Saturday night in order to get her alone to play a song he had composed in a Mexican bordello. Now, though Hal was dead and buried in Fresno, he was living proof that Old Town was no place to spend one's Saturday nights. In a sense, it was fitting that his funeral announcement had appeared on the bulletin board beneath a placard reading "HASTE MAKES WASTE."

Looking over her tulips for the last time, Freda felt like some child-murdering Medea, with unbeaten breast and unpulled hair. Not only would this beauty be lost, but the golden band which had wedded her spirit to Hal's would be severed forever. Looking out over the beds, she was suddenly aware that the wedding was less valuable to her than the wedding ring, but the drone of an aircraft helped stiffen her spine against the blandishments before her, and she lifted her gaze to the sky. Out of this welter of wilted green and gold, a new Freda would arise, no longer the career girl, but devoted wife and mother. She just hoped Paul Theaston appreciated her sacrifice.

Eastward, the spray plane was banking to commence its run. Over the squawk box, the pilot announced that he had picked up the flare, and she watched as he dropped altitude. Despite her resolution, Freda stole one last peek at the tulips, dancing and bending before the wind. . . . No, they were bending *into* the wind! As she watched in horror, the slender necks of the stalks above the air chambers arced over, focusing the blooms of the tulips toward the east, and she screamed, "Commodore! The tulips!"

"You're on course and coming . . ." the Commodore was telling the pilot, when Freda's cry brought his attention to the beds. His voice never changed tempo. "Abort mission, angel. Abort! Condition red. I say again, abort."

From one thousand yards out, the pilot replied, "Roger, base. Wilco."

He banked the little plane slowly toward the south, and Freda breathed a sigh of relief, which escaped in a gasp of horror when the down wing crumpled and fell from the plane. Too low to eject, the pilot rode his craft down. Falling in a lazy arc, the plane struck the ground nose first, cartwheeled on its remaining wing and its tail, to plunge with a rending impact and a geyser of plant stain into the very ditch that contained the Bureau's plow.

Still with unhurried haste and unperturbed pace, the Commodore switched channels and was calling, "Away, fire and rescue party. Away, fire and rescue party. Angel down, Plot area D, coordinates L-21, I say again, Plot area D, coordinates L-dash-two-one. Away, fire and rescue party."

Freda, moving toward the office and out of earshot of the Commodore, heard the beginning wail of the sirens from the Base Security Center as she entered the office. Miss Manetti, grown accustomed to greenhouse five, had not wavered in typing the cancellation of the canvas request. Freda dialed the coroner's office and said, "This is Doctor Caron. I have a dead man—"

"I know, Doctor," the duty coroner answered. "With or without a stile?"

"With stile," she answered, "and a ten-foot ladder."

"Well, I suppose that clinches the Caron-Polino theory," Commodore Minor commented as he entered the office behind her.

"Commodore, you'll have to turn in a deposition on this incident to the Navy, will you not?"

"Certainly," the Commodore replied. "It involved a civilian fatality. And I'll need your testimony as a corroborating witness. I'll have to make the statement with ten copies."

"May I offer the services of Miss Manetti? We can make the statements while the incident is still fresh in our minds. And I would like an eleventh copy as an addenda to my monograph."

"Certainly, Freda. While I make the statement, will you call Maintenance and put in a verbal requisition for a remote-

controlled bulldozer with a television viewer. And have them
sandbag the carburetor and ignition system. We'll have to tear
down the fence and scrape the area clean of tulips. If any of
those plants are left on this planet by tomorrow, I'm defecting
to Mars."

As the Commodore dictated the clincher to *An Inquiry into
Plant Communication*, Freda phoned her requisition into Maintenance. For the first time in her career, she found a flaw in
Gaynor's allegedly efficient administration of the base. "Doctor
Caron," the maintenance supervisor said, "I've got three crews
still repairing greenhouses, one crew assigned to hoist a plow
out of the drainage ditch, and now I've just got a call from Security to go hoist a plane out of the ditch. That is my last crew."

"Sir, I'm not advising you on how to handle your duties," she
snapped, "but the same hoist for the plow can be used for the
plane. They're not ten yards apart in the ditch."

"Oh," the chagrined supervisor said. "In that event, I can get
the bulldozer rigged, sandbagged, and over within the hour, but
it will take me some time to repair the fence. I can get to it before
nightfall, I think."

"See that you do," Freda snapped, and hung up.

Talk about efficiency! The first rule in the first primer on administrative techniques was: be prepared for all contingencies.
Such problems were supposed to be pretested, stress-analyzed,
and response procedures mapped in advance by computer banks.
And Charles Gaynor was going to give *her* a sanity hearing. If
she had not already decided on his execution, she would have
written her congressman, but by the time the letter arrived, she
would be complaining about a dead man.

Even as she fumed, the base messenger entered, bearing an
envelope marked "Immediate and Urgent." She tore it open and
read:

> To Doctor Freda Caron the Executive Director of the
> Bureau of Exotic Plants sends his greeting. You are hereby
> directed to report before me between the hours of 4:58 and

5:24, Tuesday, March 21, 2237, to show cause why you should not be relieved of all duties for reasons of mental and/or emotional incapacity. Hearings will be held in the presence of Bureau medical authority.

Doctor Charles C. Gaynor
Executive Director
Bureau of Exotic Plants
U.S. Department of Agriculture

She had read the oracle aright. She put the letter in her brief-case and turned to Miss Manetti to complete her portion of the deposition regarding the crash and death of the pilot. After Miss Manetti had commenced to type, Freda commented on the sad condition of the Maintenance Department to the Commodore. He shared her indignation. "The Navy would never permit such inefficiency," he said.

She accompanied the Commodore to his jeep, and they stood for a moment in silence, watching the litter bearers from the coroner's office cross the fence on their stiles, lugging their ladder with them. Commodore Minor assured her he would stop by the maintenance office to keep an eye on the scraping to see that they did not bulldoze her greenhouse to the ground. Before he saluted her good day, he sniffed the air. "Looks like the cold front's here. The Santa Ana is broken."

She thanked Commodore Minor for his efforts and returned to the office, remarking to herself on the peculiar methodology of the Navy. Commodore Minor had sniffed the air to determine if the Santa Ana was broken, while a cold wind was blowing in from the ocean, a high haze had covered the sun, and the temperature was dropping like a Caron soufflé.

Time was the essence of victory now, and she plunged into completion of *An Inquiry into Plant Communication*. She was grateful for the anodyne of work when she heard the clank of a bulldozer beyond the fence and eventually the clink of the fence itself as the shearing blade ripped into it. Above the drone of

Miss Manetti's typewriter, the heavy tread of the tractor slashing into the loam was shearing an image of beauty that had sprouted in gold from her heart.

Freda tried to avoid thinking of events outside the door, but when Miss Manetti asked for and received a well-deserved break from her typing, the operation outside was brought in to Freda in a particularly abhorrent manner. The typist had stepped outside to watch the bulldozer, and she returned with an armload of Caron tulips.

"They were so beautiful, Doctor, I picked a bunch, but look how they droop."

Freda looked down at the dead tulips, and her dream of beauty died. Singly, they had been pathetic in death. Their massed corpses produced only revulsion in her mind. Stalks which had once been gleaming and stalwart shone with a putrescent green, and the heads drooped from the girl's arms with a slimy limpness. "Oh, throw those horrid things away, Miss Manetti. In an hour they'll be smelling."

As Miss Manetti complied, moving with impunity alongside the still intact A bed to the trash bin, Freda recalled that no one had warned the typist of danger, and for her there had been none. Freda glanced through the glass pane of the door to the outside thermometer. It read sixty-eight degrees, and she stifled a gasp of dismay. The crop duster had died racing to beat a cold front which would have made his work unnecessary. The bulldozer, clanking now outside the door, after tearing down the fence, could have been replaced by three Japanese stoop gardeners working in absolute safety in the sixty-eight-degree weather. Mr. Hokada had met death in the morning, when, if he had been permitted to finish his fan-tan game, he would have been alive in the afternoon.

Haste had truly made waste!

Her thoughts swirled around the dead pilot and Mr. Hokada. Something of them would remain, she consoled herself, at least in the records of the civil courts. The two dead men, not counting Hal Polino, whom she had already counted, represented an additional two million dollars in damage suits against the Bureau, once the Caron-Polino monograph on her desk was published. Mr. Harold M. Polino, senior, would be asking at least that much, alone, if he heeded the typewritten advice of "A Friend" that he would receive in tomorrow's mail.

After an hour's break for dinner, Freda and the typist were back at work. By ten P.M. the monograph and four copies lay completed and bound before her on the desk: the original for Bureau Archives, one for NASA, one for Agriculture, one for the Government Printing Office, and one for Doctor Hans Clayborg. Four she took to the night duty officer in the administration building in the company of Miss Manetti, and signed them in for Doctor Gaynor's attention. Alone, she took Hans's copy by the post office and dropped it into the "Urgent" slot. It was past eleven when she finally crawled into bed. It had been a busy five days, she thought, and the busiest sixth was due to arrive tomorrow.

Like an executive should, Doctor Gaynor made a habit of reporting early to his office each morning, to get in a "solid" hour before breakfast. Doctor Gaynor was particularly interested in publications by scientific personnel. In fact, if a member of his "team" did not publish something at least once a year, that team member was in for a lot of good-natured chiding from Doctor Gaynor, for a part of any Bureau's prestige rested on the number of publications it submitted to the Government Printing Office. Freda went to breakfast early and stayed late, waiting to greet the administrator, but Doctor Gaynor did not show up for breakfast.

Doctor Gaynor also skipped lunch.

Somewhere in the Administrators' Translation of the Holy Bible, it was written: "What profits it an executive to gain a Bureau and lose a Cabinet post thereby?" Leaving the ladies' lounge for her hearing before Gaynor, Freda walked in doubt of the Scripture. The Bible's maxim was an exhortation to care and to keep caring; on the evidence of her feelings, the Bible was dead wrong. Not caring released energies, destroyed inhibitions, and gave one a better perspective on codes of ethics. The best administrator was the one whose symbol of authority was the second finger extended vertically from a clenched fist.

Drawing the mantle of unrighteousness about her light-green dress, Freda bounced toward the executive suite in her green-suede shoes, her buoyancy heightened by a message the sibyl had left on the wall: "Dear Freda, by a book too deep for reading, the white-haired boy is laid. A Friend."

Hauteur of such coldness lapped around Mrs. Weatherwax that Freda feared the prim but efficient secretary might crack her neck with the nod she vouchsafed when Freda entered the reception office. "As goes Weatherwax, so goes Gaynor," Freda remembered. The chill extended to the executive secretary's voice as she said, "Doctor Caron, Doctor Gaynor is presently occupied in his inner sanctum. However, Doctor Berkeley has arrived for your hearing, and I am to show you in."

As she escorted Freda to the door, Mrs. Weatherwax spoke from the corner of her mouth without moving her lips, "They intended a dart game with you as the target, but you lobbed a grenade. The tinhead's been here since midnight."

She held open the door. Her features were a model of formality, but from those ventriloquist's lips Freda heard, "Shaft the bastards, Freda!"

The psychiatrist was sitting in the straight-back chair, working a crossword puzzle attached to a clipboard. His legs were crossed, and he was half-turned to the seating device reserved for Freda in front of the desk. The device was a black-leather contour lounge so highly suggestive of a psychiatrist's couch that she imploded with fury: psychological warfare, a crude attempt at intimidation if she had ever seen one!

Instead of seating herself demurely and swinging, knees together, into position on the lounge chair, she mounted it from Berkeley's side with a free swing to her legs that offered him a quick flash of inner thighs. She sprawled indolently as she spoke without a tremor, "How's the advice to the lovelorn coming, Jim?"

"So-so." He had tensed at the whirl of legs, and he continued to force his eyes into her eyes as he said, with studied nonchalance, "Have you decided to take any action on my memo?"

"No, but I'm open to persuasion. There's a charming café in Old Town, the Mexicali, with rooms upstairs for private dining. Do you like Mexican music?"

"I could use a little right now!" he exclaimed. "Why don't I call you after the hearing?"

"Sounds wonderful, provided I'm not found incompetent. You know what happens to psychiatrists who take advantage of incompetent patients."

"Between you and me, and Gaynor's microphone, I don't think the old man's got a case against you, and I'm beginning to think so with emphasis. . . . But why the sudden change of heart toward my memo?"

"Oh, Jim," she said, "I've seen so much death and destruction this past week, three men and fifty thousand tulips, that I've been reevaluating life along Frommian lines. If I can do anything to bring a note of happiness into this world, I would like, in my little way, to do so. . . . I was thinking of you this morning, Jim, when I wiggled into my dress, thinking of your philosophy of loving. I know you've had trouble getting your program launched, and I thought to myself, everyone brings his problems to the psychiatrist, but no one stops to consider that the psychiatrist has problems. So I resolved to declare my own personal little 'Be Kind to Psychiatrists Week' and help Doctor Berkeley with his problem."

"Freda"—he was leaning forward, tense, beads of sweat beginning to ooze from his forehead despite the air-conditioner—"one of the first rules of analysis is to be honest with your analyst, so I'm putting it to you roundly: I've had a psychiatric cover on you since March fifteenth"—(Ah, Freda thought, the ides of March!)—"and some of your actions have been a little odd, not

163

particularly from my point of view, I deal in odd behavior, but from an administrative point of view, which is bad, because the weight of analysis nowadays is swinging to administrative aberrations, and some of your requisitions have been dillies, there's just no other word for it, they've been dillies, but between you and me and Charles's microphone, I'm a member of the A.M.A., and I took that Greek oath . . . Hippo . . . Hippi . . ."

"Hippocrates," Freda helped him.

"Yeah, that's the one I mean. And I'm not violating my hypocritic oath nor the A.M.A.'s Code of Ethics. Not for Charlie, I'm not! Now, with you, it's a different matter. In my clinical opinion, Freda, you're normal. . . . You're not average, but normal. . . . To tell you the truth, Freda, I have never seen a woman as normal as you in twenty years of practice. Now, about that Mexican music. . . . I have to cha-cha before I can rumba, rumba before I can tango, but after I've tangoed, I've got about the smoothest-gliding bolero you've ever known, believe me! It's sort of a cross between a waltz and a flamenco, and I can dance to that rhythm—"

He was primed, she thought. He was licking his lips in time to his hips, which were already moving to unheard mariachis, when the door of the inner sanctum opened and Doctor Gaynor advanced to his desk. It was a Doctor Gaynor Freda had never seen before.

His executive's urbanity was set like an invisible mask over his features, holding them rigid, but the eyes in the mask recoiled from an abyss, and beneath its transparency a stubble of pink whiskers showed through. The washroom wit had been correct: Gaynor was red-haired.

He brought with him a copy of *An Inquiry into Plant Communication,* holding it gingerly before him, and he placed it on the desk, squaring it with his blotter pad. He raised his eyes after the book was adjusted to his satisfaction and said, "Good morning, Doctor Caron."

"Good afternoon, Doctor Gaynor."

He glanced over at Doctor Berkeley, and still standing, said,

"James, I know your testimony will be of little value to me. In any event, the competency hearing has become a purely administrative problem, which I'm capable of conducting without assistance. You may go now."

"Thank you, Charles," Doctor Berkeley said, rising. "And I'll be seeing you, Freda."

He departed, humming "Mexicali Rose" softly to himself.

Once the door was closed, Gaynor sat down, looked at her, and said, "Doctor Caron, you must admit that I have ample grounds for finding you incapable and aberrant on the basis of your requisitions alone. You tell *me*, Doctor, where in the world am I going to find two thousand square yards of canvas and twenty-eight oversized telephone poles, squared?"

"A cancellation for that requisition is in channels," Freda said.

"Very well, strike that one! Now, the breakage: fifteen greenhouse roofs, one greenhouse fence, one mechanical plow, five hundred gallons of sodium citrate, a fence, one airplane! I dare say, Doctor, there has not been a breakage expense of such proportion since the San Pedro pile blew up." He leaned forward and tapped her monograph with chewed fingernails. "But all of our little differences vanish with this! This treatise leaves the Bureau responsible for a conservative four million dollars in lawsuits."

"That is an administrative concern, Doctor Gaynor," Freda pointed out, "superimposed onto a scientific treatise, and it has nothing whatsoever to do with the validity of the Caron-Polino experiment."

"Granted, Doctor Caron. . . . Granted! But it puts me over a barrel. If I forward this monograph with approval, I'm admitting the Bureau's responsibility. Using this, the claimants could collect in a small-claims court."

"In this instance, Doctor Gaynor, I prefer not to have your approval. Lay approval of a scientific work imparts a vulgar popularity to the treatise, endows an otherwise dignified work with the stigma of sensationalism. I suggest you forward it without approval."

Freda felt that she wasn't getting through to him. His eyes were fixed on her but not focused on her. Catatonia, she thought, and when he spoke, his voice had the hollow resonance of schizophrenia. "If I do not approve, and the work is given public recognition, which Doctor Hector assures me it will, and the theories are found to be valid, which Acoustics assures me they will, then questions will be raised in certain quarters regarding my fitness as chief of a scientific bureau, and the government's case will still be in peril. . . . Ah, yes, Freda, you and that young man—Peter Henley?—have placed me squarely between an evacuation and a transpiration."

"You knew about Mr. Henley?"

"Ah, yes. You were under a psychiatric cover. There's little on this base that escapes your executive administrator's notice. . . . I fully expect an override on the Linguistic veto in a week or ten days. . . . Now, in the psychiatric area, you must admit that there was some questionable behavior, despite Bob Berkeley's admiration for your normalcy. Yes, some odd activities there, too."

"Such as?" Freda interjected.

"Well, you *did* talk to the tulips. You whispered sweet nothings to them, in fact. There's nothing in this monograph"—he tapped her treatise again—"that says you could speak their language. That they communicated between each other, yes. That they could talk to you, no! Even an unbiased opinion might consider it rather odd of a woman that she should go around talking to flowers. Assumptions could be made, Doctor. Assumptions could be made."

"Then, such assumptions would have to include these two gentlemen."

She took the deposition from Minor and Barron from her briefcase and handed it to him. "It's hardly a reflection on my sanity, alone, when two such eminent gentlemen can join in singing 'Anchors Aweigh' with one Caron tulip."

"Oh, the Navy!" He shoved the deposition back to her with obvious distaste. She leaned forward on the couch to pick it up, and rose to sit on the chair, dragging it closer to his desk. Doctor Gaynor obviously needed the couch more than she.

"But you never mentioned that little black box you and Polino had on the hill with you," he said cagily, "when the coroner was investigating Polino's death."

"There's nothing in the standard operating procedure regarding coroner's investigations which says that I must answer questions not asked. There was no formal investigation. To them, it was an open-and-shut case of a natural death, until the little black box is mentioned in the monograph, where it is covered in full detail."

"Yes, yes. I know." He looked around him, as if expecting to find an eavesdropper, lowered his voice, and said, "Doctor Caron, let's both be reasonable. I'll drop all charges—"

"What charges? I'm here for a competency hearing."

"I don't mean it quite that way. . . . Look, I'm a man. I have hopes and fears and, yes, ambitions, like everyone else. When I started out, I wasn't particularly gifted, or talented, or intelligent. But I was shrewd! I majored in administration. People like you, and Hector, and Polino . . . Yes, even Polino. He was talking behind my back too. You were all after me. . . . And there's Berkeley, flaunting his Latin crossword puzzles in my face. . . . How's an old country boy going to compete in this league? I didn't make this system, Doctor Caron. But I could see where the power lay, at the crossroads, where decisions come together, conflict. I choose the decisions; if I'm right, I win. If I'm wrong, the man who made the decision loses—"

"Doctor Gaynor," Freda interrupted, "this is all very interesting, but what has it to do with my sanity hearing?"

"I was trying to appeal to your humanity, Doctor. I need your help. Any decision I make here is wrong. Please don't publish that treatise."

So, it was out. Now they were entering bargaining grounds. Her answer was emphatic, "Doctor Gaynor, I would not think of suppressing a revolutionary finding in the plant sciences in order to forestall possible lawsuits."

"Doctor Caron, I'll appoint you my successor, in writing. . . ."

"I appreciate your vote of confidence, Doctor Gaynor." Freda held up her hand. "But I am willing to sacrifice my position as Bureau chief for the sake of scientific truth. Why aren't you willing to match my sacrifice?"

"Doctor Caron, I can't do anything *but* administrate. All I have is my job, and a wife and three children depending upon me. Doctor Caron, think of my wife and children."

Freda thought for a moment. She did sympathize with Mrs. Gaynor, for marital reasons, and with his children, for their genealogical handicaps. She spoke: "As you say, Doctor, we're both reasonable people, although I'm here because you've disputed that fact. . . . Maybe we can work something out."

"Think, Doctor Caron," he said. "You're smart."

"Perhaps I might," she said slowly, "submit the monograph with a discretionary release. . . . I would never delay the publication myself. It's not ethical. But it could be submitted to be released at the Bureau chief's discretion."

Gaynor straightened slightly. Hope shone in his eyes. "If you were to submit it, Doctor Caron, to be released at the discretion of the executive head of this Bureau, I guarantee you that *you* would be the director who released it, after I was elevated to the Department."

"I know," she agreed. "The Caron-Polino monograph would be my guarantee. . . . But, Doctor, there are some questions I would like to ask you. If you don't choose to answer, of course, we can end the discussion here and now and send *An Inquiry into Plant Communication* on its way."

"Ask me. Ask me anything."

"Why did you take me to Washington with you, under false pretenses, and maneuver me into presenting the Flora petition."

"When I got the call from Clayborg that morning, I knew he had a trick up his sleeve. He isn't interested in perpetuating the name of Gaynor. But I am. So I had Miss Weatherwax stand by at the suggestion box and bring me whatever suggestions you submitted. I took your suggestions from there."

"But why me?"

"Clayborg loves pretty women. He knew you were my hostage to ensure his maximum effort. I knew he would strain every brain cell to get the petition through and keep you from being sacrificed. I was betting him you that he couldn't swing it. . . . He covered my ante, and lost. Maybe he isn't so damned smart, after all."

Gaynor was wrong, Freda thought. The game was still in progress, as Clayborg well knew. Hans still held a hot pair of dice. "Second question," she said. "Why do you dye your hair platinum?"

Her question startled him. He tried to smile, and he shook his head, "Now, they come, those Clayborgian questions. . . ." He leaned forward, and she noticed that he was struggling to contain tears. "All right, I'll lay it on the line!"

His hand swept back over his head, taking his hair with it, and he laid a wig on the desk top. "I've been baldheaded since I was eight—scarlet fever. All the kids used to follow me home from school, calling me 'Baldy.' Nobody loves a baldheaded boy. . . ."

"Calm yourself, Doctor Gaynor!"

He struggled for a moment, leaning forward. "Since I didn't have any hair, I had a choice of colors. I chose an outstanding color because of my job. An administrator has to be noticed, or he gets passed over in the promotions. Most of them try for a nickname . . . or sign their names with red ink. . . . Anything, to attract . . . attract . . . attention."

He was losing control again. Freda wanted to remark that he would be even more distinguishable as a baldhead, and he would have a built-in nickname, but she was sympathetic toward childhood traumas, and she could understand why he had not chosen baldness. His head was too shiny; it seemed to capture and focus the filtering sunlight through the translucent bricks behind his desk.

"Put your hair back on, Doctor," she snapped. "The glare blinds me."

As he deliberately adjusted his hairpiece, Freda relaxed. Her battles on earth were almost over. "Doctor Gaynor, I will stamp the thesis 'Hold for release' if you will assign me to the Charlie Section to relieve Doctor Theaston on Flora."

"But the Charlie Section's in quarantine. It's being hibernated next week."

"No problem. Give me a crash program."

"Doctor Caron, questions will be asked. You'll be adding thirty thousand dollars to the budget."

"Any skillful administrator can field a thirty-thousand-dollar question," she pointed out. "It would take a genius to explain away a four-million-dollar error in judgment."

Gaynor shrugged, beaten, and flicked on the intercom. "Mrs. Weatherwax, will you fill out a quarantine emergency pass detailing Doctor Freda Caron to Flora with the Charlie Section, as cystologist assigned to relieve Doctor Paul Theaston, on the Florian island of Tropica. And bring it to me as soon as you have it completed."

"Yes, sir."

He pushed another button. "Hello, Medicine, this is your chief speaking. Who is the medical officer on duty?"

"Doctor Youngblood here, sir."

"Doctor Youngblood, I'm afraid I'm going to have to ask you to work over tonight to prepare Doctor Freda Caron for transport with the Charlie Section. Do you mind?"

"Doctor Gaynor, for that one I'd stay up all night!"

Freda laughed at the doctor's spontaneous enthusiasm, and her laughter trilled as lightly as the laughter of her tulips. Doctor Gaynor, red-faced, flicked off the button and made a great to-do about searching his desk for the rubber stamp. He was searching for the inkpad when Mrs. Weatherwax entered and laid the quarantine permit on the desk before him. He glanced at it and passed it over to Freda. She read over the form, checking it for errors and finding none, as Gaynor turned back the cover of the Caron-Polino treatise and stamped the title page.

Ethically, Freda thought, she might be violating some principle, but, as Doctor Gaynor himself had said, anything that worked was right. She could figure on Clayborg keeping silence for three weeks, long enough to get her free of this noisome planet; then the juggernaut of underground science would roll. By the time Freda returned from Flora, Doctor Charles Gaynor would probably be Superintendent in Charge of Ground Tenders at Arlington Memorial Park, changing cut flowers on the Tomb of the Unknown Soldier.

He handed her *An Inquiry into Plant Communication*. Across the flyleaf was stamped, "To Be Released at the Discretion of the Bureau Director."

"Sign here," he said, pointing.

She handed him the quarantine pass.

"After you, me," she said.

Gaynor pretended amusement. "Surely you don't mistrust your Bureau Chief?" he chided her, signing. He was regaining his imperial manner.

"Not without reason," she agreed. She had not regained her subservient attitudes.

She signed the treatise, took her pass, and rose. Gaynor rose also, automatically extending his hand in the gesture of formal farewell and uttering the ritual good-bye. "Godspeed, Freda, and heaven spare you a bad trip."

She responded in kind, saying, "God's grace be yours on earth —Charlie."

As she closed the door behind her, she felt spent, with nerves sagging, and she had merely cleared the first hurdle, an earth-man. Awaiting her was a battle with titans for control of the emotion-generating capabilities of the man she intended to marry. Yet it was her own arrogance that frightened her most. Hans Clayborg had said that intellectuals did not fall in love, and she was launching her woman's intuition on a collision course with the logic of Hans Clayborg. She believed the male intellectual was capable of gonad-based obsessions.

Turning to pass through the reception office, she nodded a friendly good-bye to Mrs. Weatherwax, and Mrs. Weatherwax, nodding, flipped up her fingers in the V-for-victory sign. Freda registered a spurt of optimism at her gesture, seeing in it the final prophecy of a sibyl who had never erred. Her quarantine pass had been filled in with the spidery scrawl which identified Doctor Gaynor's executive secretary as the oracle of the ladies' lounge.

Chapter Twelve

AWAKENING AS SHE SLID FROM THE CHUTE, FREDA TUMBLED onto the grass and rolled aside to clear the exit. Lounging back on her elbows, she looked up a slope of grass to a ridge line covered with a grove of beech trees, thinking that the cameras had understated the colors of Flora. No one had told her that the grass smelled of clover, that all the clouds were nimbus clouds floating across the primal blue of all blues. The boles of the trees, grayish silver, were laid against the skyline with a palette knife, the leaves swirled with a brush, and higher on the ridge, to her right, an outcropping of granite was fringed at its base by yellow roses. From the grove a bird warbled six notes, soaring and swooping into a silence made sweeter by the sound.

Poets and painters should accompany expeditions, she thought, and composers, even dried-out newspaper reporters. NASA erred in limiting flights to Eagle Scouts who could say no more than "A-okay" or "all systems functioning."

She glanced behind her at the maze of landing struts, upward at the alloy of vanadium. The USSS *Botany* had touched down in a meadow on the side of a hill. Other chutes distended from the ship on the downward side, but she was alone, dressed in a field dress of gray permalon. She slipped out of the jacket and somersaulted over the grass, completing three flips, when she heard a voice say, "She's gone Florian, Doctor."

Captain Barron, in dress blues, was assisting Doctor Youngblood to his feet by the exit. Sprawled on the grass, Freda looked up and asked, "Where's the rest of the section?"

"They exited downslope, toward the camp, to get the headquarters crew in clothes before you go down," Barron said. "I've talked with Paul on the radio. He wants you to fly over right after lunch, before the satyrs on the continent get you."

"So he's jealous."

"Your flight will take you an hour, and Doctor Youngblood will go along to check Paul. Paul said he'd spend twenty-four hours with you, passing along records and setting up camp."

"Captain, I'd like a vocal transponder planted in my blouse with a twenty-four-hour watch on the monitor," she said.

"Are you afraid of Paul, Freda?" Doctor Youngblood asked.

"Afraid for him," she responded. "I'll be asking him leading questions, and a psychiatrist should analyze the answers."

"You have one already," Doctor Youngblood answered. "It's in the button on your field jacket."

"Are you suspicious?" Freda asked.

"No," he said. "It's recently been adopted as standard operating procedure on this planet."

Paul was waiting on the coral ledge Hal had told her about when the copter was guided in by his homing signal. In the afternoon sunlight he looked like a young Moses with his curling blond beard, his long hair, and dressed in a breech clout with a machete tied around his waist. From one hundred feet above him, she could see he was bronzed with the tan of Flora, and muscles rippled where she could not recall seeing muscles before.

He lifted her from the helicopter door, and it was a full minute before her feet touched the ground. Residual traces of her contact phobia were swept away in their reunion. Freda would have been perfectly willing to let him try for an endurance record if Doctor Youngblood's complaints about the delay finally had not persuaded Paul to lower her to the ground.

"I'm supposed to give you a physical and mental," the Doctor said. "How many fingers?"

"Two," Paul said, "but what about the earth woman? She looks a little peaked."

"Sit on the rock," the Doctor said, brandishing a rubber hammer, "and cross your legs."

"Stand clear when you tap, Doctor. I might punt you over the cliff."

Paul passed the physical, and Freda supervised the unloading of her equipment crate while Paul talked to the Doctor. Paul's crate was packed and ready to go back, and the pilot loaded it aboard.

"What about your field log?" Freda asked.

"I'll talk you into a landing," Paul told her.

After the wave-off, and the helicopter soared away to leave them standing on the three-thousand-foot level, Paul turned to her. "All you'll need for tonight is your machete. I wanted you here before sunset to show you the view from Sunset Point. It's a ten-mile hike, and I'll show you the orchids as we walk. Fall in."

He strode over the coral, barefooted, toward the orchid line in the distance, saying, "The old reefs captured the lava flow from the volcano, and once inside the ring of coral, the soil is fertile. There's a terrace of orchids above us and one below. Above the orchids is a temperate forest, above that a grassland, and then the cone. There's a lake inside the cone, and that fissure in the cliffs, over yonder, is from a stream that drains the lake. Now, these first orchids are males. They grow on the outer perimeters and near the fissures the streams cut."

"They go a-courtin' at night, I understand," Freda remarked.

Paul laughed. "That was a feedback from Hal Polino. I never took it seriously, but so much was going on that I couldn't understand, I was willing to work on anything."

"Out with it, Paul. How do they pollinate?"

"I have a theory. Basically, it has to do with the ecology of the island, and it explains why the males are stationed on the perimeters."

They were nearing the grove, and he reached down and pulled a dead stalk that had gained an isolated foothold on the coral strand but had not been able to survive. He showed her the bifurcated roots with their twin orchis, and she hefted the plant. It was stiff, brittle, and light. "I'm glad it's a plant," she said. "The Caron tulips were twixt and tween."

"They were lower on the scale," he commented, not saying

which scale he referred to, and added, "I suppose you had to destroy them."

"Yes. They were deadly," she said, as they entered the grove, following a cleanly demarked pathway of grass four feet wide. "Did you cut this path?" she asked.

"No. The groves are crisscrossed with them. The broad paths, between male and female groves, are wider, invariably six feet. The consistent width of the paths gave me my first hint of their pollination method."

Freda was as grateful as she was curious. Without the paths, it would have been difficult to maneuver through the thick stalks, some towering as high as eight feet, with tendrils trailing from above the hip swelling and coarse blades branching from the stalks below the hips. Walking behind him, she gazed up at the huge blossoms, ranging from white to pale pink.

Once he stopped and lifted her to his shoulder for a closer view of a bloom, its calyx petals folding outward to three feet in diameter. Delicate traceries of red on the corolla petals and the lip gave it the appearance of a *Cymbidium alexanderi,* save for the fact that there was a single stamen with no stigma. Its stamen was almost six inches long.

From below, Paul remarked, "The stamen's compacted with the rostellum. In the female, there's a single stigma at the oviduct, almost vestigial, although it's sensitive."

"With a single, terminal inflorescence," she said, "you should have named them cornstalk orchids."

"The hips are more pronounced on the female," he said, "so I deferred to the weaker sex."

From her perch she could look out over the fields, and in the distance she spotted a bright-red orchid. "It's beautiful from up here," she said.

"Then I'll carry you," he said, moving off with an effortless glide. On earth, she remembered, he had started and stopped by jerks when his attention was drawn to some phenomenon, but here he seemed to sweep up to a subject and over it without effort, and his physical movements had the same flowing grace.

"We can go faster," he said, "and I want to get to the point before sunset."

"You seemed to know I had to eradicate the tulips. Were you aware they were intelligent?"

"If you wish to call it that," he said. "Theirs was the intelligence of a social insect, and if they were deadly, so is a bee swarm. What pollinators did they use on earth?"

"Wasps," she said.

"Like to like," he said contemptuously. "The orchids could never adapt to earth. They only seed once a year, and then only a single seed."

"How did they get started in the grass?"

"They swung down from trees, like we did," he answered. "Ages past, they were epiphytes. When the lava covered the ground, it killed the grass but left a few tree trunks with their orchid guests. So the orchids got a foothold before the grass returned."

Without her slower pace to retard him, he was covering at least five miles an hour, and carrying her in ease and comfort. From her height, she could see a coral knob soaring fifty feet from the terrace in the distance, and Paul was making for it.

"You're easier to ride than a Tennessee walking horse," she complimented him when he finally lowered her at the base of the coral knob.

"It's hand over hand from here to the top," he said.

From the summit, in the slanting rays of the sun, they could see over the rim to the terrace below and over the orchids to the ramparts three miles distant. A waterfall soared from the tier above from a deep chasm it had cut in the coral, and she noticed that the face of the cliff seemed pitted. They were old sea grottoes, Paul explained, which became caves when the coral reef lifted.

Above the cliff soared other terraces, rising in tiers of pink to the green base of the mountain, which lifted a snowcapped cone to trailing wisps of clouds. "The sun's rays," Paul said, "glance from off the coral to tint the snow and clouds. We're a little late. The blush is beginning now. . . . Here, lie down. Cradle your head on my arms, and watch with me as I lay the day to rest."

She hoped the transponder had picked up the last sentence. Paul had gone Florian to a fare-thee-well. Flowers were growing out of his sentences. Perhaps the liquid flow of his stride she had admired on their walk over might be more aptly defined as a swish. Snuggling into the cradle formed by his deltoid and trapezius, she found the muscles harder than the coral: he might be nuts, she decided, but he wasn't fruit.

"It's beautiful," she said, falling in with Paul's mood, leading him on. "The snow and clouds look like strawberry ice cream."

He chuckled. "It will deepen to a Manhattan cocktail, and just as the sun goes down, become a cherry cordial."

Now, she thought, would be the ideal time to check his reaction to shock, as he lay musing in the sunset. "The tulips killed Hal Polino."

For a moment he was silent, and she thought him stupefied by the news, but when he spoke he said, "Now that the snowfield's incarnadined, watch the scarlet swallow the cloud tops."

Freda could feel the tranquility and beauty flowing from the sunset. Death seemed suddenly far away, remote, not merely Hal Polino's death, but all death. It was as if the island and orchids shut out thoughts of mortality. But she persisted, "Paul, I said the tulips killed Hal."

"He would have died, hereafter. . . . How did they do it? With high-frequency sound waves?"

Now it was her time to be shocked, but not into silence. "How did you guess it?"

"Their air chambers were Helmholtz resonators with high-frequency filters, and their petal configuration focused sounds. I diagramed the structure to Hal before he left and pointed out the dangers. . . . He must have been teasing them. But they didn't kill him. If he invaded their stimulus-response area knowing what I told him, he committed suicide."

So, all of Hal's fancy theories were Paul's, dressed up by Hal to impress her. No, to seduce her! He had taken Paul's ideas and run away with them. In actual fact, the Caron-Polino theory was the Caron-Theaston theory.

Swiftly she told Paul what Hal had done, and how she had used the theory to get to Flora. Paul was very tolerant, or bemused by the sunset. "We're coming to the Manhattan-cocktail hour now, Freda. . . . Let the theory stand as a monument to the boy. He was a good student and a dear friend."

"I don't know if Hal *was* your dear friend," she said with genuine indignation. "He persuaded the tulips that he and I were their mother and father and started their vibrations to working on me. He almost succeeded, too. We were going to the Mexicali Café, but he got too eager. To get a rival out of town, he rushed the experiments, and the very weapon he was using to seduce me saved me."

"Look, Freda. The clouds seem on fire!"

She looked at the fiery glow from the clouds, thinking that the orchids had not tampered with Paul's libido. He was still as romantically inclined as an oyster undergoing metamorphosis.

"It looks like the volcano is alive, at least," she said.

After the colors died, he spoke. "I wish you'd gotten to the Mexicali. It was high class, as such joints go, and Hal would have died happy."

She snuggled closer, charmed and dismayed by his answer. "Aren't you being rather generous with my favors?"

"I love you as a woman, and loved Hal as a man." He chuckled. "Love is a sharing, even if it's a three-way split."

"Did you ever go to that horrible place with him?"

"I took him there," he answered candidly. "Since he was a good assistant and bordello-minded anyway, I wanted to minimize absenteeism caused by knife whacks, Montezuma trots, cupid's pox, and all the attendant ills of the meaner cathouses."

Freda sat bolt upright and whirled on him. "Paul Theaston! I'm disgusted! Here, you courted me for a year before you even kissed my hand. And I suppose you had some little hot tamale who called you El Toro?"

His eyes twinkled at her anger. "Yes," he admitted, "but that was on another planet, and besides, the wench couldn't tango." His arm was encircling her, drawing her down to him. "I feared to hug you too hard, lest your veneer crack and cut me. . . . Look, it's cherry cordial now! . . . And your virginity frightened me. As a pragmatist, I find virgins have no practical value; but, on the other hand, I'm not the Holy Ghost."

"Well, you don't have to worry about *that* anymore!"

"You mean you're not a virgin any longer?"

"Would you be jealous if I told you I'm not sure?"

He looked at her in amazement. "I wouldn't be jealous, but I'd be damned curious. You either are or you aren't."

"I'll tell you about that later. Right now, I'm more interested in your licentiousness. And, to think, your profile was just like dad's."

"Yes, indeed," he agreed. "Since your mother was a professional, I'm sure he didn't find her at a convention of horticulturists." His other arm was around her now, and she hoped the pressure of his chest against her was jamming the transmit signals from her button. "In some circles, your parentage might meet with disapproval, but for me you represent the best of my two favorite worlds."

He was nudging her neck, kissing her, and his arms were wringing out any residual anger not spun dry by her thoughts. His implied admiration for her mother shook her, for she had never considered her mother's side of the marital arguments. Perhaps she had been as wrong in accepting her father's judgment of her mother as she had been wrong in underestimating the amorous potential of Paul Theaston.

"Darling," she whispered.

"Yes, sweet."

"Would you do something for me?"

"Yes, dearest."

"Get me off this damned rock!"

Without a word, he stood, lifting her to his shoulder, and gripping the incline of coral with his bare feet, he carried her down, saying, "I don't want you slipping and breaking a thigh bone."

As always, Paul had immaculate control. Even with his inward excitement, while balancing himself and his burden on the dangerous descent, he had not specified her arm or leg or neck; he was specifically concerned with her pelvis. On the other hand, in the excitement of their reunion and his revelation of the real Paul, she had completely forgotten the voice pickup in her button.

As night fell and the first moon of Flora rose over the mountain, they set up camp by a broad path in a male grove near trees by the stream from the fissure in the rampart and in earshot of the waterfall. "We'll weave a lattice of tendrils to shade our eyes from the second moon, which gets so bright at its zenith it can awaken a sleeper."

He showed her how to plait the tendrils, and when she had gotten the hang of the task, he said, "I'll go hustle up supper while you finish. I'll not be gone long, but don't leave the male grove. You'll be safe here."

"Safe from what?" she asked in alarm.

"A theoretical danger," he said vaguely, "something from above, I think, from the forest or from the sea grottoes in the cliff."

"If there's a threat," she said, "I'd like to know what it is. I'll be here for four months."

"There'll be no threat now if you stay among the males. After you've learned quickness with your machete you can defend yourself against anything you wish to defend against."

"How does one learn quickness?" she asked.

"You'll be adapted," he grinned, "like this."

Suddenly he was gone, vanishing into the grove as silently as a Mohawk, to leave her weaving and wondering.

Emotionally, mentally, and physically, Paul was in perfect condition; but there was the absence of records, which was unusual, even though he had promised to 'talk her into a landing.'

So far his talk had been a skimming over of facts that should have been analyzed in detail, and half-answers to whole questions.

He knew too much to say so little. He said he had warned Hal of the danger from the tulips, yet he had not mentioned the danger in his field notes to her. On their hike from the landing, he had told her that the paths had furnished a clue for a pollination theory, but he had told her nothing about the theory. Male groves were "stationed" on the perimeters, a military term. He thought he knew why the sexes were segregated, but he had not told her what his thoughts were. Now there was this theoretical threat from the forest above, or was it from the sea grottoes? And why would she "be adapted," rather than "adapt," to learn quickness. He had realigned her life with a few hammer strokes of honesty, yet there was a furtiveness in his candor when he spoke of Tropica, and his methodology had certainly grown slipshod.

He came back to her down the path bearing a stalk of sugarcane and singing an Elizabethan song with a "hey, ho, and hey nonino." Moonlight bathed his bronze with silver, and she said, "Sire, the tent is raised."

"Whet lips and tongues for a feast," he said, hacking off a section of the cane and peeling it, "and to tell me about this virginity codicil to our late marriage contract. . . . Your supper, milady."

It was a delicious cane with an edible pulp, and as he squatted before her, munching away, she found herself recounting in detail the incidents in Washington, beginning with her first dinner with Hal and finishing with her outwitting of Gaynor. Then she told him bluntly, "Hans Clayborg's theory that intellectuals didn't fall in love was out of joint with Hal's remark that you kept him out of the groves. I had the feeling the orchids might have aroused your ardor."

"Clayborg told the truth. A wise man's love is a value judgment."

"Then why did you keep Hal out of the grove?" she asked, stifling a yawn.

His answer marked him as irrevocably her soulmate. "Hal could have 'fallen in love' because his overactive hormones impaired his reason. With two males in the groves, I would have had an organization with a love-smitten, useless subordinate. I'm a scientist, not an administrator."

"Aren't you an organization man?"

"By and large, I detest organizations. Legally they're only theoretical bodies, but they squirm with genuine maggots spawned by real blowflies. . . . You're getting sleepy. Let's get in the tent."

"But I want to know what you've found out about the pollination process—"

"Tomorrow," he interrupted. "It's all abstruse deduction, and I could be wrong."

"You're never wrong, Paul, but I am sleepy."

Stretching out beside her, he stroked her hair. "No, I could be wrong. Did it ever occur to you that in the primal innocence of life there were no pollinators in Eden?"

"But I came to Eden by the back door," she said, remembering Heyburn, "chewing on an apple core."

"No, dearest," he said. "You've come in innocence, and you've entered by the servant's entrance. . . . Now, go to sleep."

His hand was stroking her hair, and a lassitude was descending over her mind. "You've got so much to tell me, Paul. You must spend tomorrow with me."

"Of course, dear Freda, I'll stay with you tomorrow."

She was drifting off to sleep, but she heard his voice whisper, from far away, "I'll never leave you. We've come to Eden to stay. Now, sleep. Sleep. Sleep."

She heard him, and she knew he was lulling her fears to lull her to sleep, lulling her with soporific sounds, suggestions, and she loved to be lulled by Paul. Drowsily she smiled and turned her lips to his good-night kiss. She knew he was manipulating her, but she did not mind. It was one thing to be manipulated at the hands of an office politician, like Gaynor; it was quite another to be manipulated by the hand of a lover.

She awakened once, when the second moon's orbit carried it above the cloud on Tropica's cone and its brightness on the snow cone filtered through the tendrils. She could hear Paul's even breathing in the moonglow beside her, and, reassured, she drifted back to sleep.

When she awakened again, it was not to certain wakefulness, for dream images impinged on her consciousness. Both as a dreamer and as a wakeful sleeper, she felt hands disrobing her, and she thought Paul had come to her, though she could not hear his breathing. "He has come for me," she thought, "my bridegroom, my beloved." But the dream imagery returned, and she lay in a chamber as vestals disrobed and anointed her, vestals of the moon goddess preparing her for a ritual sacrifice.

She was not afraid as they lifted her and bore her up temple steps, and she knew, so light was their touch, that she was being borne down the corridors of a dream, past rows of silent priests. Although the priests neither sang nor chanted, she felt the variety of their love as she was carried past them, the worshipful love of the stripling, the detached love of the kindly brother, the fatherly love of a patriarch toward his daughter. It was as if she were being wrapped in a coat of many colors, and though the wrappings bound her straitly, they bound her lightly, and they did not cover her completely.

The long procession wound along and led her, finally, to the altar of Isis. It must have been her altar, for the moon was directly behind the high priest, who stood with sacrificial knife upraised. Then, in the manner of dreams, the forms changed. She was not being draped onto an altar but bound into a fetal position, and she wanted to giggle: she was being offered up to the high priest, breech foremost.

He stood with knife upraised, and the knife was altered to a belaying pin. In the split second before the downsweep of the instrument, she knew she had been tricked. She was not being slain on the altar of Isis. The priest was an orchid, dark in the blaze of the moon, and she was a ritual sacrifice to an orchid god.

She felt a prick, but there was no death agony. In the manner of dreams, she had become a rodeo rider, aboard a bucking stallion, upside down. With each lunge upward she sank lower, rising to the thrust with a metered rhythm and falling, with an ingasp of agony at the outdrawn stamen, to the bottommost dip of the highest rollercoaster ever built. Then the ride was over and she was swaying down the fairway in a jinrikisha loaded with all the Kewpie dolls at the fair, hearing the hurdy-gurdies play and smelling the odors of hot-buttered popcorn, peanuts, and elm trees.

She awakened to sunlight and to Paul, squatting before her on the grass and hacking a casabalike melon with his machete. He looked over as she rubbed her eyes, hacked a half into two pieces, and handed her a quarter, saying, "Here, have the best breakfast you've ever eaten."

Lying out of the grove and on the grass, where he, apparently, had dragged her, she could admire the washboard configuration of his stomach, the ripple of his thigh muscles, without hindrance. Paul Theaston was stark naked.

"You have no clothes on," she commented.

"You haven't either," he said, and she didn't have.

She bit into the melon, thinking that it was easier to be honest without clothes. "You left me alone last night."

"You had *them*." He waved his hands to the orchids.

"I dreamed *they* had *me*. . . . Your friends were delightful."

"One night in Eden, and you're dreaming like a wanton. . . . But you have the body for such dreams. Come, eat breakfast on the way, and I'll take the most beautiful girl from earth to meet the most beautiful girl on Flora."

He led her down the path and entered the female grove, moving easily through the widely spaced stalks, and with such sureness that she asked, "How can you find an individual beauty among this galaxy of beauties?"

"By the color of her bloom in daylight and the odor of her perfume at night."

"Were you out here last night?"

"Yes, I patrol the groves in early morning, by the light of the second moon. By noon the plants are dormant. . . . Ah, here's the lissome lovely. . . . Freda, meet Susy."

Susy was a splendid plant, her stalk shining with the pale green of adolescence, and her bloom was deep red. Her tentacles seemed to quiver as Paul approached, guiding Freda by her arm, and the curve of the flower's hips had a boyishness that matched the freshness of her fragrance. She was at least seven feet tall. "Why, Paul, she's lovely."

"She likes you, Freda. You set her tendrils aquiver. Stand closer. Let her embrace you."

He bent forward and lifted a tendril from midway of the stalk and draped it over Freda's shoulder. It seemed to her that the leaves of the vine cupped as it touched her to massage her shoulder lightly, and the other leaves on the tendril, one by one, formed delicate suction cups which clung to her back and swept down her waist, clinging to the small of her back and coiling around her hips. Its tip fluttered lightly against her navel. Other tendrils were moving from the stalk to embrace her, and Freda moved closer, pressing against the stalk and looking up at the bloom with the awe of an artist before the Mona Lisa.

Now, all tendrils were coming into play, fluttering along her thighs and encircling her hips. She lifted her arms and folded them behind her head to give the vines more freedom with her torso. They enwreathed her, the lower tendrils sliding between her thighs and upward to weave a green cocoon that held her lightly with its suctions and caressed her with its quiverings. The leaves seemed to sense her areas most sensitive to their touch, kissing her lightly at first and then more amorously, finding zones of maximum response to become her suckling babe, her lover, her sister, her spouse; and though they stroked her cheeks and lips, they left her nostrils free to breathe in quickening gasps of delight.

Looking up at the blossom, she saw it sway backward, moving slowly at first, and downward in a sinuous arc as the vines tugged at her, trying to lift her. Sensing the orchid's intent, she stood on tiptoe, feeling the tendrils below her trunk parting for the culmination of the bloom's sweet journey, and she strained higher, so avid now for the union that she was oblivious to Paul as she would have been to a band of Indians circling the stalk with war whoops. Nearing its journey's end, the blossom slowed, and she saw the petals of its labellum opening to encompass its desire.

The petals unfolded and enwrapped her, to close again and cup her in their beauty, and in her green bower she shivered with the shivering leaves. Inside the blossom's cup, she could feel the stigma, a lark's tongue of love, fluttering, quivering, probing.

Then it touched.

As her buttocks tensed, her torso relaxed and her spine arched back as if to a sudden blow, while a shudder in her loins foretold an ecstasy unbearable. She would have torn herself from the glory loosening her thighs, but in the green rush of its caress her fear wished less to flee than her love wished to pursue. She was flung into a vortex of exquisite agony and searing rapture. Around her the tendrils shivered in joy and release, and she answered thrust with throb. Her breasts were torn from the vines' embrace by the backward snap of her arching spine, and for long moments she quivered in matching joy and release while her breasts heaved like twin roes leaping in the sunlight. Thus it was that Freda Caron, with breasts palpitant and loins tensed, found what earth had denied Hal Polino—the ultimate expression of dissonant rhythm.

Suddenly the vines grew lax; the tendrils ceased to cup and whirl. She was lowered gently, to slump backward into the grass, her legs folded around the base of the stalk, and she slept.

Paul awakened her, patting her cheeks. "Ten minutes is all you get. It's a nervous reaction." He bent down to help her to her feet. "Up, girl, those thews were also made for walking. A dip in the pool will snap you out of it. That was a classical pose. Reminded me of the statue of Leda and the swan."

"Statues again," she said, getting to her feet. "What you were watching was the Caron can-can."

"Never heard of the Caron can-can."

"Boy, you never will."

Freda moved in heavy-thighed languor behind him as he led the way down the path, pausing occasionally to lop off a sere bottom blade from a stalk. "They like it," he said. "It's like trimming toenails. The plants are very sensitive to the desire of others. Your act back there was a mirror image of your own desires, desires you repressed for no good reason. And as you get to know the orchids, you'll find you're sensitive to them, and to other human beings, in a manner you were never aware of before."

"Paul," she said suddenly, "I have a monitor planted in my jacket."

"We'll fix it," he said. "Trim a few blades with me, and save them."

She chopped, carefully avoiding the stalk, and felt the satisfaction gained from rendering a service appreciated. Inside her, some pickup system registered thanks from the orchids.

When they reached the bivouac area, Paul gathered her clothes and bound them with the stalks, using her belt, and put them under his arm. He led her toward the tree line and down a path toward the sound of rushing water, which had cut a glen through the lava. He circled east along the ravine, toward the ramparts. "There's some of the cane you ate last night." He pointed. "It's both soporific and aphrodisiac."

"That was a Clayborgian trick. . . . Why didn't you let me stay awake?"

"It was a safety measure. I feared you might not like the blind date."

They had broken through a grove of live oaks to a pool of green water and were standing on a ledge fifteen feet above the surface. Above them the waterfall poured from a crevice in the terrace above, dropped five hundred feet to a cairn of crumbled coral rubble, and roared downward to scoop out the pool above which they stood. It was thirty yards long, and they stood above its widest point, which was at least twenty yards, and it was deep. Looking downward, she could see water-carved stalagmites of lava jutting up from a sandy bottom.

Paul tossed her clothing into the pool, and they watched as, buoyed by the dry stalks, it floated down to the exit narrows and dipped once and swirled down the rapids toward the sea. "It'll be out to sea in three hours, and the husks will grow sodden and sink, and that is the end of the earthly career of Freda Caron."

"You were serious last night when you told me you were staying. Does this mean we're defecting?"

"Why not? You leave nothing on earth but bad memories and office politics."

"But what about all my equipment?"

"Crated and ready to go back. All you took was a machete. As defectors, our property will be seized. Even after probate there should be enough left to pay for the machete."

"Isn't this treason?" she asked.

"Oh, no," he said. "We're not betraying our country. By the terms of the Social Compact, a government rules only by consent of the governed. We are merely exercising our right to withdraw our consent. . . . Last one in's a bum!"

He turned and dived cleanly into the water.

It was the most delightful and uninhibited game of underwater tag she had ever played. When she tagged him, he knew he had been tagged, and with the residual oxygen from her space pill, she could stay under him for five minutes at a stretch. But once he lunged from a grotto and sent her spinning to the surface, and she knew she had been tagged. Afterward they lay on the narrow sand beach and laughed in the sunlight.

"Say, boy," she accused him, "you've been keeping secrets. What's this mysterious threat you hinted about?"

"I spoke guardedly," he said, "in order not to alarm you last night, and because the evidence is partly deductive. Apparently there was, and may still be, a tusked mammal as large as a peccary, probably with the tongue of an aardvark, which the orchids used as a pollinator, much as the tulips use a koala-shrew. They must have been permitted to dig up a few dead stalks, or stalks that couldn't defend themselves, to eat the tubers."

"Defend themselves?"

"With their tendrils. The tendrils are tentacles, and the males can tear chunks of flesh from a body with their suction leaves. But a population explosion must have occurred among the pigs, and they started to raid the orchid groves in force."

"How do you deduce this?"

"Tusk marks on the trees on the sixth level. Swaths of new growths in the orchid groves on the fifth level. The fifth level is a battleground. But over the years, the orchids learned to put the males on the perimeters, letting a few of the pigs through as pollinators, killing them when an ecological overbalance brought the pigs out in force."

"This is all deduction?" she asked.

"Not quite," he admitted. "One night I heard animal screams on this tier near the canyon's mouth, and in the morning when I investigated, I found flecks of blood on the stalks, and blood on the grass. Once, on a cliff ledge, I found a skeleton fallen from above."

"Or thrown," she said.

He nodded. "The paths were runs for the pollinators. Four feet between the female groves, because they have a shorter killing range. Six feet on the broad paths. The orchids could control them when they ran amok."

"You speak of them in the past tense," she said. "How do the orchids pollinate without them?"

"Well, they could use hand-pollination with their suction leaves."

"But they don't," she said. "Quit hedging. What else have you found?"

"The scream I heard that night. When I reached the spot where the blood was, the only orchid uprooted was a dead stalk. They had killed the pollinator while it foraged for fair game."

"Why should they turn against the animal?"

"It was dangerous and inefficient. There was no true animal-plant symbiosis, but an ecological cold war." He raised his eyes to the snow cone, and there was a steel in their grayness. "Someday, with my sons, I'm going up to the forest and show the pigs how men can kill."

She turned on her side and raised her head to him. "You are still evading my question. If the orchids are killing their pollinators, how can they pollinate without them?"

He sat up and looked down at her, his eyes burning with a zeal that reminded her, more than ever, of a young Moses, but when he spoke his voice was gentle. "Dear girl, they've found the ideal animal for their purpose. We are the pollinators of Eden."

Freda rolled onto her back and looked up at the snow cone, swept free of clouds and gleaming in the sunlight. She and Paul could establish a new race on Flora, one reared in brotherhood with nature. Awareness and pride in her fecundity gave the prospect charm, particularly for a girl who had spent most of her life in Southern California. She lamented young ladies who married organization men and went into split-level houses, never to come out again; and she herself did not care to be numbered among those living dead. But there were technical considerations.

"What of our findings? Our records would be lost to science."

"Let them," he said. "I'm tired of accumulating facts for the sake of facts. Let science be lost if it doesn't serve us."

"Very well. Out goes science, and culture too. But we have a more immediate problem. Granted the *Botany* has neither the detectors nor the manpower to find us, there is a pack of bloodhounds aboard—"

"Which would last five minutes among the groves."

"Are the orchids hostile?"

"Not unless I want them to be. In Eden, the word of Adam is law."

She had waited to spring the hardest question last. "How can

I find time to be a race mother, or the inclination, after a night out with the orchids?"

"Pollination by proxy," he answered, grinning. "Susy was the third leg of a three-legged stool."

Freda's last night on Flora was a night to remember. At Paul's suggestion, and riding on his shoulders, they spent the remainder of the morning looking for the rare bright-red bloom of an orchid lover. "The one I spotted for you yesterday was past his prime," Paul said, "but it was a rush assignment, and a man can't truly select a lover for a woman. There are so many subliminal factors involved."

After an hour's search, she found a Prince Charming among the orchids, almost in the corner of the terrace formed by the river's canyon and the sea wall. It was a gorgeous specimen, young, and fully six inches taller than its closer neighbors. Paul let her guide him over to the plant, at his suggestion, so she could look at it, get acquainted, and find food to feed her fantasies.

She tingled as she looked down on the sleeping prince, and though it was completely dormant in the sunlight, it seemed to quiver with eagerness when she laid her cheek against its petals and tweaked its pollen-engorged stamen. "Get me away from here, Paul, before this thing wakes up," she squealed in mock fright, kicking him in the ribs.

That evening for supper she ate only half a segment of the cane stalk from a portion near the roots, where the aphrodisiac qualities exceeded the soporific. They wove their canopy against the moonlight early, so she would be rested, and Paul counseled her on attitudes, banishing the old taboos and shearing away inhibitions with his words. Yet nowhere in his indoctrination did he deny the spiritual values inherent in the ritual, and he urged her to see the affair as a communion and to look upon herself as a sacred chalice for the fluid of life. He counseled her on humility, saying, "Aid the young and immature with your experience, and help the old with your strength."

Briefly he discussed their means of communication, touching tendril to tendril, and told her that an orchid needing her could find her within five hundred yards. They were bedding down within fifty yards of the chosen one because there was no point prolonging her suspense. "Once the tendrils lift you and the courtesans carry you to their prince for the night, there is no turning back. So relax and enjoy it."

So it was that she came to her second communion by moonlight and found the consummation exceeded the fantasies she had prepared for it. She was lifted to heights of adoration by her surging acolyte and lowered to rise again, and again, but now no dream images cloaked her delight, and she well knew what was up and who was down. As the third and final tidal wave bore her toward the second moon, she felt an expansiveness of psyche, a plumbing to depths never reached before, and she thought, "If this be treason . . ." but the thought was whipped to spume by nonverbalizable tremors that spun the loved and the lover into homogenized ecstasy, and she sank with a sigh into the profound sleep of repletion.

Freda was awakened to bright sunlight by the sound of bacon sizzling on a frying pan. She stretched luxuriously and turned to Paul to find him gone. Still yawning, she leaned out and looked down the path, and grabbed her machete.

Three human beings were approaching, clothed in rubber guards and masked in plastic bubbles. Two of the waddlers carried cylinders on their backs. As they advanced, they sprayed a fine mist to left and right, keeping the third man, who was armed with a rifle, between. In the split second before she acted, her mind comprehended the full horror of the scene. Sometime during hibernation they had planted a transponder under her flesh, probably in her earlobe, and they had tracked her, listening to every word she and Paul had spoken. Her words had branded her a defector, and her orchids, now white and brittle beneath the spray of liquid oxygen, were powerless to protect her as they themselves died beneath the frost.

"Murderers!" she screamed, and charged, brandishing the machete in her naked fury, as she hurled herself at the trio. She saw the central figure raise the rifle, and she swerved but swerved too late. The tranquilizing pellet struck her thigh with the impact of a truck, crushing her into oblivion.

Chapter Thirteen

"HOW MANY FINGERS?" A VOICE ASKED.

Freda focused her eyes. "Three," she said.

"What is your name?"

She was beginning to see a face behind the voice, and above the face a receding hairline. "Freda Janet Caron."

"That will be all, nurse," the doctor said. She could see him plainly now, seated on a straight-backed chair beside her couch. Beyond him was a door opening onto a white-tiled bathroom. She saw a desk with a bookshelf nailed onto the wall behind it, a bed with a lavender counterpane, and a green carpet on the floor. Turning her head, she saw a high window which admitted haze-filtered sunlight. There were bars on the window.

The doctor looked up from the pad on which he had scribbled a note and said, "Freda, my name is Doctor Campbell. I am a Platonic psychiatrist, and you are in the neuropsychiatric ward of the Institute for Space Ailments at Houston, Texas. You have suffered a traumatic episode, and I am here to help you. You have been undergoing deep analysis, under narcosis, since your arrival two days ago. Following the methods of Plato, I intend to ask you questions. Your answers will lead to self-enlightenment. Platonism holds that sanity is innate in man's mind."

"Then I must be insane!"

"Insanity is a loaded term, Freda. Let us say your attitudes need adjustment. You suffer a mild earth-alienation induced by the transference of your affections to another planet. In Freudian terms, your libido is fixated on the Planet of Flowers, but the fixation is indicative of a deeper malady still. However, Freda, your libido itself is somewhat unique, since it has an entire planet as its love-object, a condition known to the trade as 'Nymphomanic omniphilia,' meaning a passionate love of everything."

She cut through his pedantry with a question. "What's the 'deeper malady'?"

"Humanism. It's a social aberration. Basically, you're antiorganization; proindividual, anticivilization; pronature, nonaltruistic; hedonistic. Since the function of society is to function, you are similar to a left-handed screw in a machine using only right-handed screws."

"You make it sound awful, Doctor."

" 'Serious to grave' is the preferred terminology, Freda; but we know an awful lot about you, and we think we can help. Now, listen carefully to my questions and take your time answering."

Campbell's analytic technique was a subtle exercise in dialectics. He began by asking her simple questions that explored her attitudes toward status: would she prefer to be mistress of a house or a serving maid? He related his status questions to mobility relationships, which led her to defining freedom as action initiated by free will. Leading her with questions, he made her admit that pollinators in a plant-insect symbiosis did not behave with free will. "It is self-evident, then," he declared, "that your relationship with the orchids of Flora was a master-slave relationship. Does it not follow that you were either an insect or a slave?"

His name-calling aroused in her a Bloody-Grant-Clayborg reaction. "Yes," she agreed, "in the sense that a wife-husband is a mistress-slave relation and that men are infrastructures designed to support their procreative equipment."

His dialectics faltered after that remark. Doctor Campbell shied away from overt discussions of sex or any questioning of the sanctity of marriage, the logic of monogamy, or the capabilities of the male. Even as Freda answered his questions or listened to his evasions of her counterquestions, she was planning on another level.

To get released from Houston was not enough; she must get

back to Flora, to her red princes and her blond Moses. She was needed on Flora for precisely the reason she could not be used on earth. She was an unusual screw.

Doctor Campbell was in his mid-forties, a stage of life, Freda knew, when a man simultaneously sensed the approaching end and came to realize the futility of the beginnings, a time of suicide or licentious excess. Beneath the pedantry of Campbell, she sensed a man who favored excesses, one still eager to clutch life but unequipped with grappling hooks.

"Now, Freda"—he looked at his watch—"for the next nine minutes and forty-five seconds, we're permitted an informal chit-chat."

With the placebo words of the New Analysis, he was saying the recorded session was over and that off-the-record talks, to relate analyst with patient, had begun. It would serve her ends, she decided, to equip this boy with grappling hooks and provide him a few excesses to grapple.

"Oh, goody!" she said. "Now I have you for my very own."

He squelched a smile and glanced at his watch. "Yes, you have nine and a half minutes of me."

"You're such a scrupulous timekeeper, Doctor. Do you sometimes hear time's winged chariots hurrying behind you, and feel there's so much to be accomplished, so much loving to be—"

"I'm not a Frommian," he reminded her.

"Well, so many questions to be asked that you will die like a sick eagle looking at the sky?"

"Yes, Freda, I do have a sense of urgency. But the main problem in this business is that there's nothing you can put your finger on. If I could just get inside skulls, shake up a few neurons, realign a few synapses, like a mechanic can jerk out a carburetor and clean it."

He threw up his hands in despair. "It's 'now you have it, now you don't.' Once a man came to me who smoked too much. It took me three months to analyze the smoke out of him. Then he developed a tic! Well, two months and the tic yielded, but he started having migraine headaches. It took me a solid month to cure his headache. When he got up from that couch, he had not a ghost of a headache, was absolutely ticless, and would not look at a cigarette. Freda, he was in *radiant* health. He complimented me profusely, he shook my hand, he walked out of my office, down the hall, and the ungrateful bastard jumped out of the window to the alley, forty floors below. Six months' work shot to hell!"

"Relax, Doctor," Freda said. "If he had lived and smoked, he might have died of lung cancer. By the way, what is your given name?"

"James," Campbell answered, and, almost furtively, he lowered his voice. "My friends used to call me Jimmy."

"What do you mean, Jimmy—'used to call'?"

"I don't have friends anymore. I'm a father image to my patients, and the average neuro wants to kick hell out of his old man. Off the record, this is one area where you're normal. You wanted to seduce your father, but he was so fond of your mother—"

"He divorced her, Jimmy."

"Sure. She had to lock him out or die of overwork. You don't remember any of this consciously. That's where you get your libido, and, girl, you've got one that won't quit! To my knowledge, you're the first woman who ever did it to a flower, and the first case of space madness localized in the primary erogenic zone."

"Space madness!"

"Technical only." He brushed it aside. "Nonobsessive. By definition, all which is not of earth is of space. To use the lay term, you're not a neck-snapper."

Jimmy was too tense, too wrought-up, still glancing at his watch. She stirred on the couch and smiled at him. "Sort of a pelvis-twitcher, eh, Jimmy?"

He smiled. He had a beautiful smile. She said, "Light me a cigarette, will you, Jimmy?"

Lighting a cigarette might help him relax, she thought, but his hand trembled so that he could hardly find the end. To divert him, she remarked, "You know, not all my libido is fixated on Flora."

She told the truth. When she mentally superimposed an image of a red orchid around his balding head, she found she could sense the needs of others as she had on Flora, and she could pinpoint Campbell's frustrations. He had devoted his life to helping others, who had returned his aid with ingratitude, and he was terribly perplexed. Inside him a child was crying, and the oversensitive adult he had become needed assurance of his manhood. She could hear Paul saying, "Guide the young with your experience, and help the old with your strength."

When he finally handed her the cigarette, she asked, "Are you married, Jimmy?"

"Not anymore. I failed as a husband, too."

"That father image again?"

"No. Professional duties kept me from home so much, and I was detached around the house, thinking about problems, so my wife got bored."

"I should think she would be willing to make sacrifices for the honor and prestige of being the wife of a lay saint."

"A lay saint!" He took out a cigarette and lighted one for himself. "That's the first time anybody ever called me *that*."

"Although your tool might be a question, Doctor, your art is love," she said. "The moment I awakened, I felt in the presence of an old friend. Your wife did not know what flowers were at her feet. If I had been gifted with a husband such as you, not all the ills that earth inherits could have sundered us. I'm happy, Jimmy, that you're my doctor, and I can never be completely alienated from a world that has such analysts in it."

He dropped his eyes modestly, and they must have fallen on his wristwatch, for he leaped to his feet. "Enjoyed it, Freda. Books on the shelf. Read them. No correspondence. No visitors. Your nurse is Wilma Firbank, RN, and I'll send her in. Don't let her show you her judo chop."

He was gone, and not a second too soon or too late.

She walked over to the shelf above the desk and looked at the books: Jowett's *Plato*, Hegel's *Dialectical Materialism*, Krafft-Ebing's *Psychopathia Sexualis*. As she pondered the rather odd trio of volumes, she heard the key turn in her lock, and a square-shouldered, square-jawed woman of thirty entered, freshly scrubbed and wearing a starched uniform. Freda looked over and said, "You must be Miss Firbank?"

"Yes, ma'am, and I got to show you how to push some buttons, tell you about the hospital's schedule, and explain some house rules."

Freda listened, sizing the woman up. Wilma Firbank had open-faced candor, but her eyes seemed sad. Freda asked the nurse if she had been briefed on her case.

"They tell me, ma'am, you sort of fell in love with a planet. Must have been some planet."

"It was a planet of love," Freda said, "and it was glorious. Wilma, let me ask you: have you ever been loved by a man, totally, and for yourself alone?"

"No'm. I'm flatfooted and sort of waddle when I walk. Men like girls with curvy hips. Tell the truth, I kind of agree with them."

"On Flora, I was once loved by a lissome, redheaded maiden with a caress lighter than a butterfly's wings."

"Sort of reminds me of a dietician who works here, Ruby May Washington, except Ruby May's not redheaded. You'll meet her."

"I'm looking forward to meeting Ruby May Washington," Freda said, superimposing a red orchid around the sandy hair of Wilma.

In cultivating friends in high places, Freda thought, it never paid to ignore the rank and file. Wilma would have connections with the hospital's underground, and Freda's private bathroom truly rendered her incommunicado. Besides, if her plan worked, she'd need two other women. Wilma Firbank would be ideal for the top terrace on Flora. If any more pigs came down from the forest, Wilma looked perfectly capable of converting them to pork with one judo chop.

It took Freda three days to persuade her doctor to smuggle a letter out to Hans Clayborg, because Doctor Campbell's problems were far more deep-seated than she had assumed. He was terribly shy. His professional ethics had conditioned him, like Pavlov's dog, against the use of his own couch.

There were also technical problems, among them the lock on Freda's door. The lock was operated from the outside, and Campbell had to use all of his persuasive powers to get the committee to move it to the inside.

On the day after she got her lock moved inside, she had a visitor from the Great Beyond, as inmates called the outside. Hans Clayborg bounced into her room, his electric hair atingle. Ostensibly he had come to discuss defects in the Stanford-Hammersmith theory with the head psychiatrist. Actually he had come in response to Freda's letter.

They spent an excited preliminary half-hour swapping news, she of Flora and he of earth. The Caron-Polino theory, she learned, had taken the scientific world by storm. "The Caron Can-Can" had been banned from the airwaves as deleterious to the morals of the young, and Doctor Hector was new Chief of the Bureau of Exotic Plants. Doctor Gaynor was now supervisor in charge of floral arrangements at the San Diego Zoo. "I could spring you on a writ of *habeas corpus,*" Clayborg said, "but you'd have to stand trial for defection."

"Getting out of Houston isn't enough, Hans. I must get back to Flora, with your help. I want you to demonstrate mathematically that a few rungs from a human being's DNA ladder can be spliced onto the double helix of a Florian orchid to produce seeds with enough human genes to bridge the death-creation gap between universes. Show that Mendelian laws, over generations, would produce functioning human beings from the seeds who could selectively breed out the nonfunctioning orchid traits. Give me imaginary seeds, Hans, to store in real urns."

Hans lost his ebullience. "If I advanced that hypothesis, they would not put you on Flora. They'd put me in Houston. Whoever heard of human-orchid seeds?"

"I got the idea from your human corn."

"Girl, that was simply boy-talk to polarize you along a germinal axis. The idea's impossible!"

"You deal with impossibles at Santa Barbara, remember? . . . Hans, for the love of me, write a letter to the President. Tell him a union of dissimilar DNA molecules is theoretically possible—the Caron-Polino theory has laid the groundwork—and name me as field cystologist best qualified to conduct the experiment on Flora. Make the letter persuasive. Please, Hans!"

"Freda," he groaned. "I deal with impossibles, true. But I persuade presidents with possibles. I know nothing about the DNA of Florian orchids."

"There's part of a seed in my greenhouse icebox at the station. Get it and formulate a theory. When Einstein sent his letter, Roosevelt probably neither knew nor cared that $E=MC^2$, but he trusted Einstein."

"But this would be a perversion of science to serve a human want!"

"It's about time science was perverted to serving human wants! You'll pervert your knowledge to seduce an innocent girl but balk at using it to persuade a callous chief executive. Very well! Then, think of this, you acolyte of pure science: if life just happens to be an entropic function, some of you altarboys are missing a devotional by not integrating the life force into the Unified Field Theory."

"I never thought of *that*," he said in genuine amazement. For a moment he was silent, numbed by the knowledge that there was something he had not thought of, but he waved his hand in dismissal. "I cannot flaunt my disciplines and bend an entire technology to the whims of a . . . a . . ." He managed a weak smile. ". . . a nymphomanic omniphiliac. I do worship science as an abstraction, and I'll continue to, until someone shows me a better Truth."

In desperation, Freda superimposed the image of a red orchid onto the head of Hans Clayborg, and the petals fitted his flaring hair perfectly. Now she could read his mind: he was throwing up verbiage to ward her off while he considered life force as part of a unified field. But he had thrown out the words "show me," and the words were a rope with which she could hog-tie him.

"Hans," she said slowly, "I can prove to you that the poetry of the human heart holds truths as valid as the abstractions of science."

"Just how can you do that?"

"Turn the key in yonder lock," she said, "and lay your teeth on the desk."

Freda found that Doctor Campbell's father had been so weak that his son could not identify with him, so Jimmy had become his own father image and had played the role of surrogate so strongly that he had repressed the growing boy. When his problem was finally analyzed, Doctor Campbell responded to therapy with enthusiasm. His haggard look faded with his father image, and what he lost as a psychiatrist he gained as a man. Empathy was replaced by character.

At the end of six weeks, Jimmy Campbell resigned from the hospital staff to become an automobile mechanic. His last favor to Freda was to pronounce her incurable. "It won't do any good, Freda," he said, "because they'll never let the records out of this nut house, but anything you want from me, you get. We humanists must stick together."

Doctor Campbell was replaced by a Frommian named Williams who lasted only two weeks. His philosophy of love and tender care was so amplified and reinforced by his patient that he was dismissed from the staff for laying siege to a nurse who had fled him and locked herself into a linen closet. Wilma, who was becoming a reliable pipeline to the hospital's underground, told Freda that Williams left for Hollywood to become a movie producer.

He left too quickly to recommend Freda's exile to Flora, but he did leave her with some rather curious additions to her library. Even Wilma was interested enough to borrow her copy of *The Well of Loneliness*.

Her Frommian was replaced by a Freudian named Smith, who brought her a copy of *The Theory of the Neuroses*, which was invaluable in helping her to help him think that he understood himself, but he resigned under peculiar circumstances. In the intense concentration on her psyche, the hospital staff had completely ignored her soma, and halfway through her third month in Houston, Freda was found to be two months pregnant. Her Freudian, Smith, who was poorly informed outside of his field, resigned her case, thinking himself responsible.

At least that was the reason he gave her. She had her doubts. Her condition was becoming apparent to a charwoman, and Smith told her he would become a sculptor and spend the remainder of his days re-creating her torso in marble. "No arms, no heads, Freda," he told her. "Just breasts."

She bade good-bye to one more humanist, feeling he had undertaken a fitting line of work. Smith had strong Oedipus tendencies.

For three full weeks Freda suffered a hiatus in which she had no analyst at all. Wilma, through channels, kept her posted. The hospital staff, concerned by the rate at which she used up analysts and by her pregnancy, caused, the staff assumed, by a hospital employee, was bringing in a Pavlovian from Cape Cod. The Pavlovian, Wilma understood, conditioned his patients with a form of continuing shock treatment so obnoxious that they fled into sanity to escape therapy.

Doctor Watts was his name. She feared to ask him his given name. He was a New Englander carved in Midwestern Gothic, prim-lipped, sandy-haired, square-jawed, with pale blue eyes that stared through her when he spoke. He had the commanding presence of a Captain Bligh, and he was in his late sixties. His age did not put him outside of her range of effective action, but her pregnancy had turned her thoughts inward. Her awareness of the needs of others was not blunted but merely set aside as she contemplated the growing fulfillment of her love for Paul Theaston.

She hoped her baby was Paul Theaston's. Her period of hibernation between Paul and Hans left the matter in doubt. In any event, the child could have a father it could be proud of. Since she had substituted as a father image for Jimmy Campbell, it was highly unlikely that she could mother his child.

She did not even superimpose the image of an orchid on Doctor Watts, mostly because of his policy. He cultivated an obnoxiousness that stretched her understanding to such limits that she could not find the motive to comfort him, especially since she was fast losing the use of her primary means of extending comfort. The torso that had turned the Freudian to sculpture was becoming, in a word, unshapely.

Watts had read her case history carefully, listened to all the tapes, and had deduced much which Freda felt positive was not in the record. His greeting, when he entered her room, revealed the extent of his bookwork.

"You've been assigned to me, Miss Caron,"—he accented the "Miss" as he cast a scornful glance at her maternity gown—"because you acquired a taste for the florid on an alien planet which has thrown your stimulus-response reactions heavily to the response side. Fruits of your behavior are apparent from your appearance, but I'm here to help, not to pass judgment. If I were to blame you for this travesty on Christian motherhood, some of my blame might reflect on brother members of a profession devoted to alleviating human suffering, or perhaps an array of otherwise innocent male nurses, janitors, delivery boys, or whatever else might have crawled from the woodwork. I'm no namby-pamby do-gooder who blames society for the sins of its members. The sin is yours, Miss Caron."

"Aren't you being unkind, Doctor?"

"Not unkind. Truthful! The truth shall make you free, and the truth is that you've perverted every noble sentiment of womanhood to a loin-oriented pleasure principle. Repentance will help; atonement will cure. Humanists, Miss Caron, are lepers of the twenty-third century, and I'm not Saint Francis."

"Yes, Doctor Watts."

"To guard against your further depredations to our staff, I

have assigned Doctor Harold Franks as your obstetrician. Doctor Franks is eighty-eight years old."

In subsequent interviews Freda probed beneath the ice of Watts to find a vein of New Hampshire granite, stratified in layers of home, church, motherhood, and country. He resented her pregnancy as an affront to decent motherhood, but she was too involved within herself to point out a conflict between his attitude and his religious nature: motherhood, under any circumstances, could not be indecent, since it was an Act of God. Besides, she was also immersed in books on international law that Wilma brought her from the hospital library.

Hans Clayborg had a word about an Act of God when he called on her a week before the USSS *Botany* left on its final voyage to Flora. "Freda, your pregnancy ruined us. I'm convinced there is a possibility of DNA linkage in a pregnancy-pollination series between an orchid, you, an orchid, and Paul. Here are my formulae describing how the linkup could occur, but now it would take an Act of God or an edict from the President to get you to Flora. Congress would never cooperate, because Heyburn draws a big vote from legally married housewives."

"Hans, I don't think pregnancy has ruined me. By terms of the International Agreement of 1998, the spouse of a defector can choose to live with the defector."

"You and Theaston aren't married."

"The treaty allows for common-law marriages, since marriage customs differ from country to country, and I have proof of my relationship with Paul." She patted her stomach.

"Possibly," he agreed. "But what are the odds?"

"Fifty-fifty, between you and Paul."

He seemed startled. "What about the psychiatrist who put the lock on the inside?"

Freda blushed slightly, but the truth was the truth. "I was his father image, and his abreaction to his father was such that it would not make a woman pregnant."

She knew she had convinced Hans, because he grew suddenly

solicitous. He took her hand and asked gently, "How do you feel, darling?"

"Like a chorus from Euripides," she had to admit. "But you are my *deus ex machina*. I'm depending on you, Hans."

"Freda, you split me down the middle! Of course I want to help, but if you're the mother of my child, I'll never let you go to Flora. There's no woman on earth I adore as much as I—"

He was holding her hand and leaning toward her, and she was enjoying the intimacy in his voice, when suddenly he jerked back. An idea had struck him.

"There's possibility of a gene swap," he said excitedly. "It's retrograde, but it's there! If the child is mine, you'll be able to tell right away by its fully grown head of hair. All Clayborgs are born with long hair, but if the hair's a bright red, or if the baby has bright green eyes, if its fingertips are dented inward, if it has an odor of vanilla, if it has any one of these indices, get a blood test made immediately. Tell them to look for trace amounts of chlorophyll. If there is, we'll both go to Flora."

Hans was not merely trying to cheer her. His fervor was too genuine, and it made her pray that the child be Paul's. Hans had another mistress, his mind. He had completely forgot the sweet nothing he was about to whisper in her ear. Perhaps it was her pregnancy, she thought, but she craved sweet nothings.

He left her a copy of his calculations, which were as clear to her as the Goldberg Theory of Diminishing Entropy. Since she was a cystologist, she might have analyzed the equations, but at the moment she was occupied with knitting a bootee.

Days passed in tranquility toward her delivery date. Doctor Franks was a kindly old man who insisted on calling her "Mrs." He was so far advanced in age that she might have questioned his ability to deliver had not Watts thawed enough to tell her that a younger doctor would be on hand to assist. "You'll get full benefit of the civilization you reject," he said.

It was pleasant to strip and undergo inspection by Doctor

Franks. With him she felt appreciated as a noun rather than as an active verb. Despite his failing senses—he wore magnifying glasses in his spectacles' rims and had to turn the amplifier of his stethoscope to maximum to pick up the baby's heartbeat—his hands pummeled and probed with the deftness of an expert. And she enjoyed his sense of humor. Invariably he hobbled into her room, shouting in his high falsetto, "Hot-diggety-dog! Inspection time!"

Most of the time Freda sat alone, knitting, engrossed in her bodily processes, which acted as an anodyne to nostalgia. Yet she was aware always that in the far reaches of her consciousness the little winds of Flora were rustling through the groves, and the snow cone on Tropica rose silver in the sun. At night she sometimes awakened weeping for Paul, and in her dreams she was borne again between the ranks of her orchid lovers to a scarlet prince, well met by mellow-yellow moonlight.

Meanwhile, the *Botany* lifted off. Charlie Section returned to earth, and the Planet of Flowers was placed forever, by order of the United Nations, on the list of pariah planets. Outside the window, the hazy sun of summer faded to the smoky sun of autumn and merged into the leaden sun of winter. Freda, in her swelling loneliness, meditated on Time, which had carried her, in the space of three seasons, from an eager young junior executive to the stamen of an orchid on Flora and back again to the stigma of the bar sinister on earth, where she waited, incarcerated, famous to science but bearing a name that had fallen so low that a song of the same name had been barred from the airwaves.

If she had a son, she decided, she would call him Edmund, after the character in *King Lear*. A daughter she would call Florina.

As she sipped the vinegar and wine, time continued to sweep her along, into the delivery room, where masked faces floated above her in an anesthetic fog. Her last coherent thought was a prayer that the child be Paul's.

Perhaps as a part of Watts's continuing shock therapy, Freda felt, they brought the baby to her in her room, not in a bassinet but upon a white pillow. They prepared her formally, dressing her in an orchid-colored nightgown. Both Doctor Watts and Doctor Franks were in attendance, filing in ahead of the maternity nurse who carried the baby to place it in Freda's arms. Technically, she carried the pillow on which the baby rested and placed the pillow in Freda's arms.

Freda's baby was a reddish-mahogany seed in the shape of a small, elongated football, almost six inches around the girth, where its umbilicus had been carefully knotted. There was a faint blond fuzz at one end, and Freda thrilled to the knowledge that Paul Theaston had at least contributed to her baby's DNA.

"Freda," Doctor Franks piped from the foot of her bed, "the standard remark at such times is: it's a beautiful boy, or girl, as the case may be. By golly, I don't know what that is!"

Freda hardly heard him, gazing down enraptured upon the fruit of her womb. She marveled at its iridescence. She loved its faint fragrance of vanilla. She was entranced by its almost perfectly formed oval shape. It was her baby, conceived in beauty and delivered at a moment unique in the history of mankind, a nonmewling, nonpuking, no-diapers-to-clean baby which carried its own formula with it wherever it went. More important, in her arms lay a bridge between the life and death of universes, and who could deny her pride in an offspring destined for immortality?

The voice of Doctor Watts grated through the nimbus of her joy, asking, "Freda, do you feel maternal pride in *that?*"

Freda lifted glowing eyes to the psychiatrist. "Doctor Watts, every mother thinks her baby unique among the babies of the world. I've settled that argument forever."

"As an obstetrician, danged if I won't vouch for that," Doctor Franks said. "But there's one thing I'd like to check, Freda. I swear I heard a heartbeat."

While Freda held its pillow, Doctor Franks bent down and

placed his stethoscope halfway between the umbilicus and the blond fuzz and listened intently. "Heck fire! I *do* hear a heartbeat."

"Doctor Franks," Doctor Watts said, "the volume's up so high your stethoscope is picking up your wristwatch."

Watts turned to Freda with a strange gentleness in his voice. "What do you want done with it, Freda? Shall we bury it or cremate it?"

"Neither," Freda answered. "We'll plant it. But not here. Air-express it to Doctor Clayborg at Santa Barbara. He'll know how to prepare the soil. But let me hold it a little while longer."

She returned her gaze to the ovate sphere, feeling the universal adoration of all motherhood, supported by a more personal joy of recognition. It was more than the world's most unique baby she held in her arms; it was the Act of God that Clayborg had requested, and it would be followed, as the night the day, by an edict from the President.

On the pillow in her arms lay her reddish-mahogany passport to Flora.

Curtly now, Doctor Watts instructed the nurse to wrap the seed in tissue paper and send it to Santa Barbara. He dismissed the nurse and the seed and aided Doctor Franks, slightly confused, from the room. Watts quietly closed the door and locked it from the inside.

When he turned to Freda, Doctor Watts's face was no longer frozen in lines of moral rectitude. Its ice had broken, and it was twisting and untwisting as he fought to keep his composure. As if staggering under a burden, he walked over and knelt beside her bed, taking her hand and burying his face beside it in the bedclothes. Suddenly she realized he was weeping, that his stratum of New Hampshire granite had cracked. With her free hand, she twisted over and patted his head, and he looked up at her through tearstained eyes.

"Freda, forgive me. You are the Earth Mother. I've never seen such a beautiful maternal glow in the eyes of a woman, and under such adverse conditions. I have wronged you, Freda."

"Before you became a psychiatrist, Doctor Watts, what did your friends call you?"

"Ronnie."

Freda superimposed the image of a red orchid around the face lifted to her. One of his problems, as she had sensed, was deep-seated though simple: he had been weaned too early. Although his immediate reaction had been triggered by the proximity of lactose, what startled her was the depth of the Oedipus complex beneath his vein of granite. Her austere Pavlovian was in secret and in truth what she had often called him in private, a mother-lover.

Self-knowledge was not a necessary part of the therapy for Pavlovians, she recalled. All Ronnie must do was to learn new habits to replace his old, and she could retrain him in a trice. Meanwhile, he could help her with a minor but pressing problem. Bearing a seed, in Hal Polino's words, had been "no strain, no pain," but there were attendant discomforts.

"Ronnie," she said, stroking lightly the underjaw of his now radiant face, "ours is a world of reciprocal agreements. Generosity is so rare that the generous are confined to institutions and called by long Latin names. I wish to do something for you, but first you must do something for me."

"Anything, Freda. I'll do anything to atone."

What she proposed was less a reciprocal agreement than three gifts in succession, but she wanted him to think that he was contributing, and she did not want to leave the earth with any loose ends dangling. While he was bending to kiss her hand, she made a slight adjustment to her nightgown.

When Ronnie raised his eyes, one glimpse of their glow told her that her analysis of his needs had been correct. As he raised himself slightly and bent over her, she knew that earth was bidding hello to its latest humanist and farewell to its last Puritan.

FROM: The President of the United States
TO: The Commanding Officer, NASA

To his good and faithful servant, the President sends greetings. At the request of our beloved minister without portfolio, Doctor Hans Clayborg, IAS, who assumes full responsibility for any failures of this mission, you are hereby charged to release and transport Freda Janet Caron, patient, and to transport Wilma Rose Firbank, RN, and Ruby May Washington, dietician, to the planet known variously as Flora, the Flower Planet, or the Planet of Flowers. Upon arrival, you are directed to deposit the named females upon the fourth terrace of the island of Tropica, there to remain forever.

You are further directed to assign each female one machete, such machetes to be puveyed in accordance with Naval Regulation #376,854,329.

We are desirous that the long-term gains of this project shall redound to the benefit of all peoples, on earth and in the high heavens, and to the everlasting credit of the undersigned Chief Executive.

The President